Where
⊶ the ⊷
Trail Ends

Where
❦ the ❦
Trail Ends

MELANIE DOBSON

summerside
PRESS™

Summerside Press™
Minneapolis, MN 55378
www.summersidepress.com

Where the Trail Ends
© 2012 by Melanie Dobson

ISBN 978-1-60936-685-8

Scripture references are from The Holy Bible, King James Version (KJV).

Though this story is based on actual events, it is a work of fiction.

Cover design by Lookout Design | www.lookoutdesign.com
Interior design by Müllerhaus Publishing Group | www.mullerhaus.net

*Summerside Press™ is an inspirational publisher offering fresh,
irresistible books to uplift the heart and engage the mind.*

Printed in USA.

Dedication

To my daughter, Karlyn Skye

God has blessed you with such beautiful gifts—
passion, diligence, and determination.

Nothing would have stopped you
from walking the two thousand miles to Oregon.

The pitying stars shone out o'erhead,
On the heartbroken immigrants
Burying their dead.

Over the graves the long train has passed;
The last goodbye has been given,
Till the graves on the trail give up their dead
And we'll meet in the light of heaven.

Oh, beautiful stars a loving watch keep,
O'er the immigrant trail where our loved ones sleep.

FROM THE DIARY OF
MARY COLLINS PARSONS, 1852

Chapter One

September 1842

Samantha clutched Micah's hand, water splashing up both sides of the wagon as their two oxen labored to pull them and the Waldron family belongings across the swift Snake River. The wagon bumped over another rock and listed to the left. She swallowed hard. What would happen if her family's wagon tipped, as the Baylor family's wagon did two weeks past?

She'd promised Mama that she would take care of her little brother, but it hadn't been easy. Micah could swim—Papa had taken him down to the pond several times before they left Ohio—but this current would be too hard for him to fight, the river too wide for him to cross. Micah squeezed her hand, and his words trembled along with his fingers. "Are we gonna tip?"

She steadied her voice. "Papa will take care of us."

Micah's hand relaxed in hers.

Their father rode beside them on the one horse they'd purchased for their journey west, yelling at the oxen as he cracked his whip over their heads. During their five months on the trail, Papa had changed from an ordinary small-town lawyer to a passionate horseman and teamster.

They'd all changed, she supposed.

The wagon groaned from the pressure of the current, but she tried to stay calm for Micah's sake. She wished she could jump off the wagon bench into the river, to help Papa lead their supplies and live-stock to safety. But even if the river were shallow enough for her to walk safely through it, Papa would be angry if she got off the bench, and Captain Ezra Loewe, their hard-nosed wagon master, would be furious.

The captain was still fuming over her last attempt to help. How could she possibly have known that there was an entire family of rattlers lurking in that bush? When she screamed…well, at least their animals hadn't run very far. And they had eaten the snakes for supper. But instead of making herself a needed member of the Loewe party as she'd hoped, the captain had refused her further offers of assistance.

About a hundred yards ahead of them, Captain Loewe, the hand-some Jack Doyle, and most of the other sixteen men in their company worked on the grassy bank, leading teams of oxen and wagons out of the water and up to safe ground. Behind the men lay a small valley with endless brown hills that blended into the horizon. More steep climbs, deep ruts, and rugged volcanic rock for their wagon party to cross with lofty mountains towering around the fringe.

A small part of her wished this current could take her and Micah back east, toward Ohio and all they'd left behind them. She missed Grandma Emma and her cousins, her bed, and the fashionable dresses in her armoire. She missed eating just about anything other than beans, biscuits, and dried buffalo meat. But this journey—it was all a grand adventure, and there was nothing she loved more than an adventure. Mama once told her that she'd grow out of this craving, but she was eighteen now and had yet to outgrow her thirst for all things new.

Something bumped against their wagon, and Micah squeezed her hand again as the waves lapped up on both sides of them. As they lumbered forward, she prayed softly, as Mama would have done, for their safety and their supplies. Papa had caulked the box with pine tar, but nothing could stop the water from splashing over the top of the wagon box and soaking their food.

She glanced into the box behind her. It was once bulging with burlap bags and barrels filled with wheat, coffee, dried fruit, corn, and beans, but their food supply was rapidly dwindling. The wagon also held bedrolls and canvas for their tent, Papa's tools, and Mama's rosewood chest. Vinegar, hardtack, saleratus to make bread, wild onions they'd collected from the plains, loaves of sugar, candles, guns, rope, an ax, whiskey, peppermint oil, and a bottle of laudanum that they'd thankfully yet to use. They'd started out their journey with seventy-five pounds of bacon as well, but they'd had to dump most of it back on the plains when mosquitoes tried to carry it away.

Her brother kept his treasures with him in a knapsack he'd lugged all the way from Ohio. Before they left home, Papa had made it for him out of canvas cloth and wooden pole. When it wasn't propped over his shoulder, Micah slept with it close to his head or held it tightly on his lap when they crossed the rivers. He wouldn't let either her or Papa see the contents of what he'd packed.

He was small for his seven years, but sometimes her little brother could be just as stubborn as her and Papa.

Boaz, the Waldron family's wolfhound, paddled in the water below the bench. If only she could swim in the river alongside her dog and cool her skin as she cleaned off the trail dirt and mud. She wished she could help Micah get cleaned up as well. Her brother's blond hair was as long as a fur trapper's—she hadn't trimmed it since they left Ohio, to protect his neck from the bugs and the sun—and she'd stopped reminding him to wash his hands and face. If Mama were still alive, she'd be appalled to know how filthy her children were at the moment.

She could almost hear Mama reminding her to wash when they got to the other side of the river. With Papa in charge, her mother would never for a moment doubt that they would arrive safely.

Ahead of them, the Kneedler family's wagon reached the shore. Jack reached out and took the hand of Arthur Kneedler's elderly wife, helping her climb down from the wagon bench and up the muddy bank. It was late in life for Mr. and Mrs. Kneedler to be starting out in this new territory, but their son now lived in Oregon Country. She'd heard Mr. Kneedler once tell Papa that it was never too late to begin again.

The Kneedlers' dog scrambled out of the water behind the oxen and rushed up the hill. For some reason Colt wasn't fond of oxen, but many of them on this journey—animals and people alike—weren't fond of each other. Those in conflict had learned to tolerate one another for the sake of their company.

Her family's wagon would be next, the last one to arrive on the safety of the shore.

"My belly hurts," Micah said.

She ruffled his blond hair. "We'll make bean soup tonight."

He groaned. "We had that last night."

And every night for the past week, since they'd eaten the last of the dried buffalo meat. "We'll pretend it's Mama's oyster stew."

He looked down at the moccasins Papa had bought him back at Fort Hall. "I miss Mama."

She put her arm around his shoulders, giving him a quick hug. "Me too."

They had followed the Snake River for three hundred miles now, crossing it multiple times in their journey west, but the captain said they would have to leave this river at the bend. The Snake had lived up to its name, the waters snaking up and down. Ahead of them, a canyon boxed in the river as it turned north.

They'd lost the Baylors' wagon on a particularly treacherous crossing of the Snake. Bags and barrels—the entire contents of their wagon—plummeted into the river when their wheel hit a rock. They'd almost lost Mrs. Baylor along with the wagon, but Jack had grabbed her skirts from where he sat astride his horse and dragged the poor, flailing lady across the river to her anxious husband on the shore. They'd all watched with an alarming fascination as the swift current seized the Baylor family's earthly goods and swept them away.

The Baylors lasted three more days after their accident, subsisting on borrowed food and supplies from the other wagons, before they turned back East with two other trail-worn families. The rest of the company would probably never know what happened to those friends, who had become like family during the journey, but Samantha prayed every day for their safe return to Missouri. And she hoped that those who remained would reach their new home in the fertile Willamette Valley, on the west side of Oregon Country, before the winter storms began.

The traders they'd met at Fort Hall said once they left the Snake, water might be hard to find until they reached the mighty Columbia River near the end of their trail. They were a couple hundred miles west of Fort Hall now, and if everything went according to plan, they would begin their climb up the Blue Mountains in a week and be settling in the Willamette before November.

Unfortunately, little on this trip had gone according to the plan.

Samantha sighed. Even though they'd crossed the boundary line into Oregon Country, they were three weeks behind schedule. It was already the beginning of September, and the fur traders back at Fort Hall had said snow would be coming soon to the Blues. They should stay and winter at the fort, the traders said, but the men in their party cast a vote before they left. They all wanted to move ahead toward the Willamette at an even faster pace.

Few Americans had traveled over these mountains before them, and those who had done it left their wagons at Fort Hall to travel with packhorses for the last month of their journey. The traders said they were foolish to bring women and children out here, that it would be impossible for them to get their wagons over the canyons and rivers in the northwest. But their warnings hadn't deterred Captain Loewe, Papa, or the others from bringing wagons, livestock, and—according to the traders—the first American children overland. Captain Loewe, however, had left his wife back in Missouri.

A fish leaped out of the water and Samantha pointed it out to Micah, trying to distract herself from the painstakingly slow pace of their oxen. There was certainly hardship in traveling for months like this to an unknown valley, but land was free and so fertile, they were told, that if they planted vegetables first thing in the morning, they'd be ripe for supper that night. There was also triumph in conquering this overland journey that very few had attempted, moving to a land where few had been.

The oxen wrestled against the current, the water flowing up over their strong shoulders and splashing across their backs. Papa continued to urge them forward from his horse, lashing their thick coats with his switch, shouting for them to "get up," but instead of moving forward, they stopped altogether—halfway across the river.

"Come on," Samantha whispered.

On past river crossings, their company had waited for hours until one of their gentle but often stubborn oxen decided to move forward. They couldn't afford to wait here for hours—it would be dark soon, and they needed to set up their camp and cook supper while it was still light. If their oxen wouldn't budge, the thirty-two people already on shore would have to continue on and circle up for camp without them. The Waldrons would catch up once the oxen decided to move.

Boaz nipped at the hindquarters of the nigh ox, George, and he bellowed, stepping forward with Abe, the ox yoked beside him. Then they stopped again.

Jack rode back into the river, steering his horse toward their raft. Samantha couldn't see his dark brown hair under his wide-brimmed hat, but she could see the focus in his face, the strength of his arms as he guided his horse.

When he glanced over at her, she blushed.

Micah elbowed her. "Someone's sweet on you."

"Hush," she whispered.

"Papa says you're going to marry him."

She elbowed him back. "I told you to hush."

Micah tipped his hat low over his shaggy hair, but she could still see the grin on his face.

Jack whipped the oxen, yelling at them to move. Samantha winced every time the whip hit their backs. She knew it was necessary to prod them forward—an ox refused to be led—but she hated seeing any animal in pain, especially these oxen that had pulled almost two tons of weight for more than a thousand miles.

Mama believed in angels—the fiery messengers mentioned in the book of Hebrews who were sent to care for those on the road to salvation. Mama would have asked God to send these angels to help both the oxen and the men, so Samantha did as well, quietly asking God to send help in nudging the oxen forward.

The two men continued shouting, goading with their whips and sticks, but the oxen fought them, almost as if they were afraid of dangers on the other side of this river. More men joined them, trying to coax the animals to move.

Samantha breathed with relief when the oxen stepped again, heaving as they moved toward the shore. She'd spent much of this trip holding her breath, not knowing what might happen next, but with Papa and Jack and perhaps a host of angels at the helm, they would make it safely to the end of this journey.

The wagon shook, the hitch chain clanking, as the oxen tugged again. This time they didn't stop pulling until they reached the other side.

Micah hopped off the wagon with a loud cheer and waded beside Boaz through the shallow water and up the bank. Before she jumped to the ground, Samantha slipped off her moccasins and dropped them into her apron pocket. Jack dismounted, and she took his proffered hand, thanking him as she slid off the bench.

She tried to focus, dipping her feet into the blessed coolness of the river before wading to shore. "I think our oxen are afraid of you."

He laughed. "Not me as much as my stick."

"They certainly obeyed you."

He helped her climb up the muddy bank. "We had a dozen oxen back home."

She glanced over at him. "You miss your farm, don't you?"

"It was my parents' farm, not mine. And no, I don't miss it."

She stepped onto the land and turned toward him. "But you miss your family."

He released her hand with a slight bow of his head. "Very much."

She wished they had hours to linger, talk. But Jack moved away quickly, back among the company of the other men as they prodded the Waldrons' oxen forward again. Their wagon clamored, the contents banging, as the oxen heaved it up the bank.

Boaz rushed down to her, like he was needed to escort her now that Jack had gone, and she bent to pet him before they joined more than a dozen women, four children, and a swarm of animals on the flat land.

"Get that dog out of here," the captain barked behind her.

She turned around, glaring at the man down the bank. She wished Boaz would bark back.

"We're going," she said, but she didn't think he heard, as he ordered the men to stock up with water. Even after five months on this journey, she didn't believe the captain knew the name of her dog…or even Samantha's first name, for that matter. She supposed she should be glad he was keenly focused on the details of the journey rather than the names of the people and their pets, but he could at least try to be polite.

Lucille McLean waved, but Samantha thought she saw a trace of jealousy behind her friend's smile. She waved back, trying to shrug off the feeling that she'd done something wrong. It wasn't like she'd asked Jack Doyle for help off the wagon. The man did make her heart flutter a bit, but she hadn't determined whether she liked the fluttering, nor had she confided her conflicting feelings to Lucille. Her friend was convinced that she would be changing her name to Lucille *Doyle* when they reached the end of their journey.

Lucille lifted the muddy hem of her skirt, but not a single strand of blond hair escaped her pink bonnet as she moved toward Samantha. "I'll be perfectly fine if I never have to cross another river again."

Samantha grinned. "You didn't enjoy the ride?"

"Hardly." Lucille nodded toward the Waldrons' wagon as it emerged on the hill. "Did you fill your barrel with water?"

She shook her head. "Papa will fill it."

Oxen and dogs milled around the people and the contents from the wagons scattered among the sagebrush. After boxes and barrels were jostled in the river crossing, most of the emigrants wanted to repack their loads before they continued.

"I need to fill my canteen," Gerty Morrison said, holding out her two-year-old daughter to Lucille. Lucille welcomed the child into her arms.

As Gerty climbed into the back of her family's emptied wagon, wind stole over the river, rustling the canvas bonnets on the wagons. Colt barked, and Mrs. Kneedler hushed him.

Samantha scanned the barren hills around them, but she didn't see anything unusual. Several companies of Indians had followed them along their journey—curious, she supposed, about the white men and women who traveled through their lands. The captain had traded shirts and fishhooks for food, and one of the Indians had tried to barter with Papa to exchange Samantha for three horses. Fortunately, Papa declined.

Two more dogs began barking, and then one growled. Her skin prickled. If the dogs had spotted a rabbit or a prairie dog, one of them would have chased it down by now.

Something else was wrong.

Samantha didn't know exactly what happened next, but Colt charged at an ox as if it were a wolf or bear. "No!" Mr. Kneedler shouted, chasing after his dog, but it was too late.

The ox lumbered forward, no one to guide him. And then another ox followed.

Dust billowed into a maddening cloud and Samantha waved her hands in front of her face, trying to see. The oxen bellowed in unison as a thundering sound rippled across the company.

"Stampede!" someone yelled.

People scattered as the oxen pushed toward the hills. Clods of dirt flew off the ground; bows cracked as oxen broke loose of their yokes.

She couldn't see. Couldn't breathe.

All the dogs were barking now, and the oxen harnessed to the Morrisons' wagon took off after the others. Gerty screamed, and through the dust, Samantha saw Gerty peeking out of the back flap as though trying to determine whether she should jump.

Men ran toward the oxen. Lucille and the other women ran away from the wagons, their screams echoing in Samantha's ears.

Samantha ran toward her father.

"Steady," she heard Papa say as he clung to the oxbow on the lead team, his voice a controlled calm in the midst of the chaos.

"Where's Micah?" she shouted.

"Hold on to them!" Papa yelled. She reached for the bow on the other side, trying to anchor the large animals to the ground.

A child cried out from the storm of dust, and she turned around, searching for her brother. "I have to find Micah!"

"Steady," Papa said again before he looked across at her. "Go, Samantha."

A horse raced past her, and she jumped back, coughing as she scanned the chaos. She glimpsed her brother's blond hair close to a rock, but then he was gone.

"Micah!" she yelled as she tore through the confusion.

God help all of them.

Chapter Two

Alexander Clarke elbowed his way through the crowded room that smelled like musky fur and bear grease. Simon Gervais and a fellow clerk named Oliver Deloire dueled on their fiddles, while another officer pounded a beat on his drum. The sound of stomping feet overpowered the music as Fort Vancouver's young officers swung their ladies across the wooden floor.

The young women, natives of the West, loved to dance; and the officers—a combination of British, Swiss, and French Canadian—often entertained their wives and guests until long past midnight. For many of them, tonight would be the last night of dancing in Bachelor's Hall until spring, because at first light the companies of fur traders would leave to set up camp among the majestic trees of the Columbia District, harvesting thousands of pelts from the forests and creeks through both autumn and winter. Wolves, bear, silver foxes, and the most prized fur of them all, beaver—*brown gold.*

The pelts would be shipped off on the next boat arriving at Fort Vancouver from London, and this year, Alex would accompany the furs on their 17,000-mile journey down the west coast of the Americas and around Cape Horn, back to the Port of London.

Simon lowered his fiddle, catching Alex's eye before he slipped out the door.

"Aren't you gonna join us?" his friend called to him.

"As much as I would like to—" Alex knew how to dance, but

not in the stomp-your-feet, swing-your-partner way of these men. The nephew of Hudson's Bay Company's president didn't stomp.

Simon was at his side, nodding toward several women wearing long black braids and beaded buckskin dresses at the far end of the room. "Taini's been asking to dance with you."

Taini's husband had traveled into the wilderness two years ago and never returned. Taini had since made it quite clear that not only was she looking to remarry, but she wanted Alex as her husband. He had tried to make it quite clear as well that he wasn't interested in marrying her. He had already promised to marry a woman in London.

"There will be no dancing for me tonight." Alex pointed back over his shoulder. "I'm taking my dinner at the big house."

Simon's eyebrows arched. "You don't think your sweet Judith is still pining for you, do you?"

Heat crawled up Alex's skin and into his cheeks. He didn't like to talk to any of these men about his intended wife. "Pining would not become Lady Judith, but she will be faithful to our promise."

Simon laughed so hard that Alex thought he might pop one of his shirt buttons. "You clearly don't have much experience with women."

Alex looked over the heads of the men and women lined up on opposite sides of the room, traveling toward each other and then back to the wall, dancing to the muted sound of the fiddles. It was true; he didn't know much about the ways of women, but Simon didn't know Judith Heggs.

His uncle and her father had negotiated a marriage between Alex and Judith more than a decade ago. It might seem strange to those who lived at the fort, but Alex had never balked at the idea of an arranged marriage, especially since he and Judith had been such chums in their younger years. Of course, that was years ago; he was twenty-nine now, and she was twenty-four. But they plenty of time to renew their acquaintance, and marriage, he hoped, would only increase their mutual admiration and respect.

His uncle had begun mapping out Alex's life when he was eleven, and it seemed to be a good life, much better than he'd had the first decade of his life. His only act of rebellion had been to stay here a year longer than what his uncle had planned, but he had written letters to both Judith and his uncle, the esteemed Lord Neville Clarke, explaining in much detail why it was important for him to stay. During this past year, he had visited three of the company's other trading posts, until he felt confident that he understood every aspect of the business that would sustain his family.

Alex pushed open the door, a blast of night air refreshing the room. "I mustn't keep McLoughlin waiting."

Simon strung a few notes on his fiddle, a smile on his tobacco-stained lips. "You couldn't pay me enough money to spend an entire evening trying to act like a British gentleman." Simon was the son of a Umatilla woman and a French-Canadian *voyageur* who'd paddled away from Fort Vancouver when Simon was four, but the loss of his father didn't seem to bother him—at least not like the loss of Alex's father bothered Alex.

Alex smiled. "I think you would do just about anything if I paid you enough."

Laughter burst from Simon's lips like water flooding over the great falls on the Columbia.

Alex stepped out into the night and slowly crossed the grassy piazza washed gray with moonlight. Pointed palisades twenty feet high hemmed the border of their village, and the gates on both sides of the fort were locked for the night to keep thieves away from their storehouses of food and supplies.

Alex was a British gentleman known as *Lord Clarke* on the other side of the world. Nobility had been in his father's family for generations, and his uncle had told him stories of his ancestors dining with King George I. Although the blood of aristocrats flowed through him, he no longer felt much like a gentleman now that he'd been at Fort Vancouver for four years. Nor did he feel entirely comfortable in the company of trappers and laborers.

Some days he felt trapped right in between.

Most of the officers of Fort Vancouver were British gentlemen who had taken Indian women as their wives. These men liked to pretend they lived just as fine as their counterparts in Great Britain, but most hadn't been back in decades. None of them knew about the changes in fashion or politics or world affairs. News came to them six months after it occurred, with the annual arrival of the ship, and then they didn't receive news again for another year.

The person Alex respected most at the fort was Doctor John McLoughlin, the chief factor of the trading post, though everyone here called him "governor." Alex's uncle respected McLoughlin as well and had requested that Alex work directly for the governor to learn everything about the trapping-and-trading business at Fort Vancouver before Alex returned to London for his place on the Hudson's Bay Company committee.

Alex could tell by his uncle's last letter that the tide was changing. Great Britain's patriots weren't as enamored of McLoughlin's policies as they were of his ability to manage Fort Vancouver.

McLoughlin had Alex working plenty hard at the fort, but he felt neither privileged nor indentured. Over the past four years, McLoughlin had given him the opportunity to work in nearly every area of Fort Vancouver, including the kitchen, the trading post, and out at one of the trapping camps. When he returned to London, Alex would know the business of Hudson's Bay Company better than anyone else on the committee, which was exactly what his uncle planned. Then Alex could move into the role of president when Lord Neville Clarke retired.

He eyed the house in front of him, with its split staircase leading up to the grand front door. The shutters on its four front windows were olive green, the walls white. The only painted house, he'd been told, west of the Mississippi. Grapevines decorated the trellis along the wide veranda, and flowers bloomed at the base. There was a cannon at the bottom of the house and a pyramid of balls stacked beside it, but as far as he knew, the cannon had never been used. No one had ever tried to raid the trading post.

As a servant opened the door, Alex took off his fine felted beaver hat, shiny and black as the night. It was fashionable top hats such as his that had kept the workers of Hudson's Bay Company employed since 1670—a hat worth three years' wages in England.

The natives scoffed at the British men who spent so much money on top hats, but they were quite willing to trade their pelts for the wool blankets, glass beads, and firing arms that the company stored at its trading post.

The servant held out his hand, and Alex handed his hat to the man before walking down a short entryway and into the dining room. Wide mirrors reflected the light of the lamps and candles, and blue walls clad with fine paintings circled the room. It wasn't nearly as elegant as the finer dining rooms in London, but the McLoughlins' home was the finest place to dine in the entire Columbia District.

Judith might laugh at the attempt to bring a bit of refinement to the wilderness. Or perhaps she would embrace the only house in the West that attempted to offer dining in style. Either way, he was glad Judith was in London. Two officers had attempted to bring their society wives over here, but both women's minds...they became unwell with the shock.

The wilderness was no place for a white woman.

Fifteen men were already seated at a white-cloaked table, the majority of them in evening dress with silk cravats knotted around their necks. Most of the men were officers at the trading post, rotating in their invitation to dine at the chief factor's table.

There was only one man Alex did not recognize. Instead of a dark cloak, the new man wore corduroy trousers, suspenders, and a red flannel shirt like many of the traders. His brown hair was pulled back behind his ears, and stubble shadowed his thin face.

McLoughlin turned from his conversation and waved Alex forward.

"Come in," the governor's voice boomed, and all the men turned to look at Alex. He bowed his head and walked forward to shake the governor's hand.

McLoughlin's white hair was long and wild over his distinguished blue coat, his eyebrows as thick and white as his hair. His dark eyes shone with good humor tonight instead of the intensity the governor often displayed when he was overseeing the fort.

"Are the men ready to leave tomorrow?" he asked.

"More than ready," Alex replied. "They are quite eager to set up their camps in the wilderness while the sunshine is still with us."

"Excellent," McLoughlin said, as he lifted his glittering glass of water in a salute. "Marguerite just told me that she is eager, as well, for a ride in the sunshine. We just might join one of the companies in the morning."

Alex nodded politely, but his mind began to rapidly tick through everything he would need to do tonight and then early in the morning to prepare for such a ride. Madame McLoughlin, in particular, would need the best horse in the stables and all the supplies necessary to keep her comfortable while they were in the wilderness. Madame enjoyed getting out of the fort whenever possible, but when she did, she liked riding a horse padded with blankets and decorated with ribbons.

McLoughlin eyed Alex for a moment. "We don't want any fanfare," he said. "We'll only be gone for a few days."

"Of course," Alex replied with a nod, though they both knew that Alex would leave straight from dinner to attend to this new detail.

McLoughlin lifted his glass again, speaking to the entire table. "Alex, here, could run the whole fort if he weren't so anxious to return to England."

"More obligated than anxious, sir."

McLoughlin laughed. "I believe you might have a little native blood in you."

The man meant it as a compliment, but Alex's uncle would terminate the governor's position if he heard him suggest that a member of their elite family might be tainted with Indian blood.

Alex's uncle, along with the rest of British society, would be appalled to learn that many of their countrymen had taken Indian brides in this territory. Even McLoughlin had married a woman whose mother was Chippewa and father was a Swiss fur trader.

Alex had no problem with the officers or traders marrying the native women. Some of these men loved and cared for their wives for the rest of their lives. His problem was with the men who married Indian women to ensure peace or gifts or protection to hunt on native lands. They were the scoundrels who abandoned their Indian wives to return to Britain and marry English women. Or sometimes they left their Indian wives to return to the women they'd married before traveling west.

"Have a seat." McLoughlin pointed him toward a high-backed mahogany chair across the table. "The cook has prepared roasted duck, cabbage slaw, and blackberry pie."

Alex pulled out his chair beside the new man. Madame McLoughlin, as well as the other officers' wives, ate in the smaller dining room at the front of the house.

"You must be Alex Clarke," the man next to him said with a wide smile and an accent clearly not influenced by a British mother.

Alex nodded, but he groaned inwardly. The last thing he wanted to do was make polite conversation with a Yankee.

He met McLoughlin's eye across the table, and the older man smiled.

"Doctor John, here, has been telling me all about you." Alex's neighbor stuck out his hand. "I'm Tom. Tom Kneedler."

Alex shook the man's hand reluctantly. "It's a pleasure."

Alex poured a light red Italian wine into his goblet as one of the menservants brought two baskets of bread into the room—probably baked that morning in the bakery beside the governor's house—and set them on the long table. Across from them, McLoughlin reached for a piece of bread and began to butter it. "Mr. Kneedler was with the company that arrived last year."

Alex had been visiting another fort when the boats full of Americans arrived, but he'd heard the stories. Some of the men who came had to crawl up the banks from the Columbia, the *bateaux* they'd purchased from Indians battered and almost all their belongings gone. They'd begged for something to eat, a place to rest.

Tom Kneedler, he'd been told, hadn't begged for food. He'd begged for medicine for his sick wife, and the fort's surgeon, Doctor Barclay, had nursed the man's wife back to health. Alex wondered if she had survived her first year in this new country, but he didn't dare ask.

"He and his new bride went straight to the Willamette Valley and set up a homestead," McLoughlin said.

Kneedler sat up a little straighter. "Next month, I'm going to be a father."

"Congratulations," Alex replied, not knowing what else to say. The men never spoke of babies—and rarely about women—at this table. He took a long sip of his wine before he spoke again. "How long do you intend to stay?"

"My Sally loves this country as much as I do," he said. "We're planning to raise our children here, and hopefully our children will stay as well."

Alex choked on his wine, coughing as he set the goblet back on the table.

"Are you all right?" Kneedler asked.

He nodded, hiding his lips behind his napkin until the cough subsided.

"My parents are coming West too, hopefully this year."

Alex cringed. He didn't want to hear about more Americans coming or raising their children here. Almost two hundred years ago, the king of England had granted Hudson's Bay Company a charter of 1.4 million miles that drained into Hudson Bay, and the company was trying to retain this land for the queen.

So far only a handful of women, such as missionaries Narcissa Whitman and Eliza Spalding, had made it across the great mountains that divided the West from the East, but if this continued, it wouldn't be long before more American women came—bringing their children with them.

It seemed absurd to risk the lives of children by coming overland, but no voice of reason seemed capable of stopping the Americans when they put their minds to something. Alex had hoped McLoughlin would turn them away from Fort Vancouver, would stop welcoming them to his dining room table, but the governor thought it better to be friendly to the Americans than risk starting a third war with them.

One of the servants set before them platters of cabbage along with three roasted ducks stuffed with potatoes and herbs from the governor's personal garden. McLoughlin asked God's blessing over their food and discussion, and when he finished his prayer, McLoughlin turned to speak with the officer next to him.

Alex heard the governor tell the man about his great pride in the twenty-four children at the fort and the man from England who was educating them until their new teacher arrived. Alex wasn't so fond of Warren Calvert, but many of the children in the fort didn't speak English. If nothing else, Alex hoped Calvert would teach them English and prepare the boys to follow in their fathers' footsteps as trappers, clerks, and officers.

As they waited for the duck to be sliced, Kneedler leaned toward Alex. "How long have you lived in Oregon?"

"Nearly four years now." He held up his white-and-blue plate, and the servant slid a serving of duck and then cabbage on it. The salty steam from the food made his stomach growl. Until that moment he hadn't quite realized how hungry he was, but he would wait until everyone was served before he lifted his fork.

Instead of following protocol, Kneedler picked up his fork and took a bite of his duck moments after the servant put it on his plate. He didn't even seem to realize his mistake, chewing and swallowing it before he continued talking. "Doctor John has been very helpful to all of us who arrived here last year."

McLoughlin took a bite of his duck, and Alex followed suit. The meat was moist and tasted of untamed rivers and trees and everything he loved about this country. "Quite so," Alex said. "Yet there are those in London who find him to be perhaps *too* helpful."

The man's eyebrows climbed. "You don't approve of Americans coming here?"

The shake of his head was brief but clear. "I admire you and your countrymen for your courage but perhaps not your wisdom."

Kneedler sipped his wine. "What do you consider unwise?"

"Coming to a new land, and a dangerous one at that, without a viable means to support your family."

Kneedler set down his goblet. "Fourteen of us came last year, and we've all started farms."

"I find no fault with you personally, Mr. Kneedler," Alex said, studying the man. "I only wonder why Americans want to come to this new territory when there is so much good land and water east of the Rocky Mountains."

Kneedler shrugged. "There are some who want the adventure, I suppose, but most of us came looking for the Promised Land."

Alex slowly smiled. "How much milk and honey have you found here?"

Kneedler chuckled. "Not much, I suppose, but there is plenty of good soil and more than enough water to make just about any crop grow. Until this summer I never dreamed I'd be able to farm, but I've already harvested enough food to put away for the winter—with some left over for my parents when they arrive. There may not be much milk and honey, but the land is just as promising."

Alex pushed the meat across his plate. This was what he feared most—what everyone at the table feared. Everyone but the American. The small successes, the promise of opportunity, would drive a whole swarm of Americans over the mountains, and then Fort Vancouver would be expected to provide the seeds of the opportunity for all of them.

When Kneedler and his fellow travelers arrived at the fort last fall, they were half-starved and without any place to live through winter, since they had abandoned nearly all their belongings and tools on the trail. Their enthusiasm for settling in this new country had been greatly diminished—until McLoughlin provided food and supplies for them.

What if Kneedler's relatives did try to follow? And more people with them? They might start their journey full of grand ideas, but the hard reality of trail life was certain to deflate both their spirits and their supplies. Hudson's Bay Company wasn't running a poorhouse for the Colonies. They were running a business.

He glanced across the table again, at the governor laughing

with the man next to him. McLoughlin was an excellent leader and manager, fair to his workers and respected by the company's London committee. Alex's only criticism of the man was that he sometimes ran the trading post like a charity instead of a company.

Lord Neville Clarke and the others on the committee had heard rumors about the breadth of the governor's charity before Alex left England, but if they knew how much McLoughlin helped the Americans who'd arrived from over the Rockies last year, they would certainly remove him from his post. Hudson's Bay Company didn't want people to tame the land and build houses along the creeks. They wanted the rivers and forests to remain unspoiled so they could continue hunting fur.

Alex knew well McLoughlin's opinion on the subject of these Americans, or *Bostons* as some of the men called them. Not only did McLoughlin think they had a right to live in this land, he thought he had a responsibility before God to feed and clothe them in their need. When Kneedler's party arrived last year, McLoughlin supplemented their food supplies from the fort's root cellar and gave them horses and other help to settle in the Willamette.

Alex knew exactly what his uncle would say once Lord Clarke learned of this charity. If they didn't feed the Americans, they would effectively send the message that the Columbia District—or Oregon Country, as the Americans called it—was not a safe place for newcomers. This would deter all who thought they could build new homes in the West.

"More Americans will be coming soon," Kneedler said.

One of the officers lifted his cup. "If the good queen would send a shipload of families our way, we could stake claim to the entire country before your fellow countrymen do."

"It would be a rare lady who would cross the ocean to live in this wilderness," another officer said.

"It will be many years before either the Americans or the British send enough people to claim this country," Alex said before he took another bite of duck.

Kneedler grinned. "You underestimate the will and strength of our United States."

Alex set down his fork. It took a lot of nerve for Kneedler to talk about how his countrymen might live on the lands where Hudson's Bay Company worked, right in front of the man who'd cared for him and his sick wife. "I've yet to see much strength in your countrymen."

"You will, my friend." Kneedler glanced around the table, his voice confident. "And you'll see it as my countrymen come in droves."

The laughter around the table sounded more anxious than amused. None of them wanted to think about more Americans coming into the country that had been occupied jointly by the Great Britain and the United States since Spain bowed out in 1819. It made Alex want to stay here just so they could have one more Brit calling it home.

He took a long drink from his goblet. He could never admit it to anyone, even the governor, but he was a bit envious of Kneedler's freedom to come to this new land and build a home and farm for his family. The thought of going back to the drudgery of London with all its ridiculous pomp and circumstance was daunting to Alex.

Here in Fort Vancouver, the lines between laborer and officer blurred—or so it seemed to him—but in London there would be no such blurring. Nor would there be freedom to choose how he wanted to live his life. The expectations on his time would be great: long dinners, committee meetings, social events, and hours spent with his uncle at the office on Oxford Street.

Kneedler began talking to the man on the other side of him, and Alex resumed eating his cabbage.

The prevailing thought around the table was that whichever

country sent the most people here would claim the land as its own. Until last summer, none of them doubted that one day this land would be owned by the Crown. After all, the British owned all the forts, and hundreds of British men worked in trading posts across the territory.

But these Americans—

They kept coming, and no one was stopping them.

Chapter Three

Silvery moonlight slipped through the tent and spilled across the quilt Grandma Emma had patched before they left Ohio. Samantha savored the coolness of the night, almost as much as she would savor sip after sip of cold water when their company found another stream.

It was their second night of staying in what the captain called a "dry camp." She called it misery. In the aftermath of the stampede, Papa had forgotten to fill the barrel that hung on the side of their wagon, and she'd forgotten to remind him. Jack gave them some of the water that he'd replenished before the stampede, and they rationed sips in a futile attempt to quench their thirst, but they couldn't waste any on rinsing food off their dishes or the dust from their skin.

Pressing her parched lips together, she rolled over carefully so she wouldn't disturb Micah, asleep on the feather tick beside her. Even though she was exhausted, sleep evaded her. She had to think about something, anything, besides water.

Their company had left behind the Snake River three days ago. Thank God, she'd found Micah in the midst of the chaos, clutching Boaz's fur behind a rock. But not all of them had survived the stampede. Titus Morrison lost his wife along with his wagon when their oxen ran off a cliff and into the canyon.

Gerty had been twenty-four years old.

There had been no time to stop and grieve his loss—their loss.

They'd all started this journey back in Missouri as strangers, but after almost five months of travel, their party had become like a family—laughing, bickering, and overlooking flaws that had rubbed them raw the first few weeks of travel. Over the hundreds of miles, they'd learned that even if they might not like every person in the caravan, they needed one another. Desperately.

Whenever someone died along the trail, the captain said they "met the elephant." Unfortunately, "the elephant" had visited their company three times now since they'd set out from Independence, Missouri, leaving the United States behind them. Samantha prayed it was the last time. She didn't know if she could bear losing another member of their community.

The company also lost seven oxen in the stampede, including one of the Waldrons' three. The men butchered the animals that didn't go over the cliffs; the women dried the meat under the hot western sun. The meat would help sustain them, but losing an ox was devastating for all of them. They had all brought extra oxen in case one died, but it meant they wouldn't be able to carry their entire load over the Blue Mountains. Later they would have to decide what to leave behind.

Later...

A dog barked from inside their tight circle of sixteen wagons, and she forced her eyes closed and tried to sleep. Papa slept most nights under the wagon box while she and Micah slept in a canvas tent. Boaz was leashed on a rawhide strip between the wagon and their tent.

Once they arrived at their new home, she would no longer be sleeping in a tent. Instead, she might be resting on a newly carved bed beside Jack Doyle.

She rolled over, punching the lumpy pillow under her head. She wished she could muster more excitement at the thought.

Jack had been married before, when he was twenty-two, but his wife had died less than a year into their marriage. That was five years ago. Jack had told Samantha that he hadn't considered remarrying until he met her. She figured that was pretty close to a proposal.

She hadn't been sure she'd ever marry, and certainly not this soon. Before they left Ohio, Grandma Emma fretted that Samantha would not find an honorable bachelor in all of Oregon Country. Grandma wanted her to marry Reginald Poole, a man who'd once clerked in Papa's office, but the man was terribly dull. When he became an attorney, he became irritable, as well, no longer smiling at her many attempts to amuse him when he came for supper or to sit on their front porch and sip lemonade.

Lemonade.

She shook her head, trying to erase the longing for a sweet, cool drink.

Reginald would never take a wagon out to Oregon—or at least that was what he'd said when Papa asked him to consider coming on this journey. She now laughed at the thought of Reginald fording a river on horseback or killing a buffalo. His idea of a grand adventure was to stand on the sidelines, watching a parade march by during the holidays.

Samantha never liked watching parades. She'd always wanted to be in them.

Now she had paraded for more than thirteen hundred miles. When they arrived in the Willamette, she wasn't sure she'd ever want to walk anywhere again.

She'd met Jack the morning before they left Missouri. He was the charming farmer from Terre Haute, one of the two bachelors in their party if she didn't include Papa. The other, Lesley Duncan, made it perfectly clear that he was seeking wealth in the West, not a wife.

Jack hadn't officially proposed yet, but Papa thought he would once they finished their journey. The Loewe party had much to overcome before Jack and Samantha could seriously consider marriage. In the meantime, she hosted Jack most nights around their family's campfire. He brought his harmonica with him, and Papa and Micah harmonized on all manner of hymns and river songs before the accompaniment of the coyotes drowned out their singing. She never dared to sing with them, knowing her vocal inabilities might make Jack turn and run, but she enjoyed the concert each night.

While she loved adventure, she wasn't completely certain about the marriage part. Papa wanted her to marry, to make sure she and Micah would be well cared for if something happened to him. And Grandma Emma had asked him to make sure that Samantha married someone with a bit of refinement. In Papa's mind, Jack Doyle was the perfect answer to what he perceived to be a problem.

A light wind blew open the tent flap, and another dog barked. She rubbed the goose bumps on her arms. A dog or two sometimes barked during the night. It was nothing to worry about. At least, that's what she told herself. They were simply barking at the wind.

The breeze drifted into the tent and she tugged her grandmother's quilt up to her chin, trying to keep warm. When the dogs barked again, the horrible stories from the British fur traders back at Fort Hall began to play in her mind. Captain Loewe said the traders' tales were tall ones meant to deter the Americans from settling the wilderness. Neither the British nor the Americans were thrilled with emigrants from the opposing country coming to settle the land, but still their company would try.

The traders' warnings were so diverse, so absurd, even, that Samantha tried to force herself to stop listening. But in the darkest hours, she remembered them. There were stories about wolves and bears and hostile Indians, about bad water, lost pioneers, autumn snowstorms in the Blue Mountains, and a deadly disease called camp fever. They'd told them about deep canyons, volcanoes that towered in the sky, and the treacherous Columbia River that plunged over rocks and swirled in pools, trapping animals and people alike.

The traders also said that it would be impossible for their company to take wagons over the Blue Mountains; some of them had laughed to the point of hysterics when they saw the trunks in the back of their wagons along with rocking chairs, tools, bags of seed, and headboards. They'd urged Papa and the others to sell their things and continue by foot or on horseback, but few in their party sold anything of real value. They figured the traders were trying to scare them out of their prized possessions.

Captain Loewe had gathered information about other Americans who had traveled this way, and he'd been confident that they would make it with all their wagons and possessions intact. But she was pretty sure his confidence was a bluff. None of them, including the captain, had ever been over the Blues.

Shadows from the dying campfire danced on the side of the canvas tent, and Samantha tried again to pretend she wasn't thirsty. Another dog started barking, and she heard Arthur Kneedler holler at Colt to be quiet. The dogs were usually as tired as their owners during the night, but the Kneedlers' dog in particular had spent several nights barking on this journey, irritating the weary travelers while they tried to sleep.

Captain Loewe had barely tolerated the dogs up to this point. He'd tried to convince the emigrants to leave them behind, citing annoyance and the fact that the animals would need food and water when there was little to be had, but their party insisted on bringing their dogs—fifteen of them, including a shepherd dog named Sandy and her five pups who rode in the back of Doctor Rochester's wagon. The dogs were both pets and protection from wild animals.

The captain reluctantly agreed to bring dogs—probably because he had no choice if he wanted to lead this party—but he wasn't above reminding everyone how right he had been about them, especially after they caused the stampede.

She hated to think what his attitude would be like in the morning if this barking continued. In her mind, tired dogs didn't spend the night barking unless they sensed that something was wrong. Unfortunately, the captain didn't share her perspective. He thought the dogs accompanying them were a menace.

Even Boaz had seemed agitated today, sniffing and then barking as he walked beside Samantha instead of roaming the countryside. The dogs were all tied to the wagons tonight, but the two men on night watch would alert the rest of them if anything threatened the camp.

She heard the low growl of her wolfhound outside the tent, and her skin prickled. She ran her fingers across the loaded rifle that rested beside her. Boaz never growled unless something was wrong.

"Boaz," Papa called from outside the tent. "Go back to sleep."

Boaz stopped for a moment, but then he growled again. Samantha sat up and crawled carefully across the feather tick so she wouldn't wake Micah. Edging back the canvas, she stuck her hand outside, but Boaz didn't nudge it with his nose. Instead, he gave a short bark. A warning.

"Papa," she whispered, "something's wrong."

Several men began talking nearby, and then she heard Papa shuffle out from under the wagon. "I'll find out what's happening," he said.

Samantha reached for her rifle and leather possibles bag containing her balls, caps, and patches. Back home, she would have had to change from her nightdress, but out here, all the women slept in their calico dresses—all except Lucille, that is. She insisted on wearing her nightgown. Uncomfortable as it was, sleeping in a dress certainly made it easier for Samantha and the other women to slip in and out of their tents when necessary.

She strapped her possibles bag over her shoulder and folded back the canvas. "I'm coming with you."

"No," he insisted, shaking his head. "You stay here."

"But what if it's Indians?"

"Stay here, Samantha," he commanded, as if she were a dog instead of an eighteen-year-old woman who knew how to shoot a gun.

She watched through the tent opening as his shadow blended into the night. Papa had never taught her to swim like he had Micah, but when she was twelve, he taught her to shoot in the hills near their home. Until Micah was born seven years ago, he'd had no son to hunt with, so Samantha had enjoyed many hours with her father, tramping through the branches and leaves as they searched for deer or wild fowl. She'd never been able to shoot an animal and certainly not a person, but no one had ever threatened her or her family either.

After his footsteps faded away, Samantha quietly counted a full minute before climbing out of the tent. Then she untied Boaz. With her dog on one side and her gun in the other, she crept around their wagon, scanning the moonlit rocks and hills around them for danger. There weren't enough men in their company, not if there was a war party of Indians who'd come to attack. If something were wrong, they would need every able person—man and woman—to ward off a threat.

Boaz sniffed the ground and growled again.

"What's wrong?" she whispered.

The wind had calmed, but she still couldn't hear anything. The men were probably spread out, searching the area around the wagons. She wouldn't wander far, but with the men gone, someone needed to protect Micah and the other children in the wagons, along with women like Lucille who didn't know how to use a gun. Samantha would stand guard until they returned.

Boaz stopped, his eyes intent on a pile of rocks on their right. She watched him for a moment and then propped her gun on her shoulder, pointing it at the rocks. Her heart raced as she stepped toward the boulder. Walking close beside her, Boaz didn't make a sound.

Her tongue was so dry, it felt like a strip of rawhide between her teeth. She tried to swallow, but when she did, a wheezing sound escaped her. She stopped.

"Who's there?" a man shouted from behind the rock.

She held the gun in front of her. The accent was American, but the traders had regaled them all with stories about the thieves in this country. Had someone been following them to steal what they refused to sell at Fort Hall? Was he biding his time, waiting to attack the company?

It might be one of the men from their company, but she had to be certain. "Who are you?"

Another voice called out from behind the rock, this one sterner. "Tell us your name."

She swallowed and lowered her gun slowly at the sound of her father's voice.

"It's Samantha," she whispered.

Papa's tall form emerged above the rock, his voice trembling. "Good heavens, Samantha. I almost shot you."

She didn't tell him that she almost shot him as well.

A second man stood from behind the rocks—Captain Loewe. She couldn't see the color of his eyes, but she could see the fury in them.

"What are you doing out here?" he demanded, glaring first at her and then down at Boaz.

"Well, I was—"

The captain didn't let her finish.

"About to get yourself killed, that's what you're doing." The captain looked at her father. "Why isn't she in her tent?"

Her father was facing her instead of the captain. "I believe she was trying to help."

"We don't need your help," the captain said before he crouched back down behind the rock, dismissing her.

"I can shoot a gun." She turned to her father. "Tell him how well I can shoot."

"You need to stay back with the wagon," Papa insisted. He didn't say "*like I already told you,*" but she knew that was what he was thinking.

"Please, Papa!"

"If there was something out there, you've scared it away," the captain said, as if she'd done something wrong.

She didn't understand how scaring away a threatening animal or person would be bad, but she didn't dare disagree with the man. His anger could cause serious repercussions for their whole family.

"Go take care of Micah," Papa said.

She shifted on her feet, her gun resting at her side. "He's asleep and as safe as any of us."

Probably safer, since he was inside the security of their wagon circle.

"Go back, Samantha."

She clutched her gun with both hands, frustrated at being treated like a child, but she supposed she could guard their wagon while her father and the other men searched for intruders. Even if she wasn't needed to watch over Micah, she didn't really have a choice.

Turning slowly, she heard the footsteps of another man rustling through the sage. When she looked to her side, she saw Jack's profile in the dim light, and her heart fluttered. His eyes were focused on the circle of wagons; his brown hair rested over his collar.

Jack took her elbow, pointing her back toward the circle of wagons. "I'll make sure she gets back safely."

Frustration welled within her at his words, the flutter in her heart stilling. She could make it the twenty yards back to the wagon without assistance. "I don't need an escort, Jack."

"Samantha!" She could almost see Papa behind the rocks, shaking his head.

"I'm leaving," she huffed before she let Jack guide her and Boaz away from the men.

"I can shoot this gun as well as any of you," she muttered as they crossed through the grass.

"No one is saying that you can't, but we're doing our best to protect the women and children in this party, Samantha, and, well—" He stumbled over his words. "Whether you like it or not, you're one of our women. Your tramping out like this, on your own, makes it really difficult for us to do our job."

She wiggled her elbow free from Jack's grasp, and he didn't reach for her again. On nights like this, she wished she'd been born a man. Then she could go hunt or stand sentry instead of caring for Micah and cooking and washing laundry inside the circle. She hated feeling roped to the camp, like they had to rope Boaz to the wagon.

She didn't like Captain Loewe, hadn't liked him ever since he refused to stop along the Platte and let Amanda Perkins rest for an extra day after delivering her baby. Amanda had followed her baby boy to the grave, and her husband had returned to his family in Kentucky. Why couldn't Jack and Papa and the others see that the man wasn't capable of leading them safely to the Willamette?

Jack stopped walking, looking down at her in the moonlight. "I know you mean well, but I'm afraid you're going to get hurt in the process. Your father wasn't the only one who almost took a shot at you."

As she looked into his eyes, her heart softened just a bit. She knew Jack cared for her. She just wasn't sure if he understood her.

She stood a little taller. "I'm not going to get hurt."

"Samantha." He sighed. "A bullet would indeed hurt you."

She looked away, feeling silly. Why did he have to be right?

He slowly took the rawhide rope from her fingers and tied Boaz to their wagon. Then he looked down at her again, shifting back and forth on his feet. It was the first time they'd ever been alone, and for a moment she thought he might kiss her. But her brother might be awake in the tent, listening to them, and Jack seemed to know it. Instead of a kiss, he gave her a gentle pat on her arm and pointed at the canvas flap.

"Get some sleep," he whispered, his voice husky.

She watched him as he walked away, turning one last time as if he was checking to make sure she wouldn't try to sneak away. With a quick tilt of his hat, he continued on until the shadows swallowed him too.

Bending down, Samantha untied the rope around Boaz's neck, and her dog crawled through the flap with her and lay down at her feet. It was crowded, but Samantha wanted Boaz close.

She leaned back against the dog's soft gray fur, picking the cockle-burs off his coat as she waited for Papa to return. She never knew exactly how to pray, not like Mama did, but as both Micah and then Boaz slept beside her, she asked the Good Lord and His angels to keep Papa, Jack, and their entire company safe tonight—even the miserable Captain Loewe.

Chapter Four

"On to Oregon!" Captain Loewe shouted early the next morning. A gunshot followed his cry, the blast meant to rally every man, woman, and child from their bed whether or not they were ready to rise.

Samantha yawned as she opened her eyes to the first golden light of the sunrise. She'd wanted to stay awake long enough to find out what happened last night, but the darkness had wooed her to sleep before Papa returned.

Boaz stood as she sat up, and when she opened the tent flap, the morning sunlight flooded their small space along with the sweet smell of sage. If only she could walk down to a river to drink the water and wash the dust off her face and hands before she began breakfast.

She had to stop thinking about water.

"Micah," she whispered, nudging her brother's toes. "Time to get up."

He rubbed his eyes, and for a moment, she thought he might get up without a fight, but then he yanked the fur blanket over his head. "Leave me alone," he groaned.

She inched the blanket back off him. "I'm serious. We start rolling in an hour."

"The oxen can pull me in the wagon."

He grabbed for the blanket, but she refused to give it to him. Instead she tickled his feet. "You'll be hungry."

"No, I won't."

She sighed. "Suit yourself."

She slipped her soft moccasins over her bare feet and crawled outside the wagon to find Papa preparing their sheet-iron cooking stove, heating it with dried sagebrush and coals from last night's fire. Around the circle of wagons, the scent of frying meat and wild onions mixed with the dusty morning air as women prepared breakfast on their stoves.

Samantha whispered as she removed their coffeepot from a box. "What happened last night?"

Papa shook his head. "We couldn't find anything amiss."

Samantha searched the circle for the captain, but she didn't see him. Between the stampede and the disturbance during the night, his hatred of their dogs could only escalate. "Is he livid?"

"As angry as I've ever seen him."

She waited for her father to reprimand her for leaving the tent, but ever since Mama had died, he seemed to struggle to communicate with her.

He cleared his throat. "I'm proud of you for trying to help, Samantha."

She blinked, surprised at his words. "Thank you."

"But I need you to be more careful. I'm afraid—I can't lose you or Micah too."

"I'll try, Papa."

He gave a quick nod. "I'm going to tend to the animals."

She watched him walk away, outside the circle, before opening the barrel on the side of their wagon and dipping her ladle into the water Jack had given them. Taking a small sip, she savored the coolness on her tongue. Then she spooned three cups into the coffeepot to boil over the stove with a teaspoon of fresh grounds.

At least they still had coffee.

The dogs were romping around the wagons as if nothing had happened, and she wondered what had riled them up last night. The animals were just as tired as the people. There was no reason for them to be up barking unless something was wrong, but the men should have spotted the source of any trouble.

As she sipped her coffee sweetened with a bit of sugar, she crushed dried corn in a mortar and cooked it over the stove with water, sugar, and a pinch of cinnamon. Then she added small chunks of dried apples to it. The porridge was easy to prepare and had been tasty the first weeks of their journey, but she would give just about anything now to have scrambled eggs or flapjacks for breakfast. She hadn't eaten an egg since they left Missouri.

A few of their fellow emigrants—pilgrims, she liked to call them—brought chickens with them on this journey, but the animals hadn't lasted long. Others had brought cows to milk, but only three of those remained. Cows needed more water than the oxen, and it was much harder to find places for them to graze. Her father had decided not to bring more than three oxen and a horse, choosing instead to save their money and buy cows and chickens when they arrived in the Willamette.

"Good morning," Lucille said as she strolled into camp, little Katherine Morrison toddling beside her. Katherine had not left Lucille's side since Gerty handed her child to Lucille before the stampede.

Lucille didn't seem to mind her little shadow one bit. Even more than she wanted to be a wife, Lucille had once confided in Samantha, she wanted to be a mother.

Lucille held a pail in each of her hands, and Katherine clung to one of the handles. Lucille's blond hair was tucked neatly back inside the bonnet she'd somehow managed to keep a pale pink color for the past thirteen hundred miles. When they left Missouri, Lucille had been heavier than most eighteen-year-old women, but they'd all lost weight after walking fifteen or so miles every day.

In spite of the dust and lack of water, Lucille still managed to look refreshed and sprightly in the morning. She was blessed with an endearing calm and a naiveté that seemed to shield her from the storms, as a seashell protected a pearl from the ocean's waves.

"What a fine helper you have," Samantha said.

Lucille beamed down at the girl. "I don't know what I'd do without her."

Katherine gently swung one of Lucille's pails, and Samantha saw milk splash against the sides. If only Papa had brought one cow…

Lucille set the pail down. "Did you sleep well?"

"I don't think any of us slept well."

Katherine toddled toward Boaz and sat down beside the dog's belly, snuggling up against his fur.

Lucille nodded toward the center of the wagons, lowering her voice to a whisper. "The captain is having terrible fits this morning. I think he'd shoot every one of our dogs if he could."

"Well, he's not touching Boaz."

"My parents won't let him anywhere near Shep either." Lucille held out one of the pails. "I thought you might be thirsty for a little milk this morning."

Samantha reached for the pail and held it to her chest. "Did anyone ever tell you that you're the best friend ever?"

The flecks in Lucille's brown eyes flashed in the sunlight. "I believe someone did—the last time I brought her milk."

Samantha smiled. "This will be so good for Micah to drink."

Lucille arched her eyebrows. "It would be good for you to drink a little of it too. You look like the slightest breeze might blow you away, and then who would I talk to around here?"

Samantha almost said *Jack*, but she stopped herself. She and Lucille were the only unmarried women in their party, and she didn't want anything to come between them. As long as they didn't talk about Jack, everything was fine.

Lucille leaned closer. "Honestly, Samantha, you're beginning to look like an apparition. You need to eat more."

Samantha shook her head. She felt fine.

Lucille glanced over the circle of wagons again. "Have you seen Jack?"

Samantha poured the three or so cups of milk into her own pail. "Not this morning."

"I thought he might want some milk too."

"How could he not?"

"Oh, here he comes," Lucille said, waving at him as he rounded the circle.

Jack met Samantha's eyes and then looked away so quickly that she couldn't tell whether he was angry at her about last night. He stopped in front of them, tipping his hat. "A fine morning, ladies."

"Indeed." Lucille blushed as she held up the pail. "After such a rough night, Mama thought you might want some fresh milk to drink."

He glanced over at Samantha and gave her a quick wink before he took Lucille's pail. "That's awfully nice of you and your mother. I will enjoy it with my porridge."

Lucille looked concerned. "Who's making you breakfast?"

Jack laughed as he did every time Lucille offered to cook for him. "I know it's hard to believe, but I can still make breakfast on my own."

"Of course you can—"

"But Mrs. Kneedler offered to fry something up for me today—without onions, of course." Everyone knew that Mrs. Kneedler refused to eat onions because of her sour stomach. The rest of their stomachs had grown stronger from the camp food.

Jack cleared his throat as he turned toward Samantha. "How are you this morning?'

He had winked at her, so he must not be too angry. "Quite well."

"I'm glad to hear that." He glanced over at Lucille and then looked down at Katherine, who was still snuggling with Boaz. "How is she?"

Lucille's cheerful voice turned sad. "She doesn't seem to realize she's lost her mama."

"Maybe it's for the best," Jack said.

Samantha bristled. "She might be able to tolerate it, but I hardly thinking that losing her mother is for the best."

Jack looked back at Lucille and then nodded toward his wagon, two wagons down from the Waldrons'. "Would you mind if I had a word with Miss Waldron about some pressing business?"

Lucille's long eyelashes batted for just a moment before her gaze dropped to the milk pail. "Of course not."

"It'll be just a moment," he promised.

She and Jack stepped toward his wagon, and when he looked down at her with those light blue eyes, her heart seemed to skip a beat again. She wished she could make it stop doing that. It hindered her ability to think straight.

"You scared me last night," he said.

"I didn't mean to scare you or any of the men." She dug the toe of her moccasin into the dusty soil and twisted it. None of them seemed to understand that she only wanted to help. "Papa said you never found out what was upsetting the dogs."

"Some of us stayed up, guarding until dawn, but we didn't see anything unusual."

"Maybe there were Indians out there."

"If there weren't, those dogs were loud enough to bring an entire war party to us." He glanced over his shoulder and saw Lucille waiting for him. He nodded his head toward her and then looked at Boaz before turning back to Samantha, his eyes heavy with concern.

"If I were you, I'd keep him with you today," Jack warned.

"Is the captain that angry?"

He gave a slow nod of his head.

"I'll keep him close." When she glanced at Boaz again, she saw that Papa had returned. She wished both Jack and Lucille a good morning and rushed toward her family's wagon.

Papa shooed Micah out of his bed, and the three of them ate their porridge quickly before they tore down the tent and packed up the wagon. When the last bedroll was tossed into the wagon box, Samantha cinched up the canvas flap.

"On to Oregon!" the captain shouted again, and the lead wagon began to roll.

"On to Oregon," she replied with the others.

When they stopped again, she hoped it would be near water.

* * * * *

Alex saluted the fur-trapping brigade good-bye as they prepared to spread across the Columbia District like the web of a spider, ready to snare its prey. Some of the officers would lead parties north and west on horses trimmed with ribbons and bells. Others would travel across the Columbia River and trap animals in the canyons and forests along the southern shore. And the final party would row up the river in long birch-bark canoes to bring back pelts from the east.

The parties all carried metal traps, guns, and enough supplies to last for six months. Most years they didn't return with their bales of pelts until late spring, but this year McLoughlin had asked those companies who set up camp within thirty miles of the fort to return next month with their pelts. None of them knew when the annual supply ship would arrive from London, and with the decrease in pelts, they needed as much fur as possible to fill this ship.

Each year it was becoming increasingly difficult to trap the quantities of pelts they had harvested in the earlier years of Fort

Vancouver. As more people came to this territory, the animals retreated farther into the hills. For as long as Alex could remember, Hudson's Bay Company had shipped an average of 61,000 pounds of animal pelts each year to make hats and coats and an assortment of household goods. But if they didn't get more fur, this year's shipment would be an embarrassment, not only to Alex but to McLoughlin and their entire company.

McLoughlin stood on the boat landing in front of all of them, a glass of white wine in his hand. In a booming voice that commanded the attention of the voyageurs ready to embark into the wilderness, he prayed for God's blessing on their bounty and for the safety of all their people. Then he toasted them. A brigade of officers and trappers climbed into twenty-five waiting bateaux and began rowing up the Columbia River.

Alex turned to McLoughlin. The governor's gaze often intimidated those in his presence, but today it only inspired confidence in Alex. "You're in charge while I'm gone," McLoughlin said, his voice still loud for all to hear.

"Yes, sir."

"You'll need to keep an eye on Calvert until our new teacher arrives," McLoughlin reminded him. "Make sure he's doing his job."

"I shall do my best."

McLoughlin mounted his horse, swinging his leg over the side. "And make sure those children actually attend his classes."

"Of course."

McLoughlin stared down at him. "And please attempt to be nice to any other Americans who might arrive while we are gone."

"I cannot promise that."

McLoughlin lifted the reins. "Our duty remains to help those in need."

"I will try, sir," Alex said, but the words tasted sour in his mouth.

If word returned to London about his role in helping Americans, he would never be permitted to take his uncle's place as president of the committee when he returned to London next year.

McLoughlin snapped the reins, and he and Madame rode east with their party.

The remaining officers and servants walked back up the hill, toward the fort, but Alex lingered on the landing as he surveyed the calm bend of the Columbia River that led to the ocean. If only the Americans stayed away while McLoughlin was gone... Then Alex wouldn't have to choose between his future on the committee and his God-given duty to help those in need.

Chapter Five

"We found a stream!" Doctor Rochester shouted from his saddle, and cheers rippled over the company.

The moment the wagons stopped, Samantha untied the rawhide strip from around Boaz's neck, and he bolted toward the water. Just as Jack predicted, Captain Loewe ordered that every dog remain tied up when they ended their journey today. It wasn't fair, though, to punish the dogs for trying to protect them, and it certainly wasn't fair to keep them from water when they were so thirsty.

Samantha took Micah's hand and then picked up the folds of her calico dress with her free hand. They raced toward the small grove of trees that blazed golden in the sunlight.

The captain might be angry with her for stealing Boaz away to the stream, but she couldn't imagine him being any angrier than he'd been last night. Lately it seemed that he was angry about pretty much everything.

Beneath the knobbed gray trunks of the trees, a carpet of sage and dried sweetgrass stretched across the dry valley to the peaks of the Blue Mountains. Several children tumbled along the valley floor near Samantha and Micah, turning somersaults in the grass after hours of riding in a bumpy wagon.

Samantha was tempted to toss away her yellow bonnet, which had failed miserably at keeping the sun off her face, and tumble with the children, but Lucille and the other ladies—not to mention her father—would be mortified at the thought. No one frowned at her playing when she was a girl. It was only after she became an adult that the other adults began frowning. A lot.

Boaz jumped into the water, rolling to soak his gray fur. She lifted her skirt to her knees, kicked off her moccasins, and hopped into the cool water to wash away the heat and dust. Then she cupped her hand and sipped the sweetness of the stream, savoring every drop as it soothed her throat.

The earth trembled under her feet, and she turned to watch four oxen and two horses run toward the riverbank. Even though the men would only release a few at a time to avoid another stampede, the earth still felt as if it were about to open up.

She tugged Micah to the other side of the stream, and as he gulped the water beside her, his towhead glistened like the autumn leaves in the sunlight. He'd stripped down to the buckskin trousers she'd found for him at Fort Hall, and those were rolled up to his knees.

Lucille hurried down to the water next, accompanied by her mother and little Katherine and a crowd of women carrying pails and kettles that clanged beside them. The women laughed as they rushed toward the stream, and Samantha stopped for a moment, watching them with envy. She wished her mother were here to celebrate the finding of water with her. She wished they could laugh together and work together and even commiserate together as they cooked over their stove in the heat.

Mama had been much more fragile than most women in their forties, her body battered by frequent miscarriages and an unexplained illness that plagued her for years. When their doctor said the dry air out West might be good for her health, Papa began saving money to travel to Oregon Country. It had taken him less than a year to save the money for their journey, and Samantha suspected he'd been saving a lot longer than that.

When he finally had enough money, it was too late to save Mama. They buried her four months before they left Ohio.

Samantha dragged her pail through the stream and took another long sip from it.

Even if Mama had joined them on this journey, there would be no running alongside her or cooking over the stove together. The fifteen or twenty miles of walking each day would have been impossible for her, and the toll of a wagon ride, jostling and bumping for hours upon hours, would surely have taken her life.

Micah jumped from rock to rock in the stream, and Lucille sat down on a smooth rock beside Samantha while her mother and younger sister continued downstream a few yards.

Lucille dipped her ladle into the water, drinking like the others. "Oh, it's wonderful, isn't it?"

Samantha nodded, the breeze gently tangling her skirt around her knees. "The best water I've ever tasted."

Then Lucille eyed Boaz lapping the water. "The captain said to leave the dogs roped up for now."

She shrugged. "Boaz was just as thirsty as the rest of us."

Lucille splashed her face with the water. "I know Loewe isn't always the nicest man, but Papa says we have to listen to him since we voted for him to be captain."

"I didn't vote for him," Samantha muttered.

"No, but your father did."

He had; all the men had voted for Loewe back in Missouri, though some of them seemed to regret it now. She petted Boaz's wet fur. "It's not fair for Boaz to suffer because the other dogs were barking."

"This isn't about what is fair, Samantha. It's about keeping everyone safe in our company."

"And appeasing that man."

"Perhaps, but what is so wrong with keeping the peace?"

Another small herd of animals hurried to the water, and Captain Loewe's whistle sounded to gather the men for a meeting, as it did every night before he announced the evening plans and schedule for the night guard. No one could fault the captain for his leadership abilities. It was his temperament that got him into trouble.

Boaz bounded through the water with a giant splash, soaking her dress and bonnet. Micah laughed from the other side of the stream and then, with his blue eyes focused on her, trailed one of his arms through the water and doused her face.

"Oh—" she sputtered.

He laughed again. "You needed to be cooled off."

Water trailing down her cheeks, she returned his splash with her foot.

"Samantha!" he hollered at her as if she'd started the battle.

Lucille shook her head. "Sometimes, Miss Waldron, I think you are more eight than eighteen."

She put her hands on her hips. "I'm two months older than you."

Lucille shook her head again, like it wasn't possible.

Samantha winked at her friend and then splashed Micah again. This time her hem tore, and she sighed. She'd have to fix that after the evening meal.

She glanced over at her friend; Lucille was still shaking her head.

Lucille probably wished she could join in their fun after sweltering in the sun today, but she was much too refined to join in the splashing, no matter how hot she was.

Samantha turned slowly toward Lucille, a grin stealing up her face. Her friend's eyes narrowed. "Don't you even think about it."

But Samantha couldn't help thinking about it. It was her father in her, the part that couldn't resist a golden opportunity.

With a swift kick, she splattered water across Lucille's pale green traveling dress.

For a moment, the sounds of nature around her seemed to still. The rustle of the leaves quieted, and she no longer heard the gentle lapping of the stream as it flowed over the river rocks. Lucille's mother and her sister and all the women turned, watching to see how Lucille would react, to see if the water would crack the calm.

Lucille didn't crack.

Words, as useless as they were, didn't form on her lips. Instead she slowly scooped up a ladleful of the stream and she flung it at Samantha. She ducked, and Lucille gasped.

Turning, Samantha saw the elderly Prudence Kneedler behind her—gray hair sopping and water trickling down her ears and cheeks.

At first, Samantha watched Mrs. Kneedler in horror, waiting for the woman to scold her. Instead, Mrs. Kneedler lowered her pail to the water and reciprocated with her own blast.

In seconds, the entire party of women and children was splashing under the hot sun, Boaz weaving in between the arcs of water. Leave it to Boaz to begin a water fight, injecting a shot of life into their tired party.

A gun blasted from the wagons behind them, and the laughter stopped.

Women and children alike turned back toward the wagons now positioned in a perfect circle, with each tailboard butted against the front of the neighboring wagon to create a fence for the livestock as well as a makeshift fortress. It wasn't anywhere near as secure as the wooden forts they'd passed on the trail, but it was the best they could create.

The dogs they'd left behind began to bark, and Samantha shaded her eyes against the sunlight to see if something was threatening their wagons. But she couldn't see either people or animals. Perhaps the men had spotted a herd of antelope or even bison coming to the stream to drink.

She hated the thought of killing any animal, but her stomach rumbled at the thought of fresh meat for supper. It had been weeks since they'd eaten good meat—a buffalo that Jack shot near Fort Laramie.

When another shot rang out near the wagons, Samantha stepped out of the stream.

"Will you watch Micah for me?" she asked Lucille.

Lucille glanced over at the wagons and then back at Samantha. "Where are you going?"

"To find out what is happening."

"There's nothing you can do—"

"I'll be right back."

"Do be careful, Samantha."

She picked up her torn hem and hurried toward the wagons with Boaz at her side. Smoke from a campfire drifted up from the center of the circle, but no one was inside the enclosure. She didn't see any of the men out chasing a deer or buffalo, either.

Where had everyone gone?

She rushed toward the camp to retrieve her rifle from their wagon in case Indians were threatening them.

She stopped when she reached her wagon. The men were standing outside the circle, huddled together as if trying to decide what to do with a buck they'd killed. Quickly she threw open the back of their wagon's canopy to retrieve her rifle, but she jumped back at what she saw. Her father was inside the packed wagon, sitting amid their goods on Mama's prized rosewood chest. His face was the same ashen color as the trees that guarded the stream.

Her stomach seemed to plummet to her toes. Papa never missed the evening meetings.

"What is it?" she whispered.

Papa shook his head, looking down at Boaz with a sadness she didn't understand. "There's been a vote."

Her eyes widened. "What sort of vote?"

"The captain—he doesn't think it's safe for us to continue with the dogs."

"Not safe?" Her voice began to escalate. "What do you mean, it's not safe?"

He shook his head again.

Her voice quivered. "It's not safe to finish this journey *without* our dogs."

"Last night—" he began, but she interrupted him.

"Last night was an anomaly, Papa, you know that. The dogs hardly ever bark like that."

He brushed his hands on his dusty trousers and stood up, hopping over the tailboard and landing on the ground beside her. "It's not about last night. It's about the stampede at the Snake. Those dogs could have killed all of us."

She leaned against the wagon, trying to make sense of what Papa was saying. They needed their dogs. They didn't bring harm to the camp—they protected them from harm.

Another shot blasted, and she slowly turned toward the men who'd edged into a half circle. The terrible realization, the truth of what they were doing, plunged into her gut and burned like a raging fire. She didn't want to ask Papa what was happening, didn't dare believe it possible. Her voice trembled again, barely a whisper, the thought so incredulous that she could barely form the words.

"Are they—" She thought she might retch. "Is he killing our dogs?"

At Papa's nod, anger blazed through her skin and her mind raged. "But the men—you said they had to vote before he can kill our animals."

"We did vote." His gaze traveled over to their fellow travelers. "It was nine to eight."

Boaz sat up, nuzzling her dress as if he could sense her devastation. She placed her shaky hand on his wet coat. How could nine men vote to kill their guard dogs? Their shepherd dogs.

Their pets.

She understood why Titus Morrison would vote to kill the animals that killed his wife, and it was clear the captain no longer wanted the animals with them. But the other men...

She knew they were afraid of being ostracized, afraid of the captain's wrath, but how dare they affirm the man's insanity? And it was insanity.

She reached into the wagon for her gun.

"It's more than the barking," her father tried to explain. "The men at Fort Hall said—"

She didn't let him finish. "They aren't touching him."

"It's not our choice to make."

"Not our choice?" Her voice escalated. "He's our dog. My dog!"

She'd cared for Boaz for four years, from the time Papa brought him home as a puppy barely weaned. She'd coddled him, probably too much, as she raised him, but he'd been a good dog, fiercely protective of Micah and her. Boaz wouldn't let a bullet or a man touch any of them, not without a fight, and she wouldn't allow any of the men or their bullets to touch him. He hadn't been the one to cause the stampede, nor had he been up barking last night.

"If we don't allow this, they'll leave us behind," Papa pleaded, trying to make her understand. "And if they leave us behind..."

His voice trailed off, but she'd heard the stories about those who'd attempted to travel this journey alone. At Fort Hall, the traders had told them that no pioneering family could survive this trip without a caravan. Not only was there the threat of hostile Indians and wild animals, there were storms and fires and all sorts of strange illnesses. Hunger and thirst, raging rivers and steep mountains, broken axles, and exhausted oxen.

They needed each other—and their animals—to make it to the Willamette. Surely the captain wouldn't leave them behind.

But as she examined her father's face, she realized that he thought Captain Loewe would make good on his threat.

When Hiram Waldron and the other men signed the laws of their wagon train, they'd agreed to reasonable laws about what time to rise, a day of rest on the Sabbath, no swearing or drinking alcohol on their journey west. No one had said anything about killing dogs.

She pulled Boaz closer to her side, his wet head nuzzling her arm. "They aren't shooting him."

"Samantha—"

"You know it's wrong, Papa."

He raked his fingers through his hair. "Of course it's wrong, but there's nothing we can do about it."

"But Boaz...he's like family."

Papa's gaze traveled over her shoulder, and she knew that someone was behind her. She didn't dare turn around.

Her finger tightened around the barrel of her gun. If Papa couldn't stop this man, she would have to do it alone.

"Miss Waldron?"

She turned slowly, defiantly. Captain Loewe was several steps behind her, his gray eyes crazed with power. She couldn't kill an animal, but the captain—

He glared down at Boaz as if he'd instigated all the trouble. "We need your dog," the captain said, his voice a steely calm.

"My dog's name is Boaz," she said, matching the calm of his voice. Then she stepped in front of her pet to shield him from the captain and his pistol. "And he bites."

Chapter Six

"Speak some sense into your daughter," Captain Loewe demanded as he looked between father and daughter.

Samantha didn't waver. One of her hands curled around her flintlock, and the other wove through Boaz's fur.

"I've been trying to talk sense into her for almost twenty years, but sometimes good sense seems to deflect off her." Even with the resignation in Papa's tone, she heard a thread of the Waldron pride. Papa may not always agree with her, but he never stopped her from standing up for what she thought was right. And this was clearly right.

"Step away," the captain ordered her, waving his pistol like the Blackfeet Indians had waved their bows during a confrontation back in Kansas.

But even as she held his gaze, doubts bubbled up in her like the springs of soda they'd passed two days ago. What if the captain did turn their family away and force them to travel alone? What if he decided to make a spectacle of the Waldrons for their—for *her*—insubordination? Papa was only trying to protect them from harm, but Micah's heart would break as well if these men killed Boaz. He'd already lost Mama. Losing Boaz now would crush him…and it would crush her too.

Captain Loewe glanced down at her soaked dress with a bit of scorn as he repeated his command. "We need your dog, Miss Waldron."

"What are you going to do if the children get too loud at night?" She glanced back at her father. "What if Micah wakes up with nightmares, screaming in the darkness? Would you let this man kill him too?"

The captain shook his head. "That's ridiculous."

She turned back to the captain. "Boaz is a member of our family too."

He narrowed his eyes. "Do you know what rabies is?"

She stiffened. "I've heard the stories."

"If a rabid coyote bites one of our dogs and then that dog turns on the rest of us…" The captain paused.

"What does this have to do—"

"There's no cure for rabies."

She couldn't bear to look toward where the men had shot the animals. "Have any of our dogs been bitten?"

He pounded his hand into his fist. "This is the reason why women are not allowed to vote."

"Because they might make sense?"

His eyes were still on her even as he threatened her father. "If you don't force her to obey, Hiram, there will be consequences."

Papa didn't respond. Nor did Samantha cower.

The others might not stand up to this man, but she wouldn't back down. Loewe might force their family to leave the train, but he couldn't keep them from following close behind. And if they had to, the Waldron family could make it through the wilderness alone.

The thought crossed her mind of a bird separated from its flock. A hawk's choice prey.

She shook her head, refusing to entertain the thought. Saving Boaz and the remaining dogs was the right thing to do, and her father knew it. So did the rest of the men who were watching the confrontation between her and the captain.

"I'm taking your dog." The captain's words sounded more like a growl.

She glanced at her father, and he gave her the slightest nod of his approval. He didn't want them to kill Boaz either. "No, you're not."

"What are you going to do?"

She lifted her rifle. "I told you I knew how to use a gun."

"You're going to shoot me?" His head bent back, laughter punctuating his words.

"Not if you leave Boaz alone."

He eyed her for a second, as if gauging whether she was telling the truth. His eyes remained on her as he spoke. "Doyle, come here."

Her stomach turned as she watched Jack tread slowly toward her. She wished for the man who used to wink at her around the campfire when Papa was telling one of the many stories about Samantha's antics as a child, the man who'd brought her flowers when he returned from scouting trips, the man who traded a buffalo hide for a loaf of sugar at Fort Laramie for her family.

Jack was twenty-eight, two decades younger than the captain, but he was strong and smart. Surely he would stand up to this lunacy.

She rolled her shoulders back, facing him, but Jack wouldn't look at her. His hat dipped over his hazel eyes, covering his wavy brown hair and handsome face. He was built for this journey, his arms and back strong, but despite his strength, his voice was resigned. "Yes, sir."

The captain's gaze remained on her. "Miss Waldron, here, won't relinquish her animal."

Jack looked down at her, and she silently pleaded with him, begging him with her gaze to rescue her dog and her family from harm. Jack's eyes weren't harsh like the captain's, nor were they wild. They were concerned. Conflicted, even.

Surely she had an ally in him.

Instead of speaking out, Jack looked back at Captain Loewe. "I'd like a moment to speak with Samantha."

The captain shook his head. "Talking to her is not gonna do you a bit of good. She doesn't listen to reason."

Her eyes were on the captain when she stepped forward. "C'mon, Boaz."

Her dog stayed close at her side as they moved away from the wagons, as if he was the one who needed to guard her from the guns. On the other side of the wagons, she heard the shouts of children as they returned with their mothers from the stream. Some of them were laughing, oblivious to what awaited them. There may not be as much barking tonight in the camp, but she guessed there would be crying.

There were no trees or rocks for her and Jack to hide behind, not so close to the wagons. With Captain Loewe and Papa watching them, Samantha's voice dipped to a whisper. "Were you one of the nine?" she asked.

Jack's gaze dropped to the worn toes on his boots. "I wish you'd trust me to do what is right."

Her back stiffened. "What is right, Jack?"

"It's right to protect the women and children in our care from harm."

She refused to back down. "It was one dog who started the stampede, not all of them."

His eyes met hers, but this time they didn't make her heart flutter. "This is dangerous territory, Samantha. Dogs could cause another stampede or scare away some of our livestock or—"

"Or they make us lose a little sleep at night."

He crossed his arms over his chest. "This isn't because we lost sleep."

"Maybe something was out there last night. The dogs could have been warning us."

He crossed his arms over his chest. "All it takes is one dog to disrupt our entire company."

"Or one child."

"It's more than the stampede, Samantha. One of the dogs had been bitten by a coyote at Fort Hall earlier this summer. They thought he had rabies."

"I understand shooting a rabid dog, Jack, but the captain—" She huffed. "He said none of our animals have been bitten."

"But think of what could happen if they were."

"You and the others, you're afraid of what you don't know." She paused. "You're afraid of what the captain might do even though you know he's wrong."

She leaned against Boaz, who was standing as still as a statue beside her, and her lips shook as she fought back her tears. Her father had wavered in the authority of the captain, and now Jack wouldn't stand up to him either. "You've got to stop him," she said.

"I can't stop him," Jack replied with a shake of his head. "We have to keep the peace until we get to the Willamette. Then we'll go our separate ways. At least most of us will…"

She didn't allow herself to linger on the implication of his words. How could she marry a man who wouldn't fight for the dog she loved? Who wouldn't fight for her?

"You have to stop him, Jack, or I can't—"

He shook his head, backing away. "I only want to protect our party, Sam. I don't want to hurt your dog."

"Boaz," she whispered. "My dog's name is Boaz."

A scream rose up from one of the wagons, followed by the wails of a child. Samantha blinked back her tears, turning away from the man she thought she would marry.

The Captain. Jack. Even Papa, whom she adored. These men didn't know what they were doing in not consulting the women before they proceeded with this deplorable action. The husbands might be afraid of stampedes and disease, but they were clearly more afraid of their wives. Otherwise they would have told them of the decision and allowed them to say their good-byes.

She'd heard three shots as she was coming from the stream. Colt, she guessed, and two other dogs were no longer members of their party. What would happen to the remaining dogs?

The sound of crying grew louder, and a woman began to yell hysterically. She tightened her hold on Boaz's neck. It was too late to remedy what had been done. A chasm had been chiseled through their community. "This is going to destroy us," she whispered.

Jack's gaze wandered back to the circle of wagons, his voice resigned. "I'm afraid you might be right."

And it could destroy her and Jack.

The captain was gone when they returned to her family's wagon. Her father was quietly setting up the tent beside it, Micah helping him. Micah rushed to Boaz, wrapping his arms around the dog's neck. Papa nodded to Jack before Samantha climbed into the safety of the tent. She didn't know where Jack went, and at that moment, she didn't particularly care.

* * * * *

No more dogs were killed that night, but the dark shadow of despondency descended over the party as they ate their evening meal. No one sang or played music as the blazes of the campfires cooled into beds of coal. She doubted any of the company would sleep well either.

Papa let Boaz sleep in the tent, between Samantha and Micah.

"No barking," she whispered as she wrapped one of her arms over Boaz. If he caused any sort of ruckus, she would never be able to convince the men of their need for him.

Her brother reached for her hand and squeezed her fingers. "Thanks, Samantha."

She held on to his hand until his breathing stilled. Then, through the flap in the tent, she looked out at the wide sky and breathed a thank-you to the God of the wilderness for rescuing her dog.

Jack's face, so handsome and stalwart, flashed through her mind. What was she supposed to do? She couldn't marry him, not if he was one of the nine, but she didn't know how she could make Papa understand. Her father loved Boaz, but not like she did. He would think that she was being foolish if she didn't marry Jack on account of a dog.

Someone cried in one of the wagons, and she heard two other people shouting at each other.

Tomorrow their company would have to mend the chasm that cut through them like the Snake had cut through the canyon. Tomorrow they would have to continue their journey on to Oregon as a community.

Then, when they got to the Willamette, they would do as Jack said and go their separate ways.

Chapter Seven

"What do you mean, he left?" Alex exclaimed, slamming his fist on the desk.

The eleven-year-old boy in front of him jumped, and the low buzz of voices in the schoolroom stopped as the eyes of all the children focused on him.

Ever since McLoughlin left Alex to run the fort, it felt as if everything were collapsing around him. The laborers were behind in building a new warehouse for their furs to replace the one that burned down last year, the women were having trouble keeping up with the demand to make a thousand nails a day, the trading post was eerily slow this week in its business with the natives, and now the schoolteacher had disappeared.

The palisades remained stalwart around the fort, but with everything else falling down inside them, he wouldn't be shocked if they collapsed as well.

Everett stepped back. "I don't mean anything else by it, sir. I just—I saw him walking out the gate last night."

Alex took a deep breath as he tried to calm himself. He needed to concentrate on housing and inventorying this next shipment of furs instead of worrying about the school, but he had promised McLoughlin that he would make sure the children were in school. This promise was impossible without a teacher. Perhaps their Mr. Calvert had simply overslept after his late night on the other side of those gates or was ill in his bed.

"Was he carrying any sort of satchel?" Alex asked.

The boy glanced at his toes and then looked back up at him. "He was carrying a knapsack…and a couple of blankets."

Alex tried to swallow the anger that pressed against his throat. He'd suspected that Calvert was interested in a young Chinook woman who often came to the trading post with her father, but the teacher had never done anything that Alex would deem inappropriate. As long as Calvert did his job well, teaching the fort's growing bounty of children, and didn't interfere with the delicate balance of their relationship with the local Indian tribes, there had been no reason for Alex to complain.

"Return to your seat," Alex said, pointing to one of the roughly hewn desks.

He scanned the faces of the twenty-three students who ranged in age from six to fourteen years old. Many of them had the copper skin of their Indian mothers and the unkempt hair of their fur-trading fathers.

McLoughlin insisted that every one of Fort Vancouver's children receive a good education, and he'd hired Calvert for the position until the new teacher arrived with the next ship from England. McLoughlin and his wife were still traveling with the fur-trapping party, and if the fort's teacher had indeed snuck out during the night, Alex didn't have any idea what to do about the school.

He glanced out the window of the schoolhouse, examining the wide gate that opened each morning and closed at night. There was much more pressing business to attend to, but he'd promised McLoughlin that he would make sure the children attended school.

Then he looked back at Everett. "Why didn't you tell me before they locked the gate?"

"I—I figured that he was just going to see, er, a friend or someone else outside. I thought he would be back by morning."

Alex—and most of the students, for that matter—knew exactly what the boy was implying. None of the men went out at night to visit mere friends. But if he had left… No, Calvert couldn't possibly leave all these schoolchildren waiting for him. It was ludicrous.

Alex opened one of the few books on the man's desk, a copy of *Robinson Crusoe.*

His leaving may seem ludicrous, but there *was* a bit of idiocy in Calvert. He had traveled all the way from England to make his fortune in fur trading, but when he failed miserably at trapping, he'd come knocking on McLoughlin's door in June, asking about a position. They needed laborers to help erect new buildings outside the fort, but Calvert apparently believed that he was much too educated to be a common laborer.

So McLoughlin gave him the only other position that was available, due to the fact that no one else—officer, tradesman, or laborer—wanted to teach the fort's unruly children. They weren't paying Calvert the fortune he had originally sought, but he was a fairly educated man—educated quite well by the standards of this district. McLoughlin was paying a modest salary out of his personal income for Calvert to show up at six o'clock, five mornings every week, to teach these children and teach them well.

"Should we go search for him?" a girl asked. He recognized her as the daughter of one of his British clerks. He wasn't sure who her mother was.

A boy snickered. "You ain't gonna find old Cal if he don't wanna to be found."

The girl's short braids twirled when she turned toward the boy, her hands on her hips. "Maybe he's hurt or something. He might be a-needing us to find him."

Alex sighed. Calvert had obviously failed to teach those who spoke English to do so properly.

The young girl turned back, grinning up at Alex. "Maybe you could teach us?"

This time several of the boys snorted.

"We will find Calvert," he said. And when he did, he'd tan the man.

Everett sat up straighter at his desk. "Can we go look for him with you?"

"No, you return home today." With his wave, chairs grated across the wooden floor as the children sprang to their feet. Half of them were already through the door when he called out, "Tomorrow. We'll have school tomorrow!"

If Calvert returned...

All twenty-three children were gone in less than a minute's time. He wished he could motivate the men under him as quickly as he'd motivated these students. Of course, if he gave his men a day off from work, they'd evacuate just as fast.

Closing the schoolroom door, Alex marched across the piazza toward Bachelor's Hall. He didn't think living in the wilderness was good for children, but the governor disagreed. McLoughlin rarely got angry, but when he did, it was most disconcerting for all those who witnessed it. The disappearance of Calvert might be one of those times.

If Alex ran the fort, he'd find a way for all of them to go to school in the East, where they could receive a decent education. But he didn't run the fort. Or at least, not when McLoughlin was here.

He strode up to the second floor of the hall and pounded on the fourth door to his left. When no one answered, he lifted the latch to Calvert's room and pushed the door open. There were no clothes hanging from the pegs along the wall, no blankets on the narrow bed. But there was a note on the windowsill, and Alex read it quickly. Then he balled it up.

Calvert wasn't coming back, and the schoolboy was right. It

would be useless to search for him. He had gone to live among the Indians, and Alex knew that they would be moving this time of year—hunting pelts and collecting food for the winter. If Calvert married the Chinook woman, her tribe would protect him.

McLoughlin was the only one who had any hope of retrieving Calvert—if he wanted the man to return. Some natives called McLoughlin "The White-Headed Eagle," while others called him "King of the Columbia." He was a peacemaker to them, and a *tilikum*—friend. He insisted that the clerks trade fairly with the Indians, and he even ransomed children the local tribes kept as slaves, offering eight to ten wool blankets in exchange for each one.

While the Indians were civil enough to Alex, he doubted they would ever refer to him as a friend.

He heard footsteps coming up the hall and turned to see Simon Gervais.

Simon scanned the empty room. "I heard Calvert's missing."

Alex tossed the note onto the bed. "And he does not plan to return."

"The man was never cut out to be a teacher."

"Sometimes we must do things we are not cut out to do," Alex snapped.

Simon backed toward the door. "I don't condone his leaving. I'm just speaking the truth."

"McLoughlin will be furious."

"It won't be the first time."

Alex studied his friend for a moment. Simon was responsible for training the new clerks assigned to the general store. He was as educated as most of the men. "You went to school, did you not?"

"Until the fifth grade. When I wasn't working with my mother."

"You could teach them, then. Just until we find a replacement."

Simon's laughter followed Alex into the hallway.

Alex shook his head. "I was not trying to be humorous."

"I don't know the first thing about teaching children," Simon said, walking with him down the hall.

Alex shrugged. "It is much like training your clerks, I suppose."

"You don't know anything about teaching children either."

"I am well aware of that." Alex cleared his throat. "But it cannot be *that* difficult."

Calvert had taught them, after all.

"I suppose it would be quite easy." Simon laughed again. "As easy as taming a classroom full of wild horses."

They stepped onto the first floor, into the great room where the men ate during the day and danced at night. Simon pointed toward the window. "Maybe she'd like to teach."

Alex followed Simon's finger, his eyes landing on the lovely Taini walking outside. It wasn't a bad solution, except that she spoke more French than English. And they needed a man to control those children. "I would never subject a woman to that classroom."

Without a teacher, he could not keep his word to McLoughlin to keep the children in school. But he certainly couldn't educate them himself. He knew how to manage the clerks and the laborers at the fort, but he had no idea how to teach their children.

* * * * *

Before the day dawned, Boaz nudged Samantha's arm. There was a scuffling sound outside their wagon, and she sat up in the darkness, listening to footsteps and hushed whispers.

"Good boy," she whispered. Thank God, he hadn't barked once during the night.

She listened for the familiarity of her father's voice in the whispers outside, but she couldn't tell who was speaking. She scooted toward the edge of the tent, hoping to understand what was being said.

"Papa," she called out, and the voices stopped.

Her father replied, not at all in the groggy voice that usually greeted her this early in the morning. "What is it?"

"I just—" she stuttered, flustered at not knowing who else was outside their tent. "Is all well?"

"As well as it can be," he said. "Go back to sleep."

Minutes later the whispering ensued. She couldn't drift back to sleep, no matter how tired she was from the short night. The dogs hadn't kept them up, but the crying and arguing had echoed through the camp for hours.

She waited until the first light slipped over the horizon, and then she brushed her hair and braided it quickly before covering her head with her bonnet. When she stood, Boaz joined her and they carefully slipped out of the tent, trying not to wake Micah. She wouldn't wander too far away.

Fires were already smoldering inside the circle, coffeepots boiling on camp stoves and skillets bubbling with grease, but instead of the familiar morning activity, the camp was almost empty. And disturbingly quiet. Several women shuffled around the fires and stoves, but she didn't see any of the men.

She and Boaz rounded the wagons until she heard Papa's voice on the other side of one of the canopies, and she quickly crossed the circle to hear what he was saying.

"Many of us are angry right now, but we must be reasonable," Papa said.

"We made a pact back in Missouri." Captain Loewe's voice sounded strained. "We all agreed to the rules."

Someone else interrupted him. "Reasonable rules!"

"They were reasonable rules—*are* reasonable rules," the captain said, correcting himself. "But now you want mutiny."

"What we want is a new captain," Mrs. Kneedler replied.

Samantha stepped closer, wondering how the captain would respond to the older woman. "I guess I should be glad the decision isn't up to you," he said.

"Arthur—"

"Perhaps we should have a new vote," Mr. Kneedler said.

"You voted for me to be your captain, and I took and still take this role very seriously, but when people undermine me as they did yesterday…"

He didn't mention Samantha's name, but she knew he must be embarrassed, especially since the one doing the undermining had been a woman.

"It was a bad decision," another man said.

"It was a decision you voted for," the captain retorted.

"And now regret."

"Regrets won't get us to Oregon," Loewe replied. "We have to rally and get moving this morning to get through the Blue Mountains before the snow comes."

"We will move," Mr. Kneedler replied. "Once we elect a new captain."

"Wait a moment." She recognized the voice of the doctor, George Rochester. "We voted for our captain back in Missouri, and we need to stick by him. He's gotten us safely this far, and I, for one, have the confidence that he'll get us all the way to the Willamette."

"He hasn't gotten all of us here safely," Mr. Kneedler replied.

This time Jack spoke. "Those deaths weren't Loewe's fault."

"Let's not cast blame about the past," Papa said. "We must determine how we proceed from here."

Samantha shivered in the morning air and leaned back against the wagon, not wanting those on the other side to see her or Boaz.

Lucille slipped up beside her. "What are they talking about?" she whispered.

"Whether or not we should keep Loewe as our wagon master."

"Of course they should—" Lucille began, but Samantha hushed

her. Sometimes Papa acted as if she were no older than Micah, as if he had to protect her from the reality of adulthood. He'd certainly send her away if he knew she was outside.

"We agreed to do as the majority voted," the captain said.

Mrs. Kneedler spoke again. "The women should be included in the majority."

"Most of the women would have voted with me," he insisted. "Any decent mother would protect her children from the threat of another stampede, not to mention rabies."

"I believe you just said that my wife isn't a decent mother," Mr. Kneedler retorted.

"We have to think rationally," the captain continued. "We have to do what is best for everyone."

"My wife and I refuse to go on with you as captain," Mr. Kneedler said.

There was a long pause. "So be it," the captain finally said.

Papa spoke again. "You can't do this alone, Arthur."

"We won't be alone."

Samantha imagined Mr. Kneedler pointing to the heavens with his words. He liked to remind them that no matter how lonely they might feel, they were never alone.

"The Good Lord gave us each other," Papa said.

"He also warned us about bad counsel."

"You think it's been hard up until now," Captain Loewe's voice grew loud again. "It's going to be a hundred times harder, getting through those mountains."

"How would you know?" another man asked.

Lucille reached out and took Samantha's hand. Since none of them had traveled through Oregon Country before, their party had just kept traveling west, trying to follow vague directions from the traders who knew this territory.

"Maybe we should go back to Fort Hall," Titus Morrison said. "We could stay there for the winter."

Everyone was silent, the recent death of his wife heavy upon all of them. Titus might want to return east with his daughter, but Samantha knew Papa and Jack wouldn't. They'd signed up to go to the Willamette, and they wanted to be there before winter.

A drop of rain splattered on Samantha's arm, and for the first time she noticed the darkening clouds in the sky. After such a hot day yesterday, the rain would feel good. But it was also a reminder that more storms would come with the autumn—unfamiliar weather like the hailstorm they'd had on the prairie and the winds from a waterspout that had overturned several of the wagons, tearing off two canvas covers and blowing them away.

The men and women began to debate, and the moment someone called for a vote, Samantha watched Micah and his buckskin trousers slip out of the tent.

"I've got to go," she told Lucille before she hurried back across the circle, her eyes on her brother to make sure he didn't wander away.

Would the Kneedlers really continue this journey alone, without their dog? Or would Titus and some of the others return back to Fort Hall?

Hopefully Papa would talk sense into all of them. If Papa was good at anything, he was good at talking sense into just about anyone. Except his daughter.

She found Micah hovered over his knapsack, sorting through his things.

"Are you hungry?" she asked.

He looked up at her. "For scrambled eggs."

"Me too," she said. "Why don't we scramble our porridge today?"

She had breakfast prepared by the time Papa returned from the meeting. Micah picked at his scrambled porridge and drank only a few sips of his coffee. Samantha told him he needed to eat more to keep up his strength for their long walk today, but he shook his head.

She hesitated, turning to Papa. "Did you fill up the water barrel?"

"I will before we leave."

"Papa—"

"I won't forget this time."

She nodded and began gathering up their dishes in a tub to scrub them down at the river. Papa spoke. "The Kneedlers have decided to leave our company."

She put the tub down, turning back to face him. Sadness washed over her. "Can they make it on their own?"

"They won't be alone." He paused. "A few others are thinking about going with them."

Relief passed through her at first, and then her heart seemed to collapse. They'd been a community for months now.

"What about us?" she dared to ask.

"Your mama would never forgive me if I didn't keep you and Micah safe."

She stirred her porridge. "Do you think Captain Loewe is going to keep us safe?"

"No one can guarantee safety out here."

An hour later, Samantha and Lucille both cried as they hugged each other good-bye. Then Captain Loewe released his familiar cry. "On to Oregon!"

Wheels began turning as the oxen heaved the wagons forward through the valley, but this time the Kneedler family didn't follow him.

And neither did the Waldrons.

Chapter Eight

About a dozen feet ahead of Samantha, Micah walked with Papa, hand in hand. The knapsack bobbed over Micah's shoulder, and their palomino trailed behind them. Samantha smiled as she watched the boy who kept stopping to wipe the dust off the noses of their oxen so they could breathe. The boy who wanted to be just like his father.

When God created her brother, he'd lit the boy with sunshine from his light hair to the smile that radiated on his face. Samantha loved his laughter as he played with his Noah's Ark set, bobbing the animals up and down as if they were in a great flood.

Papa had carved the ten wooden animals for Micah after he was born, but he'd never had time to carve the actual ark. Micah never seemed to mind. He'd brought every one of the animals on this journey and transformed crates and boxes into his ark.

When Samantha turned twelve, Mama thought she was much too old to be off hunting and fishing. But in those hours that Papa was out stomping through the forest without her, she and Mama had grown closer. Mama had asked Samantha to care for Micah when she passed on to the Celestial City, as she liked to quote from *The Pilgrim's Progress*. Samantha promised her that she would.

Mama also wanted her to marry a man who would care for Micah as well, in case something happened to Papa. At one time, Mama thought it might be the clerk in Papa's law office—until Mama was well enough to spend an entire afternoon with the stuffy Reginald

Poole. That evening, Mama said she would never permit Samantha to marry such a disagreeable man.

A laugh bubbled on Samantha's lips at the memory. Her skin was raw from the dryness and the sun. Her legs ached. There was nothing she'd like to do more than take a bubbly bath, wrap herself in clean sheets, and sleep on a real mattress. But she was also grateful that she never married that man.

She looked beyond her father and brother to the other wagons in their party struggling up the mountain. When they left Missouri, the billowy white of the wagons' bonnets had been a symbol of their hope and determination. The canvases were now shredded and streaked with brown. They'd spent the past week felling trees and creeping over piles of rocks, uncertain whether they would ever make it to the other side.

Captain Loewe and his train of ten wagons had disappeared on the horizon five days ago, while the Waldrons traveled with the four remaining families who'd decided they no longer trusted Loewe's leadership. Eleven people were in this party including their new captain—Jack Doyle. She didn't miss Captain Loewe one bit, but she did miss Lucille and Doctor Rochester and the doctor's kind wife.

Jack was serving them faithfully as captain, but he stopped coming to the Waldrons' fire at night. Samantha didn't know if he was ashamed at how he'd handled the situation back in the valley or if he was too busy with his new responsibilities to associate with her family. Or maybe he was still angry with her. She was certainly angry with him.

She licked her lips as they climbed, wishing she could take a cup of water from their barrel. Papa had remembered to fill it, but she knew it was low again. And she couldn't ask Papa to stop the oxen anyway. Perhaps when they reached the top of this mountain, they would rest.

Wind captured the canopy of their wagon, and it flapped against the hoops. The wind tangled Samantha's skirt around her legs and blew dirt into her eyes. The traders had described the Willamette Valley to all of them—the grass and fertile soil and water. The mild temperatures and acres of wood for houses and furniture.

The Blue Mountains, though, were daunting.

As she pushed through the wind, she pretended that she was almost to the Willamette. That tonight she could bake bread for Papa and Micah and sleep in a feather bed with lots of blankets. Papa could read the family Bible by the fireplace. He'd make a new fiddle to replace the one he'd left in Ohio and play it by the fire.

As the wagons ahead of her moved toward the mountain's peak, the ground flattened. The party's wagons stopped in a narrow line. At first, Samantha thought they'd found water for the night, but Jack rode toward them with a grim look on his face.

"What is it?" Papa asked. Even though he tried to mask it, Samantha heard the worry in his voice.

"We've come to a cliff."

Papa sighed. "Any sign of water?"

Jack ground his heel into the dirt, shaking his head. "Do you think we should stop for the day?"

"We can't stop." Papa eyed the sun leaning toward the horizon. "The animals need water."

Samantha could see for miles up here, the mountaintops rippling out as if they were traveling across a giant pond. But Jack was right. Their path stopped at a cliff that sloped a good fifteen feet. Beyond that rose a mountain higher than any she'd seen yet.

Jack, Papa, and two other men fanned out to see if there was another way around this cliff and mountain, but when they returned, they announced that there was no other way. They had to lower the wagons down the cliff, and to do it, they had to lighten their loads. The heavier items would be impossible to lower with the wagons and then drag up the next mountain, especially if they wanted to take their remaining food and enough seeds to plant crops on the other side.

It had been painstakingly slow, climbing the steep mountains through the trees. At this pace, it may take them another month or even two before they got to the Willamette. There was no way they could make it before the snow.

If only the men could fell some of these giant trees or find a trail to take into a valley, they might be able to make it through the mountains before November. No one wanted to admit that they were lost, and they refused to discuss what would happen if winter arrived while they were still in the mountains.

Samantha climbed into the back of the wagon and smoothed her hands over the dark grain of her mother's rosewood chest, sniffing one last time the sweet scent that lingered in its grain. The chest had been a wedding gift from her grandfather to her mama almost twenty-five years ago. Mama had treasured it.

Before Papa and Arthur lifted it out of the wagon, Samantha took out the linens, the clothing, their family's Bible, and Mama's copy of *The Pilgrim's Progress*. She wished now that she had brought more of Mama's smaller treasures instead of the chest so they could carry them all the way.

She lifted Mama's shawl out of the chest, the shawl Mama had displayed on the formal chair in her room until she died. It was made of white wool, embroidered with lilac and green flowers, and every time Samantha looked at it, she remembered her mother's love of beauty.

She packed the heirlooms and clothing in a burlap bag and put them back into the wagon. They all knew that there would be sacrifices on this journey—they'd already given up their homes and gardens and most of their furniture. How much more would they have to give up before they arrived at their new home?

Papa stared down at the chest as if he were leaving Mama behind instead of her things.

"She would understand," Samantha whispered.

He slowly turned away, wiping his dusty sleeve over his eyes. "The important thing is that our family gets to the Willamette. Together."

She nodded, her heart warming with his words. That was exactly what Mama would have wanted.

Papa removed the extra axle he'd stored under the wagon and set it on the ground beside Mama's chest. It was either that or the tools he'd brought to farm their new land, and she knew he wasn't ready to give up their prospects for the future.

Dust clouded around them as Jack rode his horse up to their wagon and hopped off beside her. Papa turned toward the wagon and called for Micah.

Jack eyed the chest before looking at her. "I'm sorry, Samantha."

"It's not your fault," she said with a shrug. "It's a small sacrifice."

His eyebrows climbed.

"Really," she insisted.

Jack took off his hat as he studied her. The families in front and behind them were busy unloading their wagons and reorganizing, trying to determine what they could leave behind in the wilderness and what they couldn't live without. The easy smile had been erased from his face, replaced with a worry that concerned her.

"How are you?" he asked.

"At this moment—a bit sad. And worried."

"It's a tough journey for everyone."

She searched his face. "Do you know where we're going?"

He lowered his voice. "None of us know exactly where we're going."

She nodded her head. The fur traders had talked about a pass through the Blue Mountains that would take them north to the Columbia River. Once they reached the river, they could go east and spend a few days at the Whitman Mission or follow the river west to Fort Vancouver. But after searching for days, they'd yet to find anything that Jack or Papa or any of the other men considered a mountain pass.

"Do you think we're going to make it?" When Jack hesitated, she stepped closer to him. "Tell me the truth."

His gaze wandered to the rocks and trees behind her and then snapped back to her. "We'll make it."

How was she supposed to believe him when uncertainty shadowed his voice? He didn't even believe what he said.

Jack's eyes softened as he looked down at her. "You know I didn't want to hurt you back at that valley."

Her heart beat faster. "I wanted you to stand up for Boaz. And for me."

"Sometimes you have to do hard things. To protect the people you care for."

She expected her heart to flutter again at his words, but she felt empty instead.

"I have to know...." She looked straight into his eyes. "Did you vote to kill the dogs?"

He released her hand, his face hardening again as he dropped his arm to his side. For a moment, he had the look Captain Loewe wore when he had to make a difficult decision. "Does it matter how I voted?"

She nodded. "It does to me."

"You have to learn to trust me."

"Samantha," Papa called, his voice urgent.

She picked up her skirt. "I have to go."

She didn't look back at Jack as she rushed toward Papa. How could he ask her to trust him? She had to follow his leadership, at least until they reached the Willamette, but she couldn't trust him. Not if he voted to kill Boaz.

She found Papa on the other side of the wagon, scanning the trees. "What is it?" she asked.

"Have you seen Micah?"

She shook her head. "Maybe he's visiting with Mrs. Kneedler."

"I already checked their wagon."

"Where would he have gone?"

Papa turned to her, lines of worry etched across his forehead. "When did you see him last?"

She swallowed as fear clutched her heart. "He was playing with his toys under the wagon, before you went for water."

"Where is his knapsack?"

She checked under the wagon and then looked under the bonnet. "It seems to be gone."

Papa started yelling Micah's name into the woods, and Samantha ran for Jack. He quickly sent Miles Oxford and Neill Parker to the north. He and Papa went south. Arthur Kneedler stayed with the women at the train.

Samantha waited with the other women, trying to keep her mind occupied by mending her hem. Then Boaz barked, his eyes focused west. She put her needle and thread back into her sewing box and grabbed her rifle.

"Where are you going?" Mrs. Kneedler asked.

"To find my brother."

"The men are searching for him."

Samantha shook her head. "There aren't enough men."

Mr. Kneedler protested her leaving, as did the other women, but she couldn't leave her brother out there to die. Her eyes on the sun, she followed Boaz west, calling Micah's name. When they found him, she would never let him wander off again.

She kept calling his name as she and Boaz climbed over massive rocks, pushed through ferns taller than her, and then struggled to get around pine trees without wounding themselves. Boaz began to run through the pines, and she hurried to catch up with him. They stopped at the edge of the cliff.

Down in the chasm she could see Micah's blond hair, and her entire body felt paralyzed for a moment, as if she were living a nightmare.

She hoped she was in a nightmare.

Then she heard Papa calling Micah's name.

"Over here!" she shouted.

Jack sighed when he saw her, but it was no time for a lecture. She pointed down over the cliff. When Papa saw Micah, he threw a rope around one of the trees and began to descend. Jack descended after him.

When they carried him up, Micah's eyes were closed, his face bloody. She felt sick to her stomach.

Dear God, don't let him die.

She would be a better sister to him. A better mother.

"We need to get him back to camp," Jack said.

When they reached the wagons, Papa placed a blanket over the place where Mama's chest had been, and Jack set Micah inside. Samantha snapped open the medicine box, and her hands shook as she tried to read the labels on the bottles—castor oil, laudanum, whiskey, essence of peppermint.

In Ohio, Samantha would have called for their doctor, but Doctor Rochester was the only doctor in their wagon train, and he'd left with Loewe. She could act as a nurse, though. She'd spent plenty of hours caring for Mama at home whenever the fever overtook her.

She reached for the bottle of laudanum. "I'll give the medicine to him, Papa. You get some water."

When Papa left, she dabbed Micah's head with her handkerchief and drew the string to cinch the back of the canopy. She propped his head on a pillow and then unbuttoned his flannel shirt to check his bones. He was plenty bruised and scratched, but no bones seemed to be broken. She only hoped he hadn't wounded anything else on the inside.

When Papa returned with the tin cup, she held the tepid water to Micah's lips. He spit out the first sip, but when she encouraged him again to take it and the laudanum, he finally drank both of them. Samantha dipped her handkerchief into the little water that was left and wiped the water across his forehead.

Hopefully they would be at this Whitman Mission soon. Surely they would have a doctor there.

* * * * *

Alex knew when he needed help, and he wasn't too proud to ask for it. Looking across the classroom at the faces of the boys and girls, he begged the Sovereign One for wisdom. These children were intent on making his life miserable—he could see it in their faces—but he wasn't going to desist without a fight.

He picked up a piece of chalk and stared back at them. How hard could it be to teach school? If Calvert could do it, so could he—at least until McLoughlin returned. Then he could convince the governor that the children should go to Ottawa or Quebec to continue their education.

The children shouted to each other in a variety of languages, but instead of trying to quiet them, he turned around and began to write the British Oath of Allegiance on the blackboard.

I do swear that I will be faithful and bear true allegiance to Her Majesty Queen Victoria, her heirs and successors, according to law. So help me God.

The room grew quiet as he wrote, and he straightened his shoulders. He may not have gone to a traditional school when he was a child, but he had certainly spent enough time in the classrooms at

Cambridge. The children would respect him if he pretended that he knew what he was doing.

Something hit the back of his neck, and he jumped, the chalk in his hand trailing a line across the oath. He swiveled on his heels, scrutinizing the children in front of him. They were all looking at their desks, some of their heads bobbing with what appeared to be laughter.

Would it be more effective to address their behavior or ignore it?

One of the older boys lifted his hand.

Alex nodded at him. "Do you have a question?"

The boy stared at the blackboard. "I'm having trouble reading your scrawl."

Alex turned around and looked at his neatly written words. It all read perfectly clear to him. He turned back around. "What happens to be the problem with these words?"

The boy smirked. "They are in English."

Snickers filtered across the room, and he heard whispering in Cree and French. Sighing, he turned back to the board and erased his words with the sheepskin eraser. Perhaps he should start with something simpler so they could learn the mechanics of English. He could start at the very beginning: Genesis 1:1.

As he began to write the words from Scripture, he heard the loud hum of the baling press start up outside the window, preparing to compact the dozens of pelts their Indian friends had brought for trade. The sound overpowered the noise of the whispers behind him.

After he wrote out the words from Genesis, he turned back again to the students. Strange. He thought there had been more children in the room before. Perhaps he'd been distracted.

He reached for the register, but before he looked down, a young girl raised her hand.

"What is it?" he asked rather loudly, over the sound of the baling press.

She grinned. "Don't ya think we need something a little longer if we're gonna learn good English?"

He glanced back at the simple verse on the board. Perhaps she was right. The verse was short, and they desperately needed to learn the Queen's English.

He erased the first verse in Genesis and studied the board again. Then he began to write, in much smaller letters, the verses he had memorized from Psalm 23. Perhaps that would be easier to learn than the oath.

His confidence began to swell as he transcribed the verse. He may not aspire to be a teacher, but he could do this. Even though there were certainly a handful of unruly children among them, some, like this little girl, were anxious to learn. Perhaps he could make some progress in their education before McLoughlin returned.

Minutes passed as he focused on writing clearly, so the children could read his work. With a bit of flourish, he dotted the last period and whirled around to address his students.

His jaw dropped.

A dozen empty desks stared back at him. The noise of the baling press drowning out their footsteps, they'd all sneaked out of the room.

"Something a little longer..."

While he was busy writing, they'd played him for a fool.

He leaned back against his desk and glanced out the window at the horde of children racing away from the schoolhouse.

Sighing, he placed the eraser on his desk. Didn't these children know what a gift they were being offered? With a solid education, they could read and write and calculate numbers. They could succeed in this life.

He'd longed to go to school as a boy, but his mother had never been able to afford the fees. He had spent hours with an elderly neighbor, learning to read from the few books she owned, until his mother died. Then Uncle Neville brought him into his manor and hired a tutor.

He drank up those early lessons with a quenchless thirst. Even as a boy, he remembered feeling a bit like Joseph of the Bible, going from prison to palace in a day. He was suddenly Lord Neville Clarke's nephew, his honored and esteemed heir, and he was offered an education to go along with it.

Uncle Neville was thrifty with his praise, but Alex hoped he'd made the man proud. If his father were still alive, would he too be proud of the man Alex had become? Alex never knew his father.

The only father Alex had ever known left him and his mother when he was four. He barely remembered Fulton Knox, but he remembered enough to know that he didn't want to follow in the steps of a man who prized neither education nor family.

His stepfather had been an entertainer who'd charmed Alex's mother away from the life of a noblewoman, and she'd been too proud to attempt a return when Fulton left her penniless. She had been convinced that her first husband's relatives would turn her away.

But they hadn't turned away Alex. His aunt had been hesitant, but his uncle had welcomed him into his home. Without children of his own, Uncle Neville had been eager for an heir.

Perhaps if he had the blood of an entertainer, Alex thought wryly, he might have charmed these students into staying in school. Or perhaps he should have caned all of them into submission…though he doubted that even a good caning would make these ruffians obey.

He glanced out the window again. He couldn't blame them, he supposed, for wanting to be outside on this beautiful day, but even if it were pouring rain, they probably wouldn't want to learn. At least not from him. How he wished he could convince them that a good education would give them the opportunity to work with their minds instead of their hands.

He leaned back at the table, glancing down at his own hands. Sometimes he wished he knew how to work with his hands instead of directing other people to do so. He'd never admit it to anyone, but sometimes he even wished he could have the joy of planting corn or wheat like Tom Kneedler and watching it grow.

Perhaps he could teach the students the importance of using their hands and minds alike.

He raked his fingers through his trimmed hair. It was all a grand joke, the idea of Alexander Clarke trying to teach anyone. He didn't know the first thing about children, nor did he have a clue how to inspire them. He'd wanted to sneak out of the classroom long before they did.

The door opened at the back of the room and he looked up, wondering if one or more of the children had decided to return to school. But instead of a child, the lovely Taini sauntered into the room.

She slowly crossed the floor, her dark green English dress rustling with every step, and she sat at one of the front desks, folding her hands before she spoke in her father's language. "Where are your pupils?"

He answered her in rudimentary French. "They like the sunshine more than school."

Her brown eyes flashed as she tucked strands of straight black hair behind her ears. "I like the sunshine too."

He nodded, glancing out the window again.

"But I am not like them. I would also like to learn English."

He looked back at her, his pulse racing at the glance she gave him. She wasn't that much older than some of his students, having married her first husband when she was only fourteen.

She fluttered her long eyelashes, her eyes speaking as loudly as any words. Everything within him shouted, "Leave!" but he'd learned early in life that it was better to confront a problem than run from it.

He crossed his arms. "I think it is a good idea for you to learn English, but I am not a good teacher."

"You would be a good teacher for me." She laughed lightly. "Or perhaps I could teach you."

"I do not think so—"

She stood and stepped toward him, reaching for his hand. "I am a very good teacher."

He turned quickly and plucked his cloak off the stand, throwing it over his shoulder. Perhaps in this case it was better to be like Joseph in the Bible…and flee.

Chapter Nine

"Pull harder!" Jack yelled as the men tugged on the ropes that were wrapped around trees and held the Kneedlers' wagon back even as the oxen inched down the steep slope. The men had spent an hour chaining locks on the wheels and then rigging up a pulley to lower the animals and wagons to the bottom.

Micah lay on a quilt, asleep on the ground beside Samantha, as Papa helped the men with the pulley. She petted Boaz as they waited, so grateful that he'd led them to Micah. Now she prayed that rest was the best cure for her brother. And that he'd give up his penchant for exploring on his own in the wilderness.

The Kneedlers' wagon made it safely down the slope along with the Parkers' and Jack's, but the next one, owned by the Oxfords, did not. One of the oxen slipped, tripping his yoke mate, and the men had to release the ropes. The wagon splintered with an ear-shattering crash when it hit the ground below.

Silence spread over the company until Miles Oxford swore. Then she heard his wife, Betty, and their two children begin to cry.

Jack's voice rose above their cries. "We'll consolidate their supplies with ours."

Samantha surveyed the damage below them. Bags of food were split open, their contents scattered. Clothes and blankets were spread out over the ground.

The oxen bellowed with pain, and Samantha's stomach wrenched as Jack and Miles Oxford shot them.

The Waldrons' wagon was last, but Samantha looked away from the slope, toward the trees. She couldn't bear to watch Abe and George go over.

She felt Micah's forehead, and it felt like it was burning with fever. If only she had some cool water to wash him in. As she waited, she prayed that God would give her another opportunity to be a mother to Micah. If so, she promised Him, she would never let him wander off again.

Papa shouted to her, and she looked back toward the men. The oxen and their wagon had made it safely down.

Papa picked up Micah, and then Jack led the women, children, and remaining animals carefully down the steep slope.

As Papa placed Micah in the wagon, she saw the frightened look in his eyes. "We have to start moving."

She nodded. The other wagons had already gone ahead through a narrow passage in the trees, and they didn't want to be left behind. She tucked Grandmother's quilt around Micah and then kissed his forehead as she pulled a blanket over him. "We're going to make it."

As the sun began to set, she asked God to provide water. Maybe Mama could ask God to send one of His angels to guide them to a stream.

The company didn't find water, but an hour later, water found them. The skies opened up and rain poured down on them.

"Micah," she said as she prodded her sleeping brother, "it's raining."

He didn't wake, but she backed away from the wagon and opened her mouth wide, letting the skies quench her thirst. Then she opened the barrel, hoping God would fill it for them.

* * * * *

The light rain revived their tired party. For the first time in weeks, Samantha heard laughter around her. Even Mrs. Kneedler was outside dancing in the rain. Mama would have liked that—a time to dance. If she were with them, Samantha could see her dancing too.

Samantha soaked a rag in the rain and dabbed Micah's face over and over with the coolness.

Before it got dark, Samantha helped Papa carry Micah into the tent, and then she cut up pieces of jerky for Papa and for Boaz. Micah's eyes opened slightly. He seemed to listen to the rain.

"Mama?" Micah asked as the sun began to set.

Papa cleared his throat and reached for the Bible that had been in their family for a hundred years. He read from the book of Isaiah: "'Fear thou not; for I am with thee: be not dismayed; for I am thy God: I will strengthen thee; yea, I will help thee; yea, I will uphold thee with the right hand of my righteousness.'"

He closed the book. "Your mother wouldn't want us to be afraid, nor would she want us to give up."

"Did she send the rain?" Micah asked, his body shaking under the blanket.

"Perhaps she asked God to send it to us." Papa patted his shoulder. "Eliza was pretty persuasive."

Someone cleared his throat outside the tent. "Can I come in?" Jack asked.

Samantha took a deep breath.

"Come in." Papa stood up. "I need to get my bedroll ready under the wagon."

Jack removed his dripping hat, leaving it by the flap, and then he sat down on the other side of Micah, placing his hand on her brother's arm. "How are you doing?"

Micah tried to smile. "Not so bad."

"What were you doing out in that canyon by yourself?"

"Trying to help." Micah turned to her, his eyes wide. "Like Sam does."

"Out here, it's better to help in pairs." Jack didn't look at her, but she knew he meant those words even more for her than for Micah.

"Speaking of help…" He looked over at her now. "What can I do to help you?"

"Just get us to Fort Vancouver as soon as possible."

He sighed. "I'm already trying to do that."

When he started to stand, she reached out to stop him. "You did a good job today, Jack."

He shook his head. "We lost the Oxfords' wagon."

"Yes, but you managed to divide up their things into the other wagons. You got everyone over the cliff safely and found us a good place to spend the night."

He studied her for a moment. "Thank you."

After he left their tent, she leaned back against her pillow, listening to Micah's slow breathing and the steady beat of the rain.

Before they left Missouri, Papa had soaked the tent with linseed oil to repel any water. If only she could soak her heart in linseed oil as well, to ward off all the mixed feelings that penetrated it.

Did she love Jack? Did he love her? He was kind to her and Micah, and he was certainly a brave man…and a good one. But she didn't know if she could trust him, at least not enough to marry him.

Why couldn't he be honest with her about what had happened the night before their company split into two? Why couldn't he understand why it was so important for her to know the truth?

She closed her eyes, trying to sleep, but her mind kept trying to unravel the unknowns. If she didn't marry Jack, she could help Papa build their house and their farm. She could help him care for Micah.

She wanted to marry one day—she just wasn't sure she wanted to marry Jack Doyle.

* * * * *

Jack leaned his head back against the rock, his rifle propped on his lap. The glittering stars reminded him of the welcoming lights in his parents' home. His older brothers, their wives, and the seven grandchildren would gather at the farmhouse soon, preparing to help his parents harvest the grain from the fields. It was the first time that he'd ever been away for a harvest.

Two years ago, he'd heard rumblings about people beginning to travel west, and he knew, without a single thread of doubt, that he had to go. It had taken him another year to save the money and accumulate the supplies for such a journey. He'd been sad to say good-bye to his family, but ever since Jenny died, he'd wanted to leave Indiana. He thought he would leave the painful memories of losing her behind, but the memories traveled the miles with him.

He didn't know what he was doing, trying to act like a leader when he clearly was not one. Now Micah was wounded and Prudence Kneedler had been complaining of stomach pains. And she said her teeth hurt. He only hoped she hadn't contracted the camp fever the traders had mentioned back at Fort Hall. They'd said it could be deadly.

The only reason he'd agreed to lead this party as captain was because he couldn't in good conscience leave the Kneedlers or Waldrons or any of the others behind, especially since he had planned to marry Samantha when they got to the Willamette.

How could he desert the woman he'd been planning to marry?

In spite of the warnings at Fort Hall, no warring Indians or rabid coyotes had threatened their party. Back on the plains, the natives had followed them at times, and a group had swarmed their caravan once, scaring them. But the natives hadn't wanted to hurt them. They'd only wanted to trade their dried meat and pelts for tobacco and cotton shirts.

He was plenty worried about hostile Indians, but if he were honest, Jack was much more worried about grizzly bears in these mountains and the steep cliffs that hindered their path. Some place around here there was supposed to be a path through these mountains, but he didn't have any idea where it was. They'd already searched for two days, felling the smaller trees and removing rocks when necessary to clear a path, but with four wagons following him, it was difficult to search effectively. Not only was their climb rugged, he also had to look for water for the people and livestock and places to rest as well.

Now he knew why the few people who had gone before them left their wagons behind and used packhorses for this final stretch. They could get over the mountains much easier without all the supplies.

But he couldn't suggest leaving their wagons to this group—at least not yet. They were already divided about how to proceed. He didn't have Captain Loewe's persuasion or ability to lead. Even in the situation with the dogs, the captain had felt fully justified in what he was doing and was therefore confident in his decision. Jack just felt confused.

He closed his eyes.

He was confused about where to go and confused about what to do regarding Samantha. He didn't want to bring harm to her family. Why couldn't she trust him to do what was best for them? To do what was best for *her*?

Jenny always trusted him.

"Do you think we're going to make it?" Samantha had asked.

The truth was, he didn't know. He didn't know if they would make it safely across these mountains.

And he didn't know if he and Samantha could ever marry.

He hadn't asked her to become his wife, but he'd certainly thought about it. He'd hinted about it too, before the incident with the dogs. Samantha had seemed agreeable to the idea, but now everything had changed between them.

Confusion twisted his gut.

Samantha sometimes reminded him of the swift river currents that had beat up against their wagons. He wanted to be strong for his wife, his family, and he wanted to understand the woman he married. But Samantha often did things he didn't understand.

When he married again, he hoped he could recapture just a bit of the wonder he'd experienced with Jenny. He didn't expect his future wife to be like Jenny, but he wanted to love her as much as he'd loved his first wife.

He groaned in the darkness. He didn't know what he was going to do.

Weariness weighed down his eyes, and he fought against it. Only two hours remained until he'd wake the caravan to continue their journey. He had to stay awake for the sake of everyone in his care.

Something shuffled in front of him, and he sat up straighter, squinting into the darkness.

Was someone out there, watching them?

He glanced back at the four wagons, but he didn't see any movement. The animals and people alike were exhausted from another long day.

He was plenty aware of the fact that they weren't alone. He only hoped that it was just a curious coyote or a skunk coming to check out the invaders of their wilderness.

Chapter Ten

Samantha rolled over on the feather tick, trying to sleep in the midst of the noise, but then she bolted upright on her bed. Boaz was barking.

Panic seized her for a moment—the thought of someone shooting her dog because he had awakened their party. She almost hushed him but stopped when she remembered that Captain Loewe was no longer among them.

Her fear of losing Boaz was quickly replaced by another fear. He wouldn't disturb them unless something was wrong.

She couldn't see Micah sleeping in the tent beside her, but when she reached out, she could feel his arm wrapped tightly around his knapsack. His chest rose and fell, his sleep seemingly unaffected by Boaz and now the barking of the Oxford and Parker family dogs.

When Boaz began to growl, she slipped out of the tent.

She looked around their camp, at the dark branches that quivered in the mountain breeze. With all the cliffs and pine trees, there had been no clearing available for their wagons to form a circle of protection, so each wagon stood in a ragged line with rocks or tree limbs securing the wheels. Aside from the dogs' barking, the only sound was a river flowing at the base of the canyon, the water just out of their reach over a rocky cliff.

Papa was already awake, lighting a tallow candle at the foot of their wagon. When he lifted the tin box toward her, candlelight filtered through the holes and spilled a spidery web of light on the ground. Branches and leaves crunched under the footfalls of their companions as they hurried toward the Waldrons' wagon.

"Where's Jack?" Arthur asked.

"I don't know," Papa said. "He was guarding tonight."

Boaz strained at the rope leashing him to the wagon. Then something crashed in the forest, and Samantha's heart lurched. Was it an animal or a person stalking their company?

Boaz growled again, pulling against his rope until it snapped.

"Come back!" she yelled, but he listened to her as well as she listened to Papa. His gray form melded into the darkness.

Then she heard another growl, this one fiercer than any she'd heard before.

She picked up her skirt. "Boaz!"

"Don't run," Jack commanded from the other side of her tent. "It's a bear!"

Papa cocked his gun, and she climbed back into the tent to retrieve both her gun and her possibles bag. Micah lay on the bed, and she quickly kissed his forehead before climbing back out of the tent. She and Papa were having more of an adventure than she ever could have imagined, but she didn't want adventure any longer. Not if it meant someone else getting hurt.

A bear crashed through the trees, and she fell back against the wagon. In the moonlight, she could see saliva foaming around its mouth and its dark fur pulsating with anger. It bore sharp teeth and growled at them, a terrible noise that sent chills across her skin.

She hoisted her gun onto her shoulder, but her arms trembled. The bear charged at one of the oxen. A dog dove at the animal, trying to stop it, but the bear batted the dog away as if he were a fly.

She didn't know which dog it was, but when he yelped, her heart tore.

"Sam?" she heard Micah call.

"Don't move!" she yelled back at him.

"What is it?"

There was no time to reply. She pressed her rifle against her shoulder, trying to aim in the darkness. She didn't want to kill the animal, but she had to shoot to protect Micah and Papa and the others.

The bear kept moving, zigzagging across the camp toward the livestock. She couldn't shoot yet, not when she might hit a person instead.

Another dog lunged for the bear, and this time the bear turned around to see what attacked it.

"Steady!" Jack called out. "Hiram, you shoot."

Papa's gun blasted, and the bear whirled again. It seemed to forget the dog as it roared in anger. She didn't know if the bear had been hit, but as Papa reloaded, Samantha and several others took aim. She closed her eyes and shot.

The bear moved slower now, but the balls didn't stop it. Yet.

They had to stop it.

In the dim light, she reloaded her gun, shaking black powder into her barrel. Then she reached for a patch in her bag. She spit on it and rammed it along with another ball down the barrel.

Papa cried out, and she looked up. The bear reared up on its hind legs, its paws three feet above her. The sickening heat of its breath rained down on her skin, and she lifted her rifle, aiming at his head.

Her gun blasted again, and in an instant, the roaring stopped as the bear teetered on his feet. She leaped back as he toppled over.

The earth quaked under her feet; pinecones bobbed up and down. Then silence hung in the night as they all stared at the bear, the seconds crawling so slowly that it seemed like hours. She filled her rifle one more time just in case it lifted its head again.

Jack surveyed their small camp. "Is everyone all right?"

"I believe so," Mr. Kneedler said.

"Can I come out now?" Micah asked, his voice small.

"Go back to sleep," she commanded, though she knew sleep would be impossible for any of them.

Boaz shuffled up beside her, and she hugged his neck, clinging to him. Then she looked toward Papa's candle box...and Papa.

He was on the ground.

She knelt as her father rocked back and forth, balled up over his left arm.

She put her arm on his shoulder. "Did it hurt you?"

Papa looked up at her, and she could see the agony straining his face. "It's just a scratch."

"Let me see."

In the candlelight she could see the blood on his shirt, and her eyes widened in fear. "Did it bite you?"

"It all happened so fast—"

She tore back his shirt and saw the deep lacerations that shredded his skin, the blood pooling over them. Her stomach rolled. "Oh, Papa."

He clenched his teeth and groaned in pain before he spoke again. "I'll be fine."

She turned from him and dug through the wagon until she uncovered the laudanum and the bottle of whiskey. Papa didn't argue when she offered the whiskey to him. He took a long sip, and then she poured the alcohol over his wound.

His scream pierced her ears.

Micah was beside her, clinging to her arm as she tried to comfort her father, but there was nothing she could do to make Papa's pain go away. She had to clean the wound, and yet fear paralyzed her. How could she cause him more pain?

He leaned back against the wagon wheel and drifted into a blessed unconsciousness, but she still couldn't look at his arm. Micah cried beside her, and tears began to stream down her cheeks too.

Mama had only been gone a year. She couldn't think about losing Papa too.

She felt a hand on her shoulder, and she looked up to see Jack.

"Let me help you," he said.

She nodded and watched as he dabbed at Papa's arm with a dusty cloth. If only they had enough water to boil. She could clean the dirt from the cloth first and then off his arm.

Micah snuggled in beside Papa as Jack bandaged the wound with strips he made from the remains of Papa's shirt.

"Where did you learn to do that?" she asked.

He shrugged. "From taking care of the animals at home."

They worked together to move first Papa's bedroll and then Papa into the tent.

Thankfully the laudanum helped Papa sleep, but Samantha couldn't rest. Boaz lay at her side, under the wagon where Papa had been, and she listened to the peculiar sounds of the wilderness, home to fierce creatures like the bear.

Was anyone else out there, watching them? Jack told them all to rest a few hours more. Miles Oxford and Neill Parker guarded the camp for the remainder of the night while Jack slept. Papa slept as well.

In the early morning hours, the two men trekked down to the stream and retrieved water. After their party feasted on bear stew, they reserved the bear tallow for making candles and for greasing their wagon wheels. The animal's pelt was given to the Oxford family to use as a blanket.

The feast lasted for hours, but Papa never woke.

If they had stayed with Captain Loewe and the others, would the bear have attacked such a large company?

She would never know the answer to that question, but it was too late for regrets now. The Doyle party was strong. They'd worked together to defeat this bear before it destroyed them. Micah was going to recover, and so was Papa.

The Waldron family would make it safely to the Willamette before the winter storms arrived.

* * * * *

Alex dug his hand into the pocket of his cloak on the peg, but instead of touching his watch, he touched something that squirmed in his hand. He jumped back, his heart racing.

One of the laborers in the warehouse looked over at him. "Something the matter?"

He eyed the cloak. "I am not certain."

"You had some visitors while you were in the back room. Some of your pupils."

He almost said that they weren't his pupils, but until McLoughlin returned, he supposed they were. "Boys or girls?"

"One of each, I believe. They were looking for you."

"Did they ask about my cloak?"

The man shrugged. "I don't think they needed to ask. You're the only one in here with such a fine coat."

What had his students left for him?

"I will be back," he said, taking the coat by its collar. He held it away from him as he walked toward the door, his eyes focused on the squirming pocket.

When he walked outside, a cluster of four children stood to the side of the warehouse, pretending to ignore him as they whispered. He waved at them and then hurried around the corner. As soon as they were out of his sight, he threw his cloak on the pebbled pathway. A green snake slithered out of his pocket.

Clearly, they loved their new teacher.

He picked up his coat, and as he shook it upside down, he heard laughter behind him. Turning, he saw the group of students. They hurried around the side of the warehouse as he pulled on the sleeves of his cloak, but he could still hear their laughter.

Sighing, he walked slowly back to his room at Bachelor's Hall. He'd always thought that he'd like to be a father one day, a completely different kind of father from the one who'd raised him in his early years, but perhaps he would never know how to relate to children. Perhaps it was a skill that had to be taught when one was young.

It was too bad. Judith would make a fine mother, but he had no idea how to raise a child.

"Mister," a girl said as she stepped out in front of him. It was the same girl who'd asked him to write a longer passage on the board.

He stopped beside her. "Did you like the passage I wrote?"

She blushed, looking down at the ground. Pieces of her honey-brown hair were tied in two braids, but most of it was tangled around her scrawny shoulders. "I just wanted to say thank ya for trying to teach us."

He shook his head. "I failed quite miserably."

"No teacher has ever passed the test."

He bent his neck down a few inches. "Test?"

She shrugged. "Ain't no one ever gonna pass it, either."

He supposed all the teachers before him had failed as well.

"What should I do next time?" he asked.

Before she responded, the bell rang out above the fort and she ran away. He hurried toward the business gate at the front of the fort.

At least one of his pupils seemed to appreciate his effort.

The watchman, a large man of mixed Spanish and Indian descent named Daniel, was standing beside the open gate.

"Why is the bell ringing?" Alex asked Daniel.

"A messenger just arrived," Daniel said. "McLoughlin is on his way home."

Alex felt like cheering. Surely the governor would relieve him of this new duty before the children subjected him to another of their tests.

Chapter Eleven

Thankfully, Miles Oxford's saw had remained intact after the loss of his wagon, and thankfully, Jack had carried the saw with his things. On the sixteenth morning of October, with fog lingering over the treetops and veiling the mountain in their path, Samantha watched as Miles, Jack, and Neill transformed the four remaining wagons into two-wheeled oxcarts.

They'd crossed over mountains in their wagons, inched down canyons, and forded rivers and streams, but the next mountain was too steep for the tired oxen to pull their loads over it. They were to pare down their belongings once again, this time to what they could carry in these carts.

The oxen and horses that weren't pulling carts would carry bags of supplies. Many of the remaining oxen looked like they wouldn't last much longer without a grassy field to graze in for a few days and plenty of good water.

Samantha's feet were blistered and sore from climbing up and down the mountains, though she was grateful for her moccasins. Her swollen feet would no longer fit into the shoes she'd brought from Ohio. Boaz's feet were bound in buckskin, and Papa's arm was tightly wrapped. He said he wasn't in pain, but Samantha didn't believe him. He'd ridden on their palomino for the past hour, commanding the oxen to keep moving, but she'd seen him clutching his arm when he didn't realize she was watching.

She glanced around the party as they unloaded their wagons

once more. Most of them had started this journey as clean city folk, filled with unbridled optimism about their new life in the West. A thread of that optimism still ran through some of them, but they were all exhausted. Their men looked much more like vagabonds than an attorney, farmer, preacher, carpenter, and bookkeeper.

Jack and the other men had searched and searched for a better trail, but they hadn't found one. This morning they'd found the Morrison wagon, though, discarded in the trees. Then they'd found two more wagons from the Loewe party. Jack said the Doyle party could no longer travel with their wagons either.

They'd also found the remains of a horse. And a freshly dug grave.

Who else had died on the trail?

She'd averted her eyes from the grave as they passed, afraid it was Lucille they were leaving behind.

Samantha stared at the back of their wagon. They'd already had to unload almost half of their belongings along the trail. At every stop, she and Papa agonized over what was necessary to take with them, but they were learning that not everything was as necessary as they'd once thought.

Captain Loewe and the other men had thought it was a ploy when the traders back at Fort Hall encouraged them to sell their things at ridiculously low prices, but even a little money would have been much better than dumping barrels of food, tools, and furniture in the forest.

"Can we bring this?" Micah asked, holding up the elephant from his Noah's Ark set.

She glanced at her father and then back at Micah, whispering, "Only if you can carry it."

"How about this?" This time it was a camel.

"Will it fit?"

He pushed the camel into the knapsack and cinched it shut again.

Micah was still sore from his fall, but his strength had returned. She'd given him a change of clothes to add to whatever was in his sack along with a tin cup, a tin plate, and several small bags full of dried jerky, corn, and coffee. She placed his wide-brimmed hat over hair that had grown to his shoulders, and he tied his coat around the pole of his knapsack, pronouncing that he was ready to walk.

"Stay close by," she said.

He nodded.

While Micah petted Boaz, she packed their cooking stove, a buffalo pelt, and an iron skillet in their new cart. Papa's arm was still bandaged, but he added two burlap bags of seeds they would need in order to plant wheat in the Willamette, and she put in the little that remained of their flour and sugar supplies along with the dried food. He added several small bags of seeds to the cart, and she picked one of them up.

"What are these, Papa?"

His smile was strained. "Those are a surprise."

"Don't you think we've had enough surprises?"

"Not enough good ones."

She kissed his cheek before she continued packing, wrapping Grandmother's quilt and a blanket around the Waldron family Bible. She packed the tinderbox, candle box, matches, candles, a small bar of soap, and several changes of clothes for when they arrived in the Willamette. Then she added her sewing kit along with a bag of fishhooks and tobacco to trade with the Indians, their bedrolls and tent, and both a pail and a canteen for carrying water between stops.

Jack thought they must be close to the Columbia now. Once they reached the river, he said, they wouldn't have to think again about packing water with them.

She tried stacking the coffeepot on top of the cart, but it kept slipping off.

"Let me help you," Papa said. He grimaced as he tied the pot to the top of their load with a rope.

"Do you want more laudanum?" she asked.

He shook his head as he scratched his arm. "It just itches."

"We can buy more medicine at the fort."

He refused the laudanum again as he helped her cover their supplies with animal skins and a big piece of canvas from their wagon's bonnet to keep out any rain.

Samantha kissed her hand and touched the box of their wagon, their home for six months now. She said good-bye to Mama's rocking chair, their feather tick, and the water barrel. There was no longer any need for the extra wagon wheel or the other tools to repair their wagon. And they were leaving Papa's farming tools in the wagon.

Their entire journey seemed to be about leaving people and things behind. Saying good-bye.

She was ready to be in the Willamette, settling in their new home. Once they arrived, she didn't think she would want another adventure for the rest of her life. They'd walked at least eighteen hundred miles now, seeing places and things that most Americans had never seen. Perhaps she could settle down and marry and be satisfied for the rest of her life in this new place, even without her things.

She reached back into the wagon and dug through the linens until she found the shawl Mama had worn on her wedding day. Tears began to well in her eyes, and she blinked them back as she took the shawl to the oxcart, folding it gently and tucking it by one of the burlap bags. She could cry plenty after they got to the Willamette, but right now she needed her strength for another long day of walking through the mountains.

Samantha met Mrs. Kneedler resting against the oxcart that her husband had piled even higher than theirs.

"How are you feeling?" Samantha asked her.

Her hands were on her lips. "My mouth won't seem to mend."

"Are you glad you came to Oregon?" she asked the older woman.

Mrs. Kneedler blinked, her gaze traveling to the mountain ahead of them. "God refines us by fire, Samantha."

Samantha turned her head. "That doesn't answer my question."

Mrs. Kneedler paused, wiping the blood on her lips onto a handkerchief. Then she spoke again. "It was my son's and then Arthur's dream to go west, not mine."

"It's a long walk to go back home."

"I don't want to return. Through this trip, God has been sifting my heart, refining me, and, I hope, making me more like Him."

More like Him.

She pondered the woman's words as the oxen pulled the carts forward.

Had she become more like God in the past months? There were times, she supposed, when she was more patient and kind than she had been in Ohio, and more courageous too, like Christiana in *The Pilgrim's Progress*. The way to the Celestial City was hard, but Christiana and her sons gave up everything and persisted until they reached the end of their journey.

During these months, Samantha had become much less consumed with her worldly desires and things like the fine dresses she'd owned in Ohio. Her concerns now were about having enough water to drink and food to eat, taking care of her father and her brother, and staying warm on the cold nights.

But how could she become more like God?

"I'm sorry, Mrs. Kneedler, but you still didn't answer my question about whether you're glad you came," Samantha said.

Mrs. Kneedler walked slowly beside her. "I'm very glad to be able to see my son and his wife, but this journey isn't about what makes me glad. It's about what God requires of me."

Samantha shook her head. "Sometimes it seems that He requires too much of us."

Mrs. Kneedler gave her a curious look. "Are you angry at God?"

She thought for a moment. "Part of me is," she admitted. "For taking my mother away."

Mrs. Kneedler ducked under a tree branch and held it up for Samantha to walk under. "God understands your loss, child. He lost someone He loved as well."

"But God knew He would be seeing His Son again."

Mrs. Kneedler reached for her hand, squeezing it. "And you'll be seeing your mama again one day as well."

She nodded slowly. "It must make God sad to see so many of His children suffer."

"I'm sure it does sadden Him, but He knows that this life is only temporary. One day His love will conquer all the evil and pain in this world."

One day.

Mrs. Kneedler walked forward to be with her husband, and Samantha dropped back and wiped the dust off George's nose with the hem of her skirt. All three of their oxen had worked tirelessly, and now they had yet another mountain to climb.

Who knew how many mountains were on the other side?

They walked for an hour up the incline, and when Samantha squinted her eyes at the summit, she could barely see the Kneedlers' cart in front of them. The two other carts in their small party were ahead of the Kneedlers.

Papa's eyes roamed the desolate mountains around them, and he shook his head as he clutched his arm. "We have to catch up with the others."

Samantha wanted to argue with her father, but she knew he was right. They couldn't be left out here alone in these mountains. This wilderness seemed too lonesome for even Indians to roam. They would be easy prey for another grizzly or a wolf.

Papa urged the oxen onward, and the animals huffed as they continued their climb. Surely Jack would stop and wait for them at the top. He would never leave their family behind.

* * * * *

Once they got to the other side of the mountain, the Doyle party moved much faster with their oxcarts. Horses were too difficult for them to ride through the forest, and it had become too cumbersome trying to move them up and down the steep paths in a timely manner— so they released their four remaining horses into the wilderness. Jack promised there would be plenty of horses where they were going, but Samantha knew how sad he was to say good-bye to his horse.

Her father had been acting strangely the past few days. He said his arm was healing, but his thinking wasn't clear. He didn't seem concerned about anything—leaving his palomino, their shortage of food and water, the cold that enveloped them at night. He didn't even seem to care that they were almost there.

The traders had said to travel northwest through the Blue Mountains to find the Columbia River. Once they found this river, they could either find a few days' respite at the Whitman Mission to the east, or they could go west to Fort Vancouver. Then they would move on to settle in the Willamette Valley.

Her family had a small bag of beans left in their cart, and some coffee. The dried fruit was gone now, along with all their wheat. Another ox had died on the trail, and the party divided that meat among them, but if they didn't find the river soon....

Samantha found herself almost wishing that another grizzly bear would find them so they could kill him for the meat as well.

What she hoped most, though, was that Papa might be able to sleep in a mission tonight, a place with hot food, a warm fire, and strong medicine to help him get well. To help him remember his dream.

A gust of wind blasted over the hill, and Samantha shivered. She pulled the quilt tighter over her shoulders, trying to protect herself from the cold. Jack had guessed that they were a week away from Fort Vancouver now.

Once they arrived in the Willamette, she didn't think she would ever eat another bean.

Micah shivered beside her. She reached out and pulled him under the quilt with her.

"There it is!" someone shouted, racing toward the edge of the cliff in front of them.

She stepped forward with Micah, looking over the canyon. Instead of leading to another mountain, the cliff sloped into a wide river with rock walls on both sides and a treed island in the middle.

The Columbia.

Samantha shielded her eyes with her hands, studying the river's path until it curved into the bend. Then she began to cry. All they had to do now was follow the river west. Never again would they find themselves lost. This river would take them home.

The men secured the oxen away from the cliff, and Jack gathered their small party together. How he'd changed in the past month. He fit into his new role of captain like a worn boot. Jack may not have realized it, but he was a good leader.

"We need to vote," he said as they circled around him. Jack allowed anyone eighteen and over to vote, including women. "How many want to go east, to the Whitman Mission?"

Samantha wanted to get to the Willamette as much as the rest of them, but they also needed food. And medicine for Papa and Mrs. Kneedler.

She was the only one who raised her hand. The others voted to press on to the Willamette, all except Papa. He didn't vote at all.

Papa began muttering to himself, his arms trembling. She reached over and took his hand.

"It's going to be all right," she whispered, trying to pretend, as he had done the night the bear attacked him, that everything was fine.

Jack didn't seem to hear her father's mumbling. "How are you feeling, Mrs. Kneedler?"

Samantha looked back at the pale-gray color of the woman's skin. Mrs. Kneedler managed a smile, but Samantha saw the blood caked on her gums.

"Don't you worry about me," Mrs. Kneedler said.

He eyed the terrain below them. "We'll head west, then."

The party plodded slowly forward along the cliff. Samantha's feet felt as if they weighed a hundred pounds each, but she wouldn't stop. They were so close to their new home, so close to helping Papa get well again.

They walked for hours that afternoon across the high cliffs until the terrain sloped low into a valley. Jack directed Miles Oxford to lead the group down the slope and then west until they found a clearing to camp for the night. Jack said he and the others would follow.

Wind gusted over the canyon, and Samantha shivered as she and Micah began to guide the oxen into the ravine. Behind her, Papa leaned on Jack, clutching his injured arm as they descended toward the river. Samantha knew Papa must be heavy, but they didn't have any other choice. There was no other way for Papa to get down.

When she reached the bottom, Samantha turned around to look back up the trail. Papa was no longer walking. He was sitting on a rock instead.

"Wait here," she told Micah. Then she rushed back up the canyon's side.

"Hiram," Jack said, tugging on Papa's good arm, "you have to get up."

She knelt down beside her father. "Papa, you can't stay here."

His throat was raspy. "I can't move."

Jack looked down at the canyon and then back up at the clouds building above them. When his eyes met hers, she saw the fear in them.

"I'll help you," Samantha said. She strung one arm around Papa, and Jack took the other.

Micah didn't listen, but she didn't scold him, either, when he joined them. Shivering, she and Jack began to carry her father down the hill, Micah trailing behind them. She hated that he had to hear Papa's moans, hated that Papa was in such terrible pain.

The wind gusted up the canyon, and she shook again. They were so close to being at their new home. They couldn't lose him.

"Only one more week, Papa. We'll be at Fort Vancouver by then."

Neither Papa nor Jack responded to her words. She looked over at Jack, urgency pressing against her even as it prompted her forward. "We need to go to the mission."

"I—"

"No, Samantha," Papa interrupted Jack. "My journey must end here."

Chapter Twelve

By the time Jack and Samantha managed to carry Papa down to the river, the others, along with Jack's cart, were so far in the distance that they looked like specks against a golden hill that bowed into the Columbia.

Jack eyed the sky again. "There's going to be a storm."

They lowered Papa to the ground, and she reached into their cart to retrieve their buffalo pelt, draping it over him. His eyes were closed, his breathing stilled. If he knew they were there, he didn't acknowledge them. Her father, who always seemed to have an answer, no longer spoke.

She jostled his shoulder. "Wake up, Papa."

"Samantha," Jack said gently.

She ignored him, shaking Papa again. "You have to get up. We're almost to the valley."

"Samantha," Jack implored her now.

She knelt beside her father. "There is plenty of land in the valley, Papa. We're going to build a house and plant a farm. Remember your bags of seeds? You promised to surprise us."

Micah took her hand. "Why isn't he waking up?"

She blinked back the tears in her eyes. "He will. He just needs to rest."

Jack put his hand over hers, gently lifting it off her father.

"We need to speak." He glanced down at Micah, lowering his voice as if her brother couldn't hear. "In private."

She knew what he was going to say, and she didn't want to hear it.

He didn't know Papa and what a fighter he was. It may take a few days, but he would beat this infection. Hiram Waldron didn't quit.

She looked up into Jack's eyes, so full of concern. She looked away.

Didn't he have faith? Papa was one of the strongest people she knew. He may be injured, but he wasn't like the others who'd died on this journey. He would win this fight.

"I'll be right back," she told Micah, trying to keep her voice as light as she could. "You stay with Papa."

He nodded as he inched closer to Papa. Boaz sat beside him.

Trees dotted the shoreline along the river. The strip of shore that bumped against the cliffs was about twenty feet wide. She looked at the tail end of the other carts traveling over the narrow path between the trees, and she knew right then that she was saying good-bye yet again.

Jack took both her hands in his. The strength of them should have filled her with hope, made her feel protected, but they terrified her instead. "We're going to lose him, Samantha."

She ripped her hands from his, wrapping her arms around her chest. She didn't want to hear this. "You don't know—"

He leaned in closer to her. "You have to stop fighting."

Tears slipped down her cheeks.

"How do you do that, Jack?" Her entire body trembled. "How do you stop fighting for the people you love?"

He put his hand on her shoulder. "You let him go, Sam. To be with God and your mother."

Something fell on her. She lifted her face to the sky, and everything within her seemed to cave.

The snow had come.

She shook away Jack's hand, and he didn't reach for her again.

"Micah recovered quickly from his fall," she said. "He was walking again in two days."

"No one recovers from rabies."

Rabies?

The very words struck horror in her heart. "He doesn't have rabies."

His voice was resigned when he spoke again. "I'm responsible for our whole party."

"I know."

"Mrs. Kneedler is sick too." He leaned his head back, looking up at the falling snow. "And I have to get everyone to a safe place for the night. We all can't wait here until your father—"

She stopped him. "He's not going to die."

"And we don't have enough men to carry him to the fort or to the mission."

She looked to the right, at the small cow path that was supposed to take them to the mission. To her left was the path that was supposed to lead to Fort Vancouver. The carts had disappeared into the trees.

Their oxen, Abe and George, waited near Papa. They were both weak, but if she got rid of their remaining things, maybe the oxen could carry Papa in the cart.

"The carts—" she began.

Jack shook his head. "He wouldn't survive an hour in a cart."

"Then Micah and I will have to wait until he can travel."

"I can't stay with you." He looked down the path where their company had gone. "But I can't leave you and Micah here alone either."

She nodded her head solemnly. The choices out here were agonizing.

She looked over at Micah, snuggled close under the buffalo pelt with Papa. Snow iced the fur, covering it like powdered sugar. Papa didn't shake or stir. When had her father grown so old? His hair was peppered with gray, and the sun on his face made his skin look like cracked leather. "I can't leave Papa alone either."

Perhaps if he got some rest, he would be better in the morning.

"He's going to die, Samantha, and you might too if you stay here."

Her body stiffened. "He's not going to die!"

"I don't know what to do," Jack pleaded, looking up at the dark sky again. "You can't travel with your father, but with the snow…we need to find a place to set up camp tonight."

Everything seemed to collapse within her. She knew what he was saying, but as with the killing of their dogs, she couldn't comprehend it. He was asking the impossible of her.

"I can't—" She clutched her fists together. "I'm not leaving him here."

"There's no shelter here from the storm."

She looked over her shoulder, east instead of west, at the path that led away from her company. "I'll take him to the mission in the morning."

He shook his head. "It will be too late."

"No, it won't."

Jack studied her for a moment. "We can take Micah with us, just until you get to the valley."

She looked over at her brother again. Was she being selfish to keep him with her? Or was it safer for him to stay where she could watch him? The members of their company all had plenty to worry about without adding the burden of someone else to feed and care for. No one would care for him like she would. If he got lost again…she could never forgive herself.

She knew what Mama would say. Mama would tell her to keep Micah with her.

She took a deep breath. "He can help me with Papa."

"Samantha—"

She shook her head. Her mind was made up. She didn't care if Jack Doyle was angry at her or if they didn't make it to the Willamette this fall. She had to take care of her family.

"Come with us," Jack whispered one last time.

Her hands clenched her skirt in fury at him and his urging to leave her father behind. Even if Papa was going to die, she had to care for him until he was gone from this world. She would rather die than live the rest of her life knowing that she'd abandoned her father to the snow and wild animals that would surely finish what the grizzly had begun.

She shivered.

How could Jack ask this of her?

She looked at her toes, shaking her head. "I can't."

Jack unpacked her oxcart, and as the snow fell harder around him, he quickly strung the canvas over several low tree limbs in the small clearing and put their bedrolls inside. "When he—" Jack started. "When you can, follow the river east to the mission. I'll come back for you as soon as the others are safe."

She nodded. "Tell the others I said good-bye."

Jack backed away, and she knew he was angry with her. But, really, she should be the angry one. He was leaving her.

Micah hugged him and then waved as Jack walked away on the path.

Samantha collapsed against a tree, the shock of it all engulfing her. Tears bubbled up in her eyes, but she didn't cry. She had to stay strong for Micah and her father.

She was tempted to yell at Jack to wait, that she and Micah were coming with him, but she could never leave her father. Just maybe he would recover quickly, like Micah had. They could all walk to the mission in the morning.

She stepped down to the mighty Columbia and dipped her pail into the river. As much as she wished she could make a hot soup for Papa and Micah, rich with vegetables and potatoes and meat, water would have to suffice.

Never in her life would she again take for granted the life-giving power of a cup of water.

Inside the tent, Micah was playing with his wooden animals on the ground. Papa shivered under his coverings, his face beaded with sweat, and she lifted his head, spooning sips of water into his mouth. For a moment, his eyes were clear, his voice raspy. "Where did the others go?"

"They're walking down the river."

"You—you have to go with them," he said, his voice urgent.

She shook her head. "No—"

"You can't stay out here by yourself."

She pulled Micah close to her. "I'm not alone, and neither of us is leaving you."

His face strained. "My back hurts—"

"I know, Papa. We're going to get you better."

He shook his head. "It's too late."

She gave him the last of the laudanum, and then Boaz sat beside her. She snuggled into his coat. They didn't need Jack and the others. Together, the four of them would be loyal to each other. They would get Papa to a safe place.

* * * * *

Jack felt sick. He didn't have camp fever like Mrs. Kneedler, but guilt was burning his insides. He'd done the unthinkable—left behind an ailing man, a seven-year-old child, and the woman he once thought he'd marry.

He raked his fingers through his hair, clinging to his walking stick as he herded their miserable-looking party of three westward. He'd had no choice but to leave Samantha and her family, had he? It wasn't possible to get the others to safety, not with her choice to stay behind.

He had caught up with the Kneedlers, but the Oxfords and the Parkers were still ahead of them on the trail. When he found the rest of their fragmented party, perhaps they could vote to turn around. But if they went to the mission and the snow continued to fall, he feared they would all have to remain for the winter. The missionaries might not have enough food and supplies for all of them.

They might all die if they didn't continue west.

And they might still die if they didn't get to shelter soon.

He had to get the others to safety, but if something happened to Samantha—

The snow fell harder on their path and he prayed as he walked, prayed that Samantha and Micah would survive the night. That Hiram would pass on quickly so that Samantha and Micah could leave for the mission in the morning.

It was a rare woman who could survive out in this wilderness by herself, but Samantha could do it.

He only wished she had trusted him enough to come with him when he'd asked. He shouldn't be frustrated at her, not for staying to care for her father, but it was clear to all of them that Hiram was going to die. If not tonight, then soon.

He didn't want her and Micah to die as well.

He raked his hand through his hair again.

What kind of man was he? He should have kept the group together no matter what. Perhaps it wasn't too late for him to go back.

Mr. Kneedler put his hand on Jack's shoulder. "You should go find her."

He nodded. "I will, once we catch up with the others."

"Prudence and I are in God's hands."

He looked back at Mrs. Kneedler, who was supporting herself against the cart. He knew she was terribly ill, and he also knew she was praying for the Waldron family as she walked. The Kneedlers were in God's hands, perhaps, but for this season, God had entrusted them to him as well. Mrs. Kneedler might live if he got her to the fort in time.

"There was no good choice, Jack," Mr. Kneedler said. "Samantha couldn't leave him."

"Do you think they can make it to the mission?"

Jack waited, hoping the man would tell him that God would keep them safe in His hands, that He would send a host of angels to protect Samantha and her family.

"No one knows the will of God, Jack."

"It couldn't possibly be His will for them to die."

Mr. Kneedler glanced across the swift river. "Sometimes I wonder if I was foolish to bring Prudence on this journey. That I stepped ahead or even outside of what God would have me do. But I still feel like we're exactly where we're supposed to be. We must pray that Samantha is exactly where she is supposed to be and that help will come when she needs it. And that you obey His voice as well."

Two hours later, Jack and the Kneedlers stopped walking. A good inch of snow had accumulated on the ground, and darkness settled over them. There would be no catching up with their remaining party tonight.

He helped Arthur set up his tent and then quickly set up his own.

Samantha needed help now; Jack could feel it in his bones. But he couldn't be there to rescue her.

Chapter Thirteen

Samantha's candle flickered inside the tent. Papa and Micah both slept close to her, but she couldn't sleep. Instead, she opened up Mama's favorite book and read about Christian's pilgrimage. She could almost see Papa pressing ahead in the story alongside Christian, staying faithful on his journey to the Celestial City.

Christian hadn't deterred like the others to the City of Destruction. He pursued what was right. Even when his body gave out, he continued to overcome until it was time for him to cross over the river and into the Celestial City.

> *Now, now, look how the holy pilgrims ride,*
> *Clouds are their chariots, angels are their guide:*
> *Who would not here for him all hazards run,*
> *That thus provides for his when this world's done.*

Papa stirred in the candlelight, opening his eyes.

"Oh, Samantha," he murmured, his smile weak. "You're as pretty as your mother."

She shook her head. Her body was covered with dust, her hair windblown, her nose burnt from the sun. And she was tired to her core. "I'm not pretty, Papa."

"Yes, you are." Papa reached for her hand, squeezed it. "And you are strong—much stronger than your mama, and stronger than me."

Samantha tucked the quilt around his shoulders. "You need to sleep."

Samantha put down her book and opened their medical box again. The laudanum was gone, but they still had some castor oil and peppermint. Neither would heal this infection, but she wouldn't stop fighting, not until the angels came for him.

Her hands shaking, she put a few drops of the castor oil in a spoon and tried to force it between his lips.

He tossed his head. "No more."

She tried to push it back into his lips. "We have to fight, Papa."

He shook his head, his brown hair ratted around his head.

"'To every thing there is a season,'" he quoted from the book of Ecclesiastes. "'A time to be born, and a time to die.'"

Samantha stopped him. "It also says there's a time to heal, Papa. A time to laugh and dance."

"They'll be plenty of dancing in the heavens."

Tears trickled down her dusty cheeks. She wanted to keep fighting for Papa's life with everything she had—she wanted Papa to keep fighting for it—but she couldn't force Papa to live.

Perhaps it was time for her to let go. Perhaps it was time for Papa to be able to run and dance and drink from the living fountain that would never go dry.

Perhaps it was time for Papa to be well again.

Samantha put the spoon down and kissed her father's cheek, knowing that this world was almost done for him. The clouds would be Papa's chariot, the angels his guide.

The hours passed in silence. Micah slept beside her. She couldn't sleep, knowing it was probably Papa's last night with them. He stirred again and she leaned down, opening the tent flap. The snow had stopped, and hundreds of stars glittered against the night sky.

It seemed fitting to her; the stars would be Papa's chariot instead of the clouds.

"Look at this view, Papa." Samantha gently lifted his head so he could see the splendor outside. "You made it to the Columbia River."

He rested against her. "The Columbia," he said slowly. "We did it."

"Yes, we did."

She lay Papa back down to rest, but moments later he sat up again, his voice more urgent this time. "I haven't been a good father to you."

"Yes, you have."

He shook his head. "Forgive me?"

She had nothing to forgive him for, but she kissed his forehead anyway. "Of course."

"You take care of Micah, good care of him."

She looked over at her brother, asleep under the blanket. "We'll both take care of him."

Papa shook her arm with surprising strength, like he had to make Samantha understand. "You need to care for him."

She choked out, "I will, Papa. Don't worry."

"Trust in God, Samantha. He'll guide you on the right path." He lay back on the ground, the shadow of a smile on his face as his gaze wandered to the top of their tent. "Do you see her?"

"Who?"

"Eliza."

Samantha leaned against Boaz. And she wept.

* * * * *

Alex saw the Americans first. They were passengers on a bullboat made of willow poles and covered with a buffalo hide. Alex watched as the Indian guide paddled the motley group toward them on the north bank of the Columbia. They looked more like half-starved animals than humans.

Alex stayed in the background as McLoughlin stepped forward, waiting to greet the newcomers. The governor and Madame had stayed away for almost a month, enjoying the last of the sunshine before the autumn rains poured.

The McLoughlins had returned last night, and this afternoon, Alex and McLoughlin had been walking along the banks, discussing what must be done with the school. McLoughlin was furious about Calvert's departure, but he in no way planned to find him. He asked Alex to continue in his attempts to teach the children, and though Alex tried to convince him of his ineptitude as a teacher, McLoughlin wouldn't hear of it. Alex could teach in the mornings and work on his inventory in the afternoon.

One of the Indians stepped onto the bank, and McLoughlin greeted him in Chinook. Alex attempted to greet them as well, but they ignored him. Clearly, they were here to see the White-Headed Eagle.

McLoughlin nodded at the passengers. "Where do you find them?"

"At The Great Dalles," one of the Indians replied in English. "They ask me to bring them here."

McLoughlin nodded. "Very good."

An older man with determined eyes and a gaunt face stepped off the boat. His gaze was focused on McLoughlin as he rushed up the bank.

"Welcome," McLoughlin said, shaking the man's hand. "Are any of you injured?"

"No, but we are very hungry."

Alex looked back at the raft. There were three men and a woman crowded into it, their faces muddy and their clothing soaked. Surely their guides had helped them portage around the rapids instead of going over them.

"What is your name?" McLoughlin asked the man who stood beside him on the bank.

"Loewe." He stood up a little straighter. "My name is Captain Ezra Loewe."

"Where do you come from?"

"Originally from the Commonwealth of Virginia, but our wagon train left Missouri, at the beginning of May."

McLoughlin motioned toward the hill behind the river. "We are on the way back to Fort Vancouver. We can feed you and your party there."

The man reached out, stopping him. "There are more behind us."

McLoughlin hesitated, as if he was afraid to ask. "How many more?"

Loewe swallowed, his voice not quite as strong. "Almost thirty."

Alex stepped closer to the man, eyeing the few barrels on the raft. "Will your remaining supplies be arriving soon as well?"

Loewe shook his head. "We had to leave almost everything back in the mountains."

Alex suppressed his groan.

Instead of chastising him, McLoughlin clapped the captain on the back. "We have plenty to share with you."

The man sighed with relief.

Alex could almost imagine the letter Loewe would send to his friends and family back home.

Come to Oregon Country. The British will take good care of you.

* * * * *

Samantha woke at first light and slowly put the medicine bottles back into the box. Papa wouldn't need them any longer. Micah slept as she put a blanket over her father's face. Then she untied the flap on the tent.

Flakes of snow clung to the ground, but the sky was a crisp blue this morning. She wrapped Mama's shawl around her shoulders, and as she prepared the morning fire, Boaz hurried up into the trees behind their tent.

She'd tried to help Papa, tried to save her entire family, but she had failed. Mama's body rested back in Ohio, and now Papa's remains would stay in this new country.

She glanced back at the tent where her brother still slept. She may have failed her parents, but she wouldn't, she couldn't, fail Micah. She'd promised Mama long ago and now she'd promised Papa that she'd keep him safe.

Maybe she should have sent him on with the others to Fort Vancouver. God forgive her if it was selfishness or even pride that had kept him here.

Twenty minutes later the coffee began to brew, but Boaz still hadn't returned. She called his name as she squinted into the trees. In that moment, she couldn't bear to think about losing her beloved dog on the same day she lost her father.

She sat on a log, her hands shaking as she poured herself a mug of black coffee. She had to press on, for Micah's sake. There was no time to stop and mourn their loss. They would have to grieve later.

Something rustled in the grass, and she turned and saw Boaz, a brown rabbit in his jaws. When Boaz dropped the rabbit at her feet, she clung to his neck for a moment, grateful beyond words that he had returned to her. They were going to make it to Fort Vancouver and then on to the Willamette. And the three of them were going to make it together.

They could try to find the mission, but her heart wasn't calling her east. It was calling her west, where Papa wanted them to go. Jack and the others would be traveling along the river. If she and Micah hurried, perhaps they could rejoin the other members of their party before nightfall.

She quickly cleaned the rabbit and cooked it in a stew. Then she woke her brother.

He stared at the blanket that covered Papa's body. "Why won't Papa wake up?" he asked.

She hesitated, breathing deeply before she spoke. "He went to be with Jesus."

Micah sat quietly for a few moments. "Is he with Mama?"

She nodded.

His voice shook. "I should be happy for him, shouldn't I?"

"I suppose we should."

His eyes welled with tears. "But I'm not very happy at all."

She pulled him close to her, and they grieved together at the loss of a man who'd loved them both, a man who'd left them a legacy of perseverance and strength. They would press on like Papa had done so many times.

She stood up beside him, offering her hand. "We're going to finish this journey for him."

Micah took her hand.

The stew tasted bland without vegetables or seasoning, but it was all they had. Micah didn't complain about the meal, and she was long past caring much about taste, concerning herself more with sustenance. The rabbit would carry them through the day.

Her heart broke as she lifted Papa's body from the tent, moving it carefully toward the cliff. They had no shovel to bury him with, so she and Micah gathered rocks and sticks from the banks of the river.

Her hands trembled again as she placed the first rock on the blanket that covered him. Micah added an armful of leaves.

They worked until the blanket was completely covered, and then she unpacked their Bible from the oxcart. She and Micah held hands as she read from it: "'And God shall wipe away all tears from their eyes; and there shall be no more death, neither sorrow, nor crying, neither shall there be any more pain: for the former things are passed away.'"

When she finished reading, she glanced down at her little brother. Then she wiped away the tears from his eyes.

Neither Mama nor Papa were in pain, but she and Micah… they were in a world of it.

Micah tugged on her hand. "Can you read Mama's verse?"

She nodded, but she didn't need to turn to the verse in Psalms. She'd quoted it often to Mama in the days before she died. "'God is our refuge and strength, a very present help in trouble.'"

Her brother clung to her as they walked away from the grave. They needed His help. Desperately.

Chapter Fourteen

"On to Oregon," Samantha said, with as much confidence as she could muster.

It had been their cry almost every morning since they'd left Missouri, and she wasn't going to quit. Not until they found either their party or Fort Vancouver.

Micah held up the pole of his knapsack and repeated her words.

She turned one last time for a glimpse over her shoulder, but she could no longer see the ground where they'd laid her father to rest. His body was only a shell, his soul gone to a better place, but she still hated that she hadn't been able to bury him in a grave.

Samantha held Micah's hand as they followed Boaz along with Abe and George down the Columbia River. They had no choice but to keep moving forward. Papa had made it to Oregon just like he wanted, but the ending of his story wasn't what any of them had anticipated. The trail ahead may have felt impossible, but she wouldn't stop moving, nor would she stop fighting. She and Micah would carry his legacy into this new country.

> When trouble, like a gloomy cloud,
> Has gathered thick and thundered loud,
> He near my soul has always stood—
> His lovingkindness, O how good!

She sang the hymn softly as she walked. And then she prayed to the One who stood near her soul.

Please help me…help me get my brother to safety.

There was little strength left in her, but she didn't care what happened to her anymore. Her parents were gone, and even though she was no longer angry with Jack, she knew she could never marry him. It was too late for her to return to Ohio, at least until next spring, but perhaps she could find work with a family in the Willamette and Micah could attend school. She wouldn't fail Mama again.

At this moment, with her feet screaming in pain and her belly aching for good food, she longed for the rhythm of a normal life. Perhaps she should have married Reginald and stayed in Ohio. If she had, Papa might not have left either…and he would still be alive.

She trudged behind the oxen across the soggy path. Her moccasins and ankles were covered in mud, the hem of her skirt torn and filthy. She clung to a tree as she inched around a wide puddle that looked more like a pond. Her hands covered with chips of bark and pine needles, she knelt down to the icy stream and rinsed them off.

Micah slogged through the mud puddle in his bare feet and trousers. There was no sense in trying to coax him around the water. They both looked more like hogs that had been rolling in their pens than two determined emigrants intent on starting a new life.

Hopefully Jack and the others weren't too far down the path. Most of them had a bulky cart like she and Micah. If they walked fast enough, surely they could catch up to them.

The sunshine had melted the snow, and the farther they walked, the more spectacular the scenery became. Rock walls shot up on the left of the narrow path, the steep cliffs towering above them. Water tumbled down the cliffs and poured into rocky streams that dumped into the river.

Micah hopped over a log and then turned back to look at her. "I'm hungry."

She ruffled his hair. "I know. Me too."

He rubbed his stomach. "If you could eat anything you wanted, what would it be?"

She thought for a moment. "Hot corn with butter. Mama's fried chicken. And lemonade."

He smiled. "I'd eat ice cream."

She laughed. "It's too cold for ice cream."

He looked at her as if she were crazy. "It's never too cold for ice cream."

"I suppose not."

He hopped over another log. "Remember when Papa bought strawberry ice cream for us at the fair?"

She remembered it well. Mama's health had rallied a year ago in July. Papa celebrated by treating them all to a day at their county fair, where they'd enjoyed the exhibits, animal shows, and foods she'd never seen in her entire life.

She'd never forget the taste of that ice cream. It had been a golden day—their time with both Mama and Papa, the sweet strawberries, the simple joy of eating something cold on a hot day—a day she'd taken for granted. She never could have dreamed that the following July they would be traversing rivers and walking hundreds of miles across the Great Plains, living on beans and dried meat. She never could have imagined heat like she'd experienced this summer, nor could she imagine tramping through cold, wet mud as they were today. And both of their parents gone.

Papa had been so excited when the doctor said that Oregon Country, with its fresh air and open spaces, might be a good place for Mama to get well again. Not only did he want Mama well, but Papa craved adventure, free land to farm, and a vast wilderness to hunt. He was also convinced that the people of Oregon would one day need his services as an attorney.

Even Mama had seemed enthusiastic about the possibilities of this new life, until her illness returned...and then stole her away. Papa was still determined to go to Oregon, maybe even more so after Mama's death. They sold their belongings not long after they buried her and traveled to Missouri to buy a wagon and supplies. He never seemed to look back.

She brushed her hands over her eyes.

She'd wanted to come to Oregon almost as much as Papa... for the adventure and also so she, Micah, and Papa could learn how to be a family. And they had relied on each other and loved each other for six months.

God had given all of them a gift.

"Whoa," she shouted.

The oxen and Boaz stopped at her command. Their path continued left through the forest, but through the trees she saw a wide plain of flat land leading to the river. Tall posts from almost a dozen tepees towered in the air, and she saw specks of people milling near the water. There would surely be food in the Indian village and maybe a place to rest, but she remembered well how that Indian man had looked at her back on the plains—the one who offered Papa three horses for her.

There were friendly Indians at Fort Hall, but the traders had told them about some tribes who held people captive as slaves. If they refused to release her and Micah, Jack may never find them on their return. She didn't know if these Indians were friendly or not, and she couldn't risk something else terrible happening to her brother.

They had to keep moving west.

Micah waved his arms over his head and shouted, "Hello!"

"Hush, Micah." She pulled his arms down. "Not all Indians are friendly like the ones at Fort Hall."

Micah tugged on her hand, pulling her toward the village. "Maybe they're cooking salmon for supper." He turned toward her, pleading with his eyes. "Please, Sam."

She kissed the top of his head. "It won't be long now before we'll be at the fort."

Boaz barked, and she turned. His eyes were focused on the trees to their immediate left.

"What is it?" she whispered, scanning the branches.

The oxen hauled the cart slowly ahead of her. If there was a predator nearby, they didn't seem to sense it.

A branch cracked in the trees, and Boaz growled. She reached for the whip.

"Get up," she commanded, snapping the whip over their oxen's heads.

They all needed to keep walking.

* * * * *

Jack sat on an animal fur and sipped a watery soup from a cone-shaped basket. The wooden strips were gummed together with some sort of resinous substance to hold in the liquid. Across the smoldering fire were the Kneedlers, and to their right were two Indian men wearing deerskin tunics embroidered with porcupine quills and tan leggings. Their black hair had been pulled back by twists of leather around their foreheads, and they smelled like grease.

The men studied him closely as they ate soup from their baskets, and fear snaked through his skin. Where they just waiting until they slept to kill them? Or were they planning something else?

An icy rain had replaced the snow, pattering against the leather covering overhead. Mrs. Kneedler had drunk about a gallon of river water before she fell asleep on the fur that she shared with her husband, her mouth continuing to bleed even as she rested. They needed to get to the fort quickly and find Doctor Rochester or another doctor to care for her.

Jack's mind raced. The Indian who'd welcomed them to the village knew enough broken English to explain that the Oxfords and Parkers had left that morning with their supplies and two Indian guides to raft downriver.

Using hand motions and a few English words, Jack asked the man if their guides could take him, the Kneedlers, and their supplies down the river as well, the next morning. The man pointed at their remaining oxen, and Jack agreed to the trade for their transportation. The sooner he could get the Kneedlers to Fort Vancouver, the sooner he could return for Samantha and her family.

His entire body ached. His shoulders, his legs. He'd been up for most of the night, worried about Samantha and Micah. He would never be able to forgive himself if something happened to them. He hoped she would follow his advice and go to the mission, but knowing Samantha...

Samantha would do what she wanted to do.

"How long do you think it will take us to reach Fort Vancouver on the river?" Mr. Kneedler asked.

Jack had tried to ask the Indian man the same question but hadn't gotten an answer. "Maybe two or three days."

"So we'll have to stop and camp on the way."

Jack nodded. They would also have to portage their supplies around the larger rapids, but he would explain that later.

"You need to get some rest," Mr. Kneedler said.

He shook his head. "I can't sleep."

He looked down again at Mrs. Kneedler, resting peacefully by her husband. He hoped they would all make it safely to the fort—the Kneedlers, Samantha, Micah, and even Hiram—but he also knew that life in this world was only a vapor.

Jenny had left his life long before she should have. Samantha and the others might go as well. He'd told Samantha that she had to let go of her father, but he'd fought for Jenny just like Samantha was fighting for her father.

Even though he'd fought hard, there had been nothing he could do to save his wife.

Sometimes you had to let go.

He looked back toward the opening, at the supplies they'd left outside. Then he looked at the two Indians still watching them.

They'd lost five horses on their journey, stolen at night by Indians, he assumed. If these men didn't kill them, would they steal from them while they slept?

He forced his eyes closed. He couldn't do everything—get the Kneedlers safe to the fort, watch over their things, go back for Samantha.

It was still hours until nightfall, but he needed to sleep, even if these Indians rummaged through their things, even if they planned to take his life.

If he awoke in the morning, he needed strength to get to the fort and then return for Samantha and her brother.

* * * * *

The cold rain drizzled at first, soaking the pelt that Samantha stretched over her head, and then it assailed her and Micah with torrents of stinging drops, like needles piercing her skin. The sun hadn't started dipping behind the cliffs yet, but she and Micah were shivering. They kept slipping in the mud, and the oxen were slipping as well as they tried to pull their cart along the path that narrowed again to the riverbank.

It was useless, she decided, to continue slogging through the downpour. If they didn't stop, they would be too sick to continue in the morning.

Micah helped her set up the tent in the rain, under a giant pine tree that sheltered them from part of the storm. She hauled her gun and their wet things into the tent. Her stomach groaned, hunger clouding her mind. It would be impossible to build a fire tonight, and they couldn't eat the pinto beans raw.

Surely Jack and the others couldn't be too far ahead. They would try to sleep and then find the rest of their party tomorrow. Boaz wandered off into the trees and the oxen grazed on the grass. At least some of them could eat tonight.

Micah snuggled up against her. "I'm still hungry, Sam."

"Me too." She brushed back his hair like Mama used to do with her when she was a girl. "We'll find something to eat first thing in the morning."

A shadow moved on the other side of her canvas. At first she thought it was Boaz, but then she realized it was a person.

She reached for her gun. They didn't have much left to steal, but she understood what it was like to be desperate.

"What is it?" Micah asked as she moved to the flap.

"I'm sure it's nothing," she whispered. "But I need to check on Boaz."

Praying silently, she inched back the flap. She was the only one left to care for Micah, and she desperately needed God to send His angels to help keep him safe.

She glanced around the side of the tent and then scanned the gray valley and river in front of them, but there was no one there except George and Abe, who lapped water from the river.

She looked down, and at her feet was some sort of bag made of an animal hide. She opened it, and inside was what the traders had called *pemmican*—a mixture of meat pounded into a powder and mixed with melted animal fat. It may have looked unsavory, but she'd been told that it sustained the trappers for months at time. There was just enough in the bag for two people.

She looked out at the river again and then at the thin line of trees on both sides of her.

Who had brought them food?

"Thank you," she whispered in case someone was listening.

Her stomach groaned again as she brought the food inside. Micah didn't even ask where she'd found the food. With a shout of glee, he dove toward the pemmican and ate rapidly.

Boaz returned an hour later, and she hoped he had found food as well. He curled up beside the flap to sleep, and as she tucked a blanket around Micah's slight body, she thanked God for the messenger He'd sent to provide for them.

Rain seeped under the canvas sides of the tent, puddling up around their bedrolls, but with the pemmican settling in her stomach, exhaustion began to lure her into a deep sleep.

In the morning they would catch up with the others.

Chapter Fifteen

Fog swallowed up the rain as it drifted through the canyon, scaling the cliffs and clinging to the colorful leaves. She and Micah sang together as they rolled up their bedrolls and then the canvas of their tent to pack in their cart. No one out here cared if she sang off-key

They quickly ate the remaining pemmican, and then she urged Micah, Boaz, and the oxen along the path. Jack and the others would likely stop and fish or hunt soon for food. Today they would surely find them on this path.

The gorge was cold, but when the fog lifted, sunshine spilled light over the rocks and trees. She and Micah had plenty of water from the river, and after the sun dried the wood, she would make a fire and cook beans. Their supply of beans could last two or three more days. Then she would buy food from the fort with the gold Papa left them.

Her body ached and her spirit was depleted, but she continued to draw strength from the beauty around her. The Columbia roared and splashed like the frothy milk in Lucille's pail as it bounded over rocks and logs. Gentle streams meandered beside the mighty river, trickling through the trees and across the narrow path that she, Micah, and Boaz hiked.

The trees dwindled to shrubs along their path, and above them, a waterfall cascaded like a glittering ribbon down the cliff. Until this week, she'd never known that so many shades of color existed in nature. The rich colors of autumn mixed with vivid greens, blazing against the charcoal wall of volcanic rock.

She picked up her skirt and waded through another shallow stream blocking their path. Micah stopped walking in the midst of the stream, staring out at the river.

"Come along," she prodded.

He shook his head. "I think those are boats."

Turning, she followed his gaze across the water and saw two rafts paddling down the wide river, traveling west. Fear paralyzed her at first, hoping the Indians didn't see them, but as she watched the rafts, she slowly realized that there were stark white faces among the copper-colored ones. It was their company, being guided down the river by Indians.

Panicking, she began to wave her arms, trying to shout above the din of the waterfall. "Hello!"

"Hello!" Micah echoed beside her, waving his arms as he jumped up and down in the stream. If only one of them saw her or Micah. If only they could direct their rafts over to the shore…

Jack and the others, they would carry all of them to safety. If they yelled loud enough surely Jack would hear them. But the rafts floated on, her and Micah's screams drowned out by the roar of the falls.

She and Micah didn't stop shouting or waving their arms until the rafts faded into the distance. Then Samantha collapsed onto the riverbank.

There would be no catching up to the rest of their company.

She and Micah were alone.

* * * * *

Alex shut the door of the schoolroom and momentarily thought about putting a lock on the door. Then he laughed at himself. The schoolhouse was the one place in all of Fort Vancouver that thieves would probably avoid. There were only books, slates, and chalk inside, and the fort's children seemed to evade all three quite well.

After observing Alex's final attempt at teaching yesterday, McLoughlin quickly concurred that Alex was not gifted as an instructor. He could manage the clerks and oversee the inventory, but the governor told Alex that he was in no way supposed to go into the classroom again. Alex was quite willing to obey that command. And the students were certainly pleased about it.

Someone shouted his name, and he turned to see Simon rushing across the piazza.

When Simon reached him, the man bent over, clutching his knees as he caught his breath.

"What is it?" Alex asked.

Simon took several more breaths before he stood. "We have visitors."

"More Americans?"

Simon nodded, his black eyes flashing in the light.

"Where's McLoughlin?"

"Henry said he went to check on the livestock."

Alex sighed. It would take a good half hour for a messenger to run to the barns and maybe another hour for McLoughlin to return. "I shall take care of it."

"They're just outside the front gate."

Alex walked slowly toward the entrance.

Captain Loewe and his company had spent the night outside the gates and left with ample supplies that McLoughlin provided for them. They promised to reimburse McLoughlin his expenses, but Alex doubted the governor would receive any of his money. McLoughlin didn't seem concerned. He didn't even ask for collateral in the event that they reneged on their loan.

Ezra Loewe had said more Americans might come, and apparently he was right. After this party arrived, how many more would follow?

Alex stepped outside the palisades and saw an elderly woman being supported on both sides by an elderly man and a rugged-looking younger man with long brown hair.

Alex looked back and forth between the men. "Which of you is the leader?"

The younger man stepped forward. His clothing was soaked, his face streaked with mud and sweat. In his eyes was the same determination of Ezra Loewe, but Alex saw disappointment in them as well. And humility.

The man reached out his hand. "I'm Jack Doyle."

Alex hesitated, staring at the man's hand for a moment before he shook it.

"These are my friends, Prudence and Arthur Kneedler."

Alex examined the gray-haired woman still leaning against her husband. Her mouth was bleeding.

"My wife seems to have caught camp fever," Mr. Kneedler said.

"Our surgeon can examine her." He motioned to Simon. "Could you escort them to Doctor Barclay's office?"

"Of course."

Alex stopped them. "Is your son Tom Kneedler?"

Mr. Kneedler nodded.

"He and his wife are waiting for you in the valley."

Mrs. Kneedler lifted her head, her eyes sparkling. "Thank you," she murmured.

As they walked away, Doyle turned back to Alex. "We're looking for the other members of our party. Families by the name of Oxford and Parker."

"A man named Ezra Loewe passed through here several days

ago with his company, but I do not know the names of the people with him."

Doyle shook his head. "These families would have come later, yesterday perhaps."

"They did not stop at the fort," Alex said. "Perhaps they went on to the Willamette."

Doyle teetered on his feet for a moment and then righted himself again. "We're going to the Willamette as well."

Alex looked down around the man's feet. "Where are your things?"

"Down by the riverbank, but we don't have much food left. We were hoping to purchase some food and perhaps lodging for the night."

"Do you have livestock?"

He shook his head. "We traded them for transportation on the river."

Alex studied Doyle's gaunt face. He may not want the Americans here, but this man clearly needed food. And McLoughlin would insist that they feed the man and his friends. "You must be hungry."

Doyle nodded.

He hesitated for a moment, but he knew what McLoughlin would want him to do. "Come along," he instructed. "We will feed you."

Doyle looked back down at the river. "I can't stay. I have to return for the rest of our party."

"How far back are they?"

"I'm—I don't know."

Alex turned to the Indian guide, talking in the local jargon that blended French, English, and Indian dialects into one language. "Did you bring them from The Dalles?"

"They were ten miles west of the Great Dalles," the guide said.

Alex turned back to Doyle. "Did you stop at one of the missions?"

"The father was ill...he was going to die." Doyle's words had begun to slur.

"If they went east, they might have found help."

"That's what I told her…but she doesn't listen." He stumbled again, catching himself on one of the palisades.

Alex shouted at two men near him—the blacksmith and one of the mill workers. They rushed to the surgeon's office and retrieved a stretcher. With Mrs. Kneedler resting at the office, they helped Doyle to an empty room in Bachelor's Hall.

He had no fever, but he was clearly unwell…either from lack of sleep or perhaps from the fear of what happened to the rest of his party.

Doyle sat up suddenly, looking around the room. "I have to go find her."

Alex put his hand on the man's shoulder. "In the morning, my friend."

* * * * *

Samantha swatted the rump of the lead ox. "Get up," she commanded before she changed her mind. George wandered slowly forward, seemingly confused about why he should move without his yoke.

George and Abe had been faithful companions since they'd left Missouri—patient, gentle, and determined. Even when they were set free each night, they never ran away.

She wished she could take them with her all the way to the Willamette, but the trail along the river had narrowed to a footpath. It was impossible for an oxcart to traverse it and almost impossible to herd their oxen through it.

Hunger plagued her stomach. She should slaughter one of the oxen and eat him. Jack and the other men in their company would do it with little regret; even Papa had been practical about their need to eat. But she couldn't kill either of these animals. They had more than earned the right to enjoy the rest of their lives in this new country.

George and Abe wandered back through the crevice that led into a valley. Tears were silly, especially after all she'd lost, but they came anyway. The animals had been part of the Waldron family for almost seven months.

Now she, Micah, and Boaz would have to carry the most essential supplies with them.

She strapped Micah's bedroll and several changes of clothes to his back with cords. He hiked his knapsack over his shoulder with a bright smile, and Samantha didn't know how he continued to smile.

Perhaps he would stop smiling if he understood the direness of their circumstances, but she wouldn't educate him on what would happen if they didn't make it to the fort soon. Or the fact that Fort Vancouver was located on the north side of the river and she had no idea how to cross it. She needed Micah's smile to keep walking.

What remained of their dried beans and ground coffee was on Boaz's back. Samantha's possibles bag was strapped over her shoulder, her flintlock rifle in her hands, and she carried her clothes and bedroll on her back along with the bag of Papa's gold, their coffeepot, and a ladle wrapped in her grandmother's quilt.

She took a small bag of the fishhooks to trade with the Indians if necessary and one of the bags of seeds Papa had coddled for the entire journey. She didn't know if the seeds were fruit or vegetables, but she would plant them in memory of Papa. His last surprise.

The other seeds, she left in the cart.

She brushed her hands over their family's Bible and Mama's copy of *The Pilgrim's Progress* before she wrapped them in Mama's shawl. They couldn't carry much now, but she would be back to get their heirlooms. Maybe in the spring.

She left the cart as close to the rock cliffs as possible, the tent canvas and then a mass of branches protecting their things. Stepping away, she breathed deeply of the cool air. She needed the air to revive her, strengthen her. She didn't know how many more days they would have to walk, but she couldn't let anything stop her from getting the three of them to their new home.

That evening, she and Micah found blackberry bushes in a canyon. The few berries that remained were dry and shriveled, but they ate them anyway before unrolling their bedding under a giant fir tree. She built a fire from the branches Micah gathered and cooked beans in the coffeepot for their supper. Then they slept in front of the fire, she on one side of Micah and Boaz on the other, huddled together under the quilt to keep from freezing in the frigid air.

Never in her life had she felt such cold. It stole through her skin, stowing itself deep inside her bones. If only she could fall asleep. It would take away the chill for a few hours.

She shivered beside her brother, praying for rest for her tired body and relief from the cold. She didn't want to move, afraid to wake Micah as the hours crawled by.

They should have brought a heavier blanket for them to sleep under, should have packed more food in their wagon.

They should have stayed in Ohio instead of coming to Oregon.

She didn't want to feel anger toward her father, but it bubbled inside her anyway, unwelcomed. Papa had brought them on this journey, and then he had left them alone to freeze to death in the wilderness. It wasn't his fault that the bear attacked him, that he'd died, but she was still angry with him for leaving when they needed him so much.

She rolled over, squeezing her eyes closed, but the more she wanted to sleep, the more sleep seemed to evade her. She shivered again, and suddenly her blanket felt heavier over her body. Warmer. She reached up on top of the quilt, but her fingers brushed over the coarse fur of a pelt instead.

Confused, she ran her fingers over the fur again. Had she somehow forgotten that she'd brought a pelt? Or was she losing her mind?

Something rustled in the trees, and she realized that someone had come to their side and placed the covering over her and Micah, like Mama would have done.

"Who are you?" she whispered to the wilderness.

The hoot of an owl was her only answer.

Fear rose within her at the thought of someone following her, but it subsided just as quickly, turning into thankfulness as the warmth lured her to sleep.

"Thank you," she whispered again as she faded away.

Chapter Sixteen

Jack tried to stand by his bed, but his legs shook in rebellion. It was so frustrating, being bedridden at this outpost when Samantha and Micah might be lost in the wilderness.

He'd hoped that either the Oxford or Parker families would come to the fort so he could ask them to return for the Waldrons, but the rest of the Doyle party never arrived. It seemed they had gone on to the Willamette before winter immobilized them.

They should have told Jack they were going on their own, but perhaps they thought he'd taken the Waldrons and Kneedlers to the mission. He supposed he couldn't blame them for not turning back on the trail. They'd come so far, pushing their animals and families incredibly hard in order to set up a home before winter.

Mr. Kneedler said that his wife was recovering quickly, and for that Jack was grateful. Instead of calling her ailment "camp fever" as the traders had done, Doctor Barclay called it "scurvy." Many of the sailors who arrived at the fort had this scurvy, and he insisted that fruits and vegetables were the cure, including the onions Mrs. Kneedler had avoided on the trail. Their hosts took some of their choice produce from the root cellar and mashed it for her to eat.

Doctor Barclay also said that Mrs. Kneedler had arrived just in time. Another few days without the garden food and her symptoms would have proved fatal.

Jack clung to the poster on the bed as he tried to step forward. He'd already been in bed for at least two days, and when he woke each morning, he promised himself he would find the Waldron family that very day. Unfortunately his body didn't concur with his determination. Even though he insisted he was ready, Doctor McLoughlin refused him the use of any of their boats until he was well enough to walk down to the wharf on his own.

He took a step. Today he would go back across the river and search for Samantha and her family.

He walked slowly out of Bachelor's Hall and surveyed the dozens of buildings in the enclave around him. The fort looked like a village, with its wooden two-story buildings clustered together and the long hall behind him. The red-and-blue Union Flag flew over a long piazza that stretched out in the middle of the buildings. There was a tall three-legged belfry and a fancy white-painted house to the right. One of the buildings was made of brick and stone, and at the corner of the fort was a tall wooden bastion.

He asked a man for the location of the mess hall, and the man pointed him to the last door of Bachelor's Hall. When Jack opened it, he smelled the aroma of sausage. He took a plate of sausage and potato cakes gratefully. The food didn't remain long on his plate.

Alexander Clarke strolled up to him, the man Doctor McLoughlin told him was second in command.

"Your health is improving," Alex said.

Jack nodded. "I'm leaving today."

Alex studied him for a moment, like he was trying to determine the true state of Jack's health. "I'm going to visit one of our fur parties this morning. On the other south side of the Columbia."

Jack's heart sped up. "May I join you?"

"McLoughlin does not think you are well enough to travel."

"I can assure you that I'm much better than the people we left behind."

"I leave in an hour," Alex said. "We will spend the night with a trapping party on the other side of the river, and if you are well in the morning, you can continue on your search."

"I'll be well enough." Jack glanced around the room at all the men of mixed blood mingling among the British men. "Aren't you afraid of having Indians live with you?"

Alex's eyebrows slid up. "Why would I be afraid of them?"

He shrugged. "They may hurt you."

Alex shook his head. "We are not afraid of Indians in the West, my friend. They rely on our supplies at the trading posts, and we rely on the pelts they bring in to trade."

Jack scanned the mess hall one more time, at those with dark, light, and tan skin laughing together.

Perhaps he didn't have to fear them either.

* * * * *

The gorge's looming cliffs had tapered into rolling hills and then flat land with bald eagles circling and screeching above them. Towering to their south was a majestic snow-covered peak that climbed into the heavens, and Samantha assumed it was the volcano the trappers had called the White Giant. Mount Hood.

The mountains in this new territory weren't like those they'd passed on the trip. The mountains they'd passed a thousand miles ago were clustered together along the edge of the path, forming a valley down the middle of them. The white peaks in this country were more pronounced, rising to triumph over this unspoiled land in bold declaration that they'd conquered it first.

Samantha didn't know who was helping them along their way, but whoever was following them brought them exactly what she and Micah needed. Like when God sent manna to the Israelites, their messenger was bringing them just enough food to sustain them each day.

She'd attempted to fish with their hooks to no avail, but two nights back, she'd wrapped a few of their fishhooks in a leaf and left it beside her as she slept. Her gift was gone in the morning, and last night, their guardian angel left them two salmon to roast.

There were only enough beans in her pack for one more meal. She and Micah had already drunk all the coffee as they struggled to stay alert during this final stretch. She didn't know how much longer they had to walk until they reached the end of this trail, but she wouldn't stop now. Her strength had been renewed with the food.

The animal fur was draped over Micah's head and tucked around his body. A piece of canvas hung over her cape in an attempt to ward off the rain, but even when the water drenched her face and dress, she hardly noticed the wet any longer. It was part of their journey now, like her torn clothing and muddy skin, like the hunger pangs that gnawed at her gut.

A small band of darker clouds clustered over the ridge ahead of them. They'd seemed to leave the fierce thunderstorms back on the plains, but there would be no escaping any storm that raged through this valley.

Micah held her hand as they walked, and she didn't let go. They'd left Papa five days ago now. They had to be close to the trail's end.

If she could just get Micah across the river to Fort Vancouver. The British may not want them there, but surely they would help her and her brother, like the traders helped their company at Fort Hall. She would pay them, of course, for food and lodging with Papa's gold. Just until she could find a way to build a home for her and Micah.

And she would build a home here. Now that they were in Oregon, she wouldn't return east. She would do what Papa had desired—what she had once desired as well—and settle in this new country. She and Micah would be all right.

Across the river, smoke curled into the sky, and her heart began to race as she watched it. The smoke could be from another Indian village. Or it could be...

Her heart raced faster.

Had they reached Fort Vancouver?

She leaned down, picking up her brother. As hungry and tired as she was, she was afraid it was a mirage. "Do you see it?"

He scanned the shore on the other side of the river. "It looks like a town."

Her heart lightened. "I think so too."

She scanned the riverfront and the island that stretched between her and the far bank. There were no rapids in this stretch of the Columbia, but the river was much too wide and the current too strong to cross without a boat or a raft. If she still had their ax, she could attempt to build one, but she carried her rifle instead of tools.

As Micah slipped down to the edge of the river, she sat on a smooth rock. Boaz rested at her feet, and she stared at the wide gulf between them and what she hoped was Fort Vancouver. Pulling her knees to her chest, her body rebelled against her. She had walked two thousand miles now, up mountains and across canyons, through streams and down hills so steep she'd needed a rope to keep her from sliding to the bottom.

They'd battled the winds on the plains, negotiated with Indians, battled the bear, lost Papa, Gerty Morrison, Amanda Perkins, the Perkins' baby, and whoever had been buried back in the Blues.

She'd been more hungry and thirsty than she had ever imagined she could be, more wet and cold than she'd thought possible to survive. They'd crossed countless rivers and streams, and now they had one last river crossing.

But she didn't know how to get them to the other side.

After seven months of traveling, the Columbia was all that separated them from a hearty fire and a roof, from hot food and dry clothes and a warm room to sleep in. How she wanted to sleep in a real bed tonight. The journey wouldn't be truly over, not until they reached the Willamette, but if they could rest at this fort and replenish their supplies, they could make it to the valley before winter.

The dark clouds were drawing closer. Any second now, the skies would open up and release their fury, and they would have no choice but to endure this storm like they'd done with the many storms before it.

"Samantha," Micah called from the riverside, motioning for her to join him.

She looked up. "What is it?"

"I found something."

"Not now—"

Micah rushed to her side, tugging on her hand. "Come and see it."

She didn't want to move, but he seemed so excited about his find. Slowly she moved her sore feet to the ground, breathing deeply. His fingers clutched her hand, and his gentle urgency propelled her forward. She rose and stumbled toward the tall grasses and mounds of volcanic rock at the water's edge.

Micah pushed back the grass, and hidden below, along the shoreline, were two boats—one a birch-bark canoe and the other a bateau. She stared at the boats in shock.

Had their guardian angel somehow managed to hide boats for them as well?

Micah helped her flip the canoe and then he lifted out a paddle, holding it up with a grin, as if he'd found a pot of gold. "I can be Noah."

She tilted her head. "Who am I?"

"A giraffe."

She clapped her hands together. "Just what I wanted to be."

He pretended to dip his paddle into the water, excited about the ride. Even after all these miles, he was still enthusiastic about their journey, the way she had been months ago when everything seemed like a grand adventure, back when she thought Papa would get her safely to the Willamette and she and Jack would work together to build a home of their own.

She eyed the long bateau and its polished oars. With its flat bottom, the bateau might be less likely to tip on the ride over, but she'd never been in one before. Of course, she'd only ridden in a canoe twice, on the pond back home, but at least she knew how to paddle.

Her muscles may be aching, but she would get them across this river. Then she would rest. If their angel hadn't brought the boats, perhaps someone from the fort could help her return it to the shore.

She set her pack on the sand and pointed at Micah's knapsack. "Let's strap that on your back so you don't lose it."

"What about my bedroll?"

"Just set it on the bottom of the boat."

Micah eyed her pack. "Can I help you carry something across the river?"

"You have enough to carry—"

He interrupted her. "Papa told me to help you."

She sighed. "Why don't you get Papa's seeds?"

After she secured her gun on her back, she checked the possibles bag at her side to make sure it was cinched shut. She glanced up at the dark sky and then back down at Micah, who was rifling through her bag. "You'll have to get the seeds later."

His blue eyes grew wide. "But—"

She shook her head. "We need to go."

She quickly secured the cords so that Micah's knapsack would stay on his back, and then he handed her a paddle. Boaz hesitated, but she coaxed him into the center of the boat, praying he would keep still. With God's help, she could get all of them safely across the river.

Micah climbed into the boat as she set her bag on the bottom.

Then she took off the moccasin from her left foot. Balancing with the oar, she pushed the boat out into the river, her toes and calf stinging from the chill. Then she carefully stepped back into the canoe.

A raindrop fell on her face, and she brushed it off. If they hurried…surely, they could make it across the river before the storm.

Lifting her paddle, she prepared to row them away from the shore. But then another raindrop followed, and then another. She looked up at the black clouds hovering above them. The downpour hadn't started yet, but it would soon, probably followed by wind funneling through the gorge.

Sighing, she put her paddle down. As much as she longed to be inside the dry walls of the fort tonight, sipping a hot cup of tea or soup, as much as she didn't want to disappoint Micah, it was just too dangerous to cross the river in a storm. The hot soup and dry bed would have to wait. They would wait under the shelter of the trees until the rain passed.

She slowly eased her left leg over the side of the canoe again, preparing to stand, when something snarled behind her. The hairs on her arms prickled at the same time Boaz's back arched. Then Boaz growled at the trees.

Samantha swung her gun around her as she turned. An animal was perched on a rock, snarling, twenty yards from them, but she didn't know what kind. Its coat was a dark brown color and it was smaller than a bear, but the sound it made was just as terrible.

She pointed her gun.

Memories of the grizzly attack rushed back to her. The chaos and gunshots. The gash on Papa's arm. This animal may not be as big as that bear, but it seemed just as angry.

The thought of killing it sickened her for only a moment. She would kill this animal if she had to, to protect her brother. But if the animal charged and she missed, there would be no time to reload.

She kept her eyes on the animal, her gun propped onto her shoulder. "Stay in the boat, Micah."

"What is it?" His voice trembled.

"I don't know."

The animal sprang off the rock, raging toward them. She took one shot and then tossed her gun into the canoe. Grabbing her paddle, she pushed the canoe away from the shore.

The animal splashed behind them, but she didn't turn around. With every stroke, she prayed that God would get them safely to the other side.

* * * * *

Alex crept forward cautiously along the rocks, scanning the south shore of the river to see who had shot a gun. The company men used traps to catch animals. They would only shoot if there was danger.

A dark cloud settled over the river valley, the sprinkles of rain a precursor to a storm. He couldn't see far, but ten yards ahead of him, some sort of animal paddled in the river.

Alex stopped at the shoreline, his skin crawling.

The animal was a wolverine.

He swung his pistol in front of him, preparing to shoot. A wolverine was a reasonably small animal, but it could be unpredictable and dangerous. A wounded wolverine could easily kill a grown man.

When the animal saw Alex, it turned quickly and swam back to shore. It stumbled erratically toward Alex, blood dripping down its side, and then it lunged, snapping at him.

Alex pulled the trigger of his gun and shot the animal through the head.

After it dropped to the ground, Alex slid his pistol back into the holster and walked carefully toward it. He expected to see another bullet wound in its fur, but instead there was an arrow in the animal's side.

Strange.

Who had fired the first gunshot, and who had shot an arrow?

Storms didn't last long in the Columbia District. He'd wait for it to pass before he took his canoe across the river. The bigger bateau he'd leave at the river's edge, waiting to bring back Jack Doyle and the people he'd set out this morning to find.

Rain fell harder now, drenching his overcoat as he pushed back the grass along the shore. He expected to see both boats where they had left them last night. Instead only the bateau remained.

He stared at it for a moment. Had someone stolen his canoe?

His gaze wandered across the wide river. Apparently someone had taken it and now was out on the river, trying to paddle his canoe to the other side.

He groaned. Didn't they know they couldn't canoe in a downpour? The canoe would fill up and—

Something rustled in the trees behind him, and he removed his pistol again. Turning, he aimed his gun, but it wasn't an animal emerging from the trees. It was a young woman, part native and part European, hurrying toward him. Her light brown hair was braided, and she wore a fringed dress of white buckskin and a long necklace of blue beads.

She pointed at the river. "A woman and child are on that boat."

He groaned, looking out across the water and then back at her. "What are they doing?"

"They need your help."

He kicked a pile of stones, and they scattered toward the water. "Of course they do."

The Americans always needed help.

She pushed him forward. "Quickly."

He left the wolverine on the bank and began to row the bateau through the rain. Experienced officers and trappers alike had died on the mighty Columbia, people who knew what they were doing. The Columbia was fifty-five miles of peril as it descended to the Pacific Ocean through narrow channels and raging cataracts. Going out on it in a downpour like this was akin to suicide.

He dragged his paddle through water that battered the sides of his boat. Wind pressed against his body, trying to push him back. The rain fell so hard now that it almost blinded him, but he kept rowing in the direction where he'd seen the canoe last.

Water splashed over the sides of the bateau, and he stopped to quickly bail it out. Then he pushed forward again.

The problem with stupid decisions, like crossing the Columbia in a rainstorm, was that not only did people risk their own lives, they risked the lives of all those around them.

He saw them again to his left—a white woman, a child, and a dog.

He never would have rowed out in the Columbia in a storm, but he couldn't leave a woman and child on the river alone.

Chapter Seventeen

It felt as though she were trying to stir tar—thick, heavy, and black as night.

No matter how hard Samantha tried to paddle the canoe forward, toward the fort, the current dragged them farther west. They'd floated past the island in the river's center now, the far shore evading them. And the sky had filled their boat in its fury.

She couldn't see the shoreline in the rain, but it couldn't be far. She wouldn't stop paddling, no matter how much it hurt. If nothing else, she could get close enough that Micah and Boaz could swim to the shore. If it was shallow enough, she could wade.

Her soaked hair clung to her face, and her dress felt as heavy as the canoe. They'd come so far. They couldn't drown now.

The boat began to list.

God, help us.

Only He could send help for them one more time.

"If we tip, I want you to hold on to the canoe," she called out.

Micah nodded his head.

"We're going to be all right," she said, desperately wanting it to be true.

She dug the paddle back into the river, trying to get them to the shore. The canoe rolled slowly to the right, and her stomach rolled with it.

"Take off your pack," she yelled at Micah, but it was too late.

Boaz jumped into the river and Micah tumbled over. She screamed when Micah's head went under.

Then the canoe dumped her and her pack into the frigid water.

Clutching the wooden side of the canoe, she inched down the side, trying to get to Micah. Her pack began to sink, and she reached for it. If she could hold it with one hand, she could get Micah with the other.

Her brother splashed in the water, his hands flailing as he gasped for breath. Samantha grabbed her pack, holding it with the same hand that held the canoe, and she grasped for Micah but couldn't reach him.

If she let go of the canoe, they would both drown.

Boaz swam to his side, and Micah clung to his fur. But their tired dog was struggling too. His head dipped under the water and then popped out again, Micah clutching his neck. She grabbed for him again, but he and Boaz were floating away, far from her grasp.

She eyed the pack in her hand. It contained Papa's bag of gold. Everything they had to start over.

But it wouldn't be worth having one piece of gold if Micah drowned in the river.

She let go of her pack, let go of the canoe, and dove toward her brother. But before she reached him, a hand appeared suddenly out of the haze, and she gasped.

The hand dipped into the water, and she watched in fascination and horror as it plucked up Micah's knapsack and Micah along with it.

There was a boat. And a man. She couldn't see the man's face, but Micah was in the boat with him. Her brother was safe.

A wave washed over her, and she reached back for the tip of the canoe. She looked around her for her pack, for Papa's gold, but it was gone.

Her hands started slipping.

"Do not let go," the man commanded her.

Her fingernails clung to the bark.

"I cannot lift you out of the water," the man said with an accent, his voice calm. "We will capsize."

Her hands slipped again. She was so tired, she didn't know how much longer she could hang on. "I can't swim."

He rowed closer to her, just out of her reach. "Do not pull us over."

Her teeth chattered. "What—what do I do?"

"Hold on to the side of my boat. I will row us all to shore."

She held out one of her hands, reaching for the boat. It leaned toward her, a little too far.

"Steady," the man commanded.

She clutched the back of the boat. Her entire body was shaking, and she kicked her bare feet under the water, trying to stay warm. Her moccasins were gone, and her dress was so heavy.

Peace flooded over her in the midst of her panic. If she didn't make it to the other side, it would be all right. Perhaps Jesus would meet her on the other side of this river, like He had Christian in Mama's book. Papa would be there too, and Mama and Grandfather. And maybe their guardian angel would meet her at the pearled gates.

Perhaps she should let go.

"You must kick," the man said.

"I am kicking."

"Kick harder," he growled.

She drew every bit of strength she had left in her, pushing her legs like she never had, to get them to the other side. "I am kicking harder."

He dumped some of the water in his boat back into the river. "We must cross here," he said, as if she were a child.

Her teeth kept chattering. "I'm trying."

She could let go and save Micah's life, but if she died, Micah would be alone out here in the wilderness. She wasn't ready to die, not yet, nor did she want Micah to die, but her heavy skirt weighed them all down, threatening to sink their boat or pull her to the bottom.

With one hand, she reached down to her frayed dress and began to tug. She'd spent much of her journey trying to keep her dress stitched together. Now she hoped it would come apart. She yanked at what she hoped was a seam, and the dress tore. Then she tugged again until another piece came off.

She could move now, without the material strangling her legs. She kicked on the right side of the boat as the man paddled on the left. She could no longer feel the coldness in her body, but she wouldn't stop. Not until Micah was safe on the other side.

The current pushed hard against them, but she kicked until her feet hit the muddy bottom of the river. Then she let go.

The man banked the boat on the shore while she crawled up onto the grass, collapsing on the soggy land. The rain was gone—she hadn't even noticed when it went away—but the sky was still dark. It would pour on them again soon.

Micah hopped out of the boat and rushed to her, wrapping his arms around her neck. She hugged him and then looked at the man pulling the boat farther up onto the shore. She couldn't see his face under his soaked hat. He was tall and wore a long black overcoat that seemed to keep out the rain.

The man walked toward her, carrying his hat in his hands. His brown hair was neatly trimmed, his face smooth. It had been months since she'd seen a clean-shaven man.

"Thank you," she whispered.

His green eyes sparked with anger, his British accent strong. "I have seen a lot during my years along the Columbia, miss, but I have never seen anything so stupid—"

"Stupid?"

"Do you know what might have happened?"

Her voice quivered. "I think I have an idea."

"You could have been killed. Both of you. This is not Boston."

She stiffened. "I've never been to Boston."

"You are no longer in the safety of the United States."

It took every ounce of strength she had, but she sat up straight. "Nor are you in England."

He tossed Micah the knapsack and cocked his head at it. "I hope you have a little money in there."

Their money. Her heart sank within her as she scanned the foggy expanse of the river. The gold. Her clothes. Grandma Emma's quilt. It was all gone.

"Are you the woman Jack Doyle went back for?"

Her head tilted toward him. "When did he go?"

"He started walking early this morning."

She wiped the water off her face. "I didn't see him."

Alex sighed. "Let's get you and your son to the fort."

"He's not—"

Micah stopped her. "Let me help."

She glanced at Micah beside her and then up at the man. If he thought Micah was her son, so be it. She was practically his mother.

Her arms behind her, she pushed up on the ground. Micah reached for her hand as she tried to stand, but her legs wobbled and she felt back on the sand. Her gaze fell to her shredded skirt, her muddy skin exposed under the pieces that remained. She tried to cover her legs, but there wasn't quite enough material.

The man didn't seem to notice her bare legs. He offered her his hand, and she eyed it for a moment, not wanting to accept any more help from a man who obviously despised her. But she had no choice, not if she wanted to stand. Reluctantly she took it.

He helped her to her feet, and the mud oozed through her toes as she scanned the shore for Boaz. He couldn't be far away.

The man pointed up a small hill. "We have a long walk to the fort."

She didn't move. "I can't go yet."

"Why in heaven not?"

It hurt to talk, but she pushed the words out. "Our dog was in the boat."

The man turned, scanning the water with her. "He can swim, can't he?"

"Of course," she whispered.

"What is his name?"

This time Micah spoke. "Boaz."

The man returned to the water and began calling Boaz's name. Micah joined him, and they moved down the shore together, calling out.

She collapsed back on the wet grass. If only she could shout with them, search the shoreline, but the cold water seemed to have stolen her voice along with her ability to stand. Boaz had to be nearby. He may have been tired, but he would have made it to shore. She didn't think she could bear to lose him as well.

Then she heard a bark and Boaz was there in front of her, licking her hand. She rocked toward him, shivering again as she hugged his neck.

The man was in front of her now, but she could barely see him. A curtain seemed to be slipping over her eyes. He took off his black frock coat. "Wear this."

She shook her head. "I can't—"

He didn't listen to her, dropping it over her shoulders instead. "You must stay warm."

She didn't know if she would ever be warm again, but the heavy coat stopped her shivering.

"Do you think you can walk?" she heard him ask. She started to nod when she realized he was talking to Micah. Then, without another word, he lifted her off her feet.

She sank into this man's chest as if he were an anchor, holding her steady in this strange new land.

* * * * *

The Waldrons' oxcart was hidden back against a cliff, their oxen grazing nearby, but there was no sign of Samantha, Micah, or Hiram.

When Jack first came across the river with Alex, they'd spent the night with a fur-trading party tucked back in the wilderness.

Had Samantha passed him that night, or had she gone east to the mission for help? He leaned back against a tree. He would keep hiking until he reached the mission, and if they weren't there, he would return to the fort to see if they'd arrived while he was gone.

As he watched the rapids on the river, the feeling was there again. In the past three days he'd been searching for the Waldrons, he kept feeling like someone was watching him. He turned again, scanning the trees behind him.

This time he caught a glimpse of blue among the browns and greens.

"Who are you?" he called. The blue was gone, but he knew that someone was there. He stepped forward. "Why are you following me?"

He waited for another minute, but no one answered.

He called out again. "Do you know what happened to the woman and boy?"

Seconds passed, and then a young woman stepped out from behind a tree.

She was no older than seventeen or eighteen, and she was the prettiest woman Jack had ever seen. Her skin was tan, and she wore her hair in a braid like the Indian women who had fed them in the village before they canoed down the Columbia. Except those women all had dark hair. This lady's hair was a golden-brown, and she wore a bow strapped over her white buckskin dress, a quiver of arrows at her side, and a long necklace made of blue beads.

Her brown eyes sparkled in the sunlight as she searched his face. "Why are you looking for them?"

"They were part of my company—" He stuttered under the intensity of her eyes and his surprise at how well she spoke English. "The father was ill."

She pointed down the river. "I buried him, about twenty miles back."

He'd guessed that Hiram had passed on, but the thought of his death still saddened him. "Did you see the woman and the boy?"

She nodded.

"Where did they go?"

"They crossed the Columbia down near Fort Vancouver."

He took a deep breath of relief. "They are safe."

"If God wills it."

He leaned back against the tree. If only he knew what God willed. It would make this journey so much easier. They would know when to cling and when to let go. Everything, he discovered, needed to be held with an open hand. His wife, Jenny. Then Samantha and her family. As much as he wanted to keep them safe, he could not. Not if God allowed them to go.

It would take him another three days to journey back to Fort Vancouver, to find out whether Samantha and Micah were safe. Until then, he would have to trust in God, like he'd wanted Samantha to trust in him.

He stepped forward, lifting the canvas off the cart and digging through it.

"What are you doing?" the woman asked.

He turned back to her. "I'll take a few things to the fort for them."

He retrieved the Waldrons' family Bible, a bag of Hiram's prized seeds, their mama's shawl. Clothes for both Samantha and Micah and the shoes they'd saved for when they reached the valley. He tucked as much as he could into his pack, but he couldn't carry all of it.

"I will help you," the woman said, taking the Bible, Micah's clothes, and some of the seeds. He hesitated for a moment. Some of the Indians on their journey had stolen from them, but this woman already knew where the cart was located. She could have taken their supplies at any time.

She didn't have any sort of pack, but she picked up the items and wrapped them in one of the animal furs. Then she carried it in her arms.

They turned on the path and silently began the walk west as the sun dipped low behind the clouds.

In the next hour rain came again unannounced, as it had done often during the past three days, and wind tunneled up the gorge. Last night he'd slept on his bedroll, under the stars, but he wouldn't get much sleep tonight if the rain continued.

He would have to say good-bye to this beautiful woman and walk through the night. If the rain stopped in the morning, he would rest.

A narrow canyon cut through the rock walls, and the woman motioned him toward a path that led away from the river. "We need to get out of this storm," she said.

He hesitated at the junction.

Was she leading him to an entire tribe of Indians? An ambush? He'd heard the stories, but he had little to give the Indians except his life.

Then again, he'd heard that some of the tribes sacrificed humans to their gods.

She stopped and turned toward him. "My name is Aliyah."

"I'm Jack. Jack Doyle."

"You can trust me, Jack Doyle."

But he wasn't certain that he could.

She began walking again and he followed several feet behind her so she wouldn't run with Samantha's things. And if necessary, so he could run the other way.

With the wind and rain spilling over him, he followed this beautiful woman into the woods.

* * * * *

Alex tapped on the corner of his desk in the warehouse. He dipped the nib of his pen into the inkstand and began to record the fort's inventory in the leather-bound journal called the daybook.

McLoughlin had given him this responsibility when Alex returned to Fort Vancouver last year after his work at Fort Colville, and it was one of his favorite duties, reflecting on all that had been trapped, made, and traded inside the fort each week as he pored over the blotters of the individual clerks and then recorded the final number in the daybook.

The front door opened, and Simon walked into the room and sat on the edge of Alex's desk. "So tell me about her."

He didn't look up. "About whom?"

"About the American woman you rescued from the sea."

He finished writing his line in the ledger. "I found her on the Columbia, not the sea."

Simon leaned down. "Why didn't you tell me you rescued a lady?"

He dipped the nib again. "I guessed you would find out that information on your own."

"What is her name?"

He glanced up at his friend. "She was drowning in the Columbia. I did not stop to ask."

"Maddox said she had her son with her."

"That is correct."

"Taini will be jealous."

He set his pen in the marble stand. "She has no reason to be jealous. As you well know, my affections are promised elsewhere."

"Is this woman pretty?'

Alex sighed. "Did I mention that she was drowning?"

"Maddox said you carried her a whole mile back to the fort."

"Maddox exaggerates."

"Do you think she's still married?"

The boy had said his father had died, but Alex hated the thought of the other men finding out about an unmarried white woman at the fort. They hadn't seen one in so long that the dozens of desperate men would parade past her room just to stare.

"Is her husband coming for her?" Simon prompted again.

"I am not certain."

Simon didn't blink. "But he might be gone."

"He might be…"

Simon had the courtesy to look forlorn at the possibility, if only for a moment. "No woman remains widowed for long around here."

"The captain of her party has gone to look for her. If her husband is deceased, he will surely marry her when he returns."

Simon smiled again. "Maybe he won't return."

What would Jack Doyle do when he didn't find the Waldron family on the trail? Or what if something impeded his return? The fort wasn't the sort of place for a white woman with any kind of refinement. The Indian wives spent most of their days in their apartments, washing laundry for the unmarried men, pounding out hundreds of nails for the new buildings, or stitching clothing for both officers and laborers. It was a lonely life, he supposed, for any woman.

Simon's eyes sparked. "For the first time in a long time, I'm glad you've promised yourself to old Judith."

Alex nodded toward the door. "Do you not have something to occupy your time at the Sale Shop?"

Simon hopped off his desk. "Everyone seems to be trapping furs right now instead of trading them. And no one's spending their money."

"Perhaps you should become a trapper."

"Not me," Simon said as he backed toward the door. "I'd miss civilization."

When Simon left, Alex stood up and walked toward the window. He could see McLoughlin's house from his office, the white a beacon against the brown wood of all the other buildings except the powder magazine, which was built of brick and stone.

Doctor Barclay had said no medication or garden food would cure the American woman. She needed rest. Madame McLoughlin had personally overtaken the care of Mrs. Waldron and her son.

He'd rescued them from the river. His job was done. Yet he couldn't help but wonder about her story.

Doyle had known she and Micah were back on the trail, yet why did the Americans leave them behind?

Madame McLoughlin would probably think he was interfering—and Simon would think he was speculating—if he paid the woman a visit, but there was nothing wrong with inquiring about her health, was there?

That's what a gentleman would do.

Chapter Eighteen

Alex stepped over the dog that had lain vigilant in Samantha Waldron's doorway since Alex carried her into this room four days past. Madame McLoughlin said Mrs. Waldron had awakened only twice since she arrived, asking about Micah. After her swim in the frigid Columbia, it was a miracle that she was alive at all.

Boaz watched him closely but didn't move. Mrs. Waldron's son was below in the courtyard, rolling a wooden hoop with a stick alongside two of Alex's former pupils.

He hadn't meant to be so harsh with Micah's mother. Now that his head was much clearer—and after speaking with Micah—he realized she had also been protecting her son from the wolverine instead of needlessly risking his life. But back on that shore, with adrenaline pumping through his veins, nothing had been clear.

With Madame McLoughlin's vigilance, he hoped Mrs. Waldron would recover soon. Alex wished someone from her company remained to welcome her when she finally woke, but the Kneedlers had left several days earlier for the Willamette, the governor's mules laden with plenty of fruits and vegetables to carry them the remaining distance to their son.

Alex sat in the chair beside Mrs. Waldron, gazing at her pretty face. She barely looked old enough to marry, much less have a son as old as Micah.

Compassion warred with his sensibilities, but he couldn't seem to help himself. She'd lost her husband on the trail, and she'd lost everything else in this district except her son and the small bag that he carried.

He wondered at her story, what her life was like before she began the long journey west. He'd tried to talk to Micah about their history when they walked back to the fort, but the boy didn't talk much except to say that his father had died and to ask when his mother would wake up.

Alex's anger at her had tempered, but it still infuriated him to think about her and her husband bringing a child all the way over those treacherous mountains. He loved everything about the Columbia District, but nothing was safe here.

Why had she risked so much to come?

Mrs. Waldron shifted on the bed, and her hand slipped over the side.

He glanced over his shoulder, back at the open door, to see if someone was there to return her arm, but no one except Boaz was in sight. Sighing, he reached down and took her hand. It was so light, frail. With his heavy coat over her, he hadn't realized how frail she was when he carried her back to the fort.

How had she survived walking two thousand miles, up and down the treacherous mountains? It was a miracle that the Columbia hadn't whisked her away. If the rest of her body was as fragile as her hand, the smallest of breezes could probably pick her up.

He placed her hand back under the blanket.

Her body might not look strong, but there was an extraordinary strength in her. No other woman that he knew would have kicked as she did across the river. If she'd panicked, he hadn't noticed. She'd pressed ahead with fervor to save herself and her son, and once Micah was safe, she collapsed.

He thought again about his betrothed, the picture of London society and fashion. What would Judith do if her canoe tipped?

The scenario never would have happened, of course. Judith was horribly afraid of the water. She might have starved before she'd board a canoe.

He shook his head. He shouldn't compare this woman to his future wife.

Mrs. Waldron's hand slipped off the bed again, and he reached for it. When he took her hand, she turned her head, her eyes opening slowly at first and then widening in surprise.

He bolted up out of the chair, staring at her.

What was he supposed to do now?

* * * * *

Samantha blinked at the man towering over her.

Where had she seen him before? His dark brown hair and side-burns were neatly trimmed, his piercing green eyes quite serious as he studied her.

Perhaps she'd met him on their journey.

Her heart began to race as she scanned the room, struggling to remember who he was. And where she was.

A fire blazed in the hearth, and a thick blanket kept her warm. It was all she'd imagined it would be like when she was finally home, but the last she remembered, she and Micah had been walking on a path by the Columbia.

How had she gotten here?

She blinked at the man and tried to inch herself up on the pillows. "Where's Micah?"

He pointed toward the window. "He is playing with the other children."

A smile crept up her face as she eased back into the pillows. Playing. Her brother hadn't played with other children in such a long time.

"And Boaz?"

The man glanced back at the door, and her dog lifted his head.

She closed her eyes again for a moment, trying to remember how she got here. There had been a canoe and lots of water. She'd been kicking, and she'd felt so weak. Someone picked her up. Someone strong.

A man.

Her eyes flashed open again. Was it this man standing over her? The one holding her hand?

Memories flooded back to her. She'd sunk deep into this man's chest, letting him carry her the last steps of their journey. What must he think of her? So weak that she couldn't even walk to the fort. So cold. She'd thought she could never be warm again.

But now, as he held her hand, she felt plenty warm.

He dropped her hand onto the covers, as if he'd forgotten that he was holding it.

"You're the one who rescued us," she whispered.

The slightest of smiles played on his lips. "I believe you gave me no choice."

Her gaze wandered back to the window as she remembered his harsh words after they got to the shore, the lecture he'd given her about taking Micah across the river. He'd called Micah her son.

Micah was small for his seven years, but she shuddered to think that she looked old enough to have even a four- or a five-year-old. The trail must have aged her, although she didn't know how she appeared now. She hadn't looked in a glass for seven months...or maybe it was longer.

How long had she been at the fort?

The memory of losing Papa washed over her as well. They'd had to leave his body, covered in rocks and sticks on the trail.

This man was right. She never should have come to Oregon.

Boaz nudged her hand, his tail thumping against the side of her bed, and she reached for him. His gray fur was wonderfully dry. He'd worked so hard at getting them there, protecting them. She knew he would have carried them across the river if he could have.

She looked back up at the man. He looked very proper in his black broadcloth suit and knotted cravat. His green eyes were strong, almost severe, but she saw kindness in them too.

"Where is Jack?" she asked.

"He went to search for you."

A breath of relief escaped from her lips. Jack hadn't left them on the trail to die. "When did he leave?"

"Three days past."

"How long have I been here?"

"Three days as well."

She should be ready to walk another thousand miles, but she wasn't sure if she could cross the room to the window. "Did the others make it?"

He nodded. "Some of them came here, but they have already gone on to the Willamette Valley."

Without her.

She thought back to the grave she'd seen in the Blues. "Was there a woman named Lucille McLean with them?"

He shook his head. "I do not know."

He studied her, and she couldn't read what was behind the intensity of his stare.

"Alex," another man called from the open doorway, "McLoughlin is looking for you."

He stepped away from her bed.

"Thank you for rescuing me," she said again.

He paused at the doorway, looking back at her one more time.

This time he said she was welcome.

* * * * *

The cave was hidden far back in the ravine. Aliyah lit a tallow candle inside the entrance and led Jack through a narrow passage until they reached a large room.

Furs were strewn across the rocky floor, and colorful shells and porcupine quills hung along the walls. Herbs were strung between two poles, and chopped wood was stacked neatly at the side. In the middle of the room was a stone pit dusted with ashes.

Aliyah stacked several pieces of wood in the pit and lit some dried leaves to start the fire. The smoke curled up into the darkness.

Jack admired some of the sketches on the rocks, drawings of people and animals. "Did you draw these?"

She nodded. "It makes it feel more like home."

He set his pack on one of the furs. "Where is the rest of your tribe?"

"A long way from here." She tossed him a fur blanket. "You need to dry your clothes, Jack Doyle."

He glanced around the room, shadows from the fire dancing on the wall. It was cool in the cave, but at least they were out of the rain.

She pointed to the back of the cave. "You can change there."

He moved into the darkness and peeled off his sopping trousers and jacket that had done little to repel the rain. After he dried his skin with the blanket, he wrapped it around his waist and lingered in the shadows.

He could see Aliyah's lovely form adding more wood to the fire. How had he gotten here, alone in a cave with this elegant native woman? She hadn't as much as smiled at him, but in her brown eyes he saw honesty and trust.

Aliyah disappeared into the darkness on the opposite side of the cave, and with the fur blanket wrapped around him, he returned slowly to the center to warm himself by the fire. When she returned, she was wearing a blue calico dress.

His thoughts tangled together, confused. Was this woman English or Indian? And did it matter? Back in Terre Haute, it would matter very much, but perhaps not so much out here.

She hung his clothes on a line and then used two sticks to place hot rocks from the fire into a leather bag filled with water. She crumbled herbs into the bag, and after it steeped, she poured the hot drink into a hollowed gourd and handed it to him. It tasted like raspberries and black tea.

She sipped from her gourd and then eyed his pack. "Did you bring food from the fort?"

He nodded. "Dried salmon and sea biscuits." He glanced around the room again but didn't see any food hanging among the herbs. "Would you like some?"

A smile crept up her slender face, lighting her eyes. "Just the dried salmon, please."

He laughed. "You've had the biscuits before, haven't you?"

She nodded. "The trappers may call them biscuits, but they don't taste anything like the biscuits my mother used to make."

He leaned forward, wanting to hear more of her story. How did such a woman end up living in a cave alone?

She tore up the salmon and added it to another water bag. Before she put the hot rocks inside the bag, she left the fire for a moment and returned with two purple-skinned vegetables.

"Are those turnips?" he asked.

She shook her head as she put them in the water with the salmon. "They are called *wapatos*."

"I've never heard of wapatos."

She shrugged. "They grow wild in the valleys."

They waited quietly as the meal cooked, and then she spooned out the cooked wapatos to eat on the tin plate he retrieved from his pack.

The vegetables tasted to him like potatoes, and after they were gone, they both sipped the salmon soup from the bag.

The meal might have been miserly in any other circumstance, but it satisfied him. Or maybe his contentment came from the fire and the dry cave and the woman who shared supper with him.

He leaned back against a rock that was covered with a coarse wolf pelt. "How did you find Samantha and her brother?"

She shrugged. "I saw them when I was out gathering moss. I followed them to make sure they were safe."

"You helped them, didn't you?"

"Of course." She sounded insulted.

A wave of guilt crossed over him again. "Why did you help them?"

"I had a son once." Her gaze wandered to the fire. "And I was all alone, like her."

Her words washed over him in the silence, a hundred questions playing on his tongue. Where had she come from, and what happened to her boy? Then he wondered how she had helped the Waldrons and why she'd followed him through the gorge.

Instead he asked, "How old are you, Aliyah?"

"Twenty-three."

He studied her face again, her slender nose and tanned skin. She looked so much younger, but there was a maturity in her eyes that the unmarried women in their wagon train didn't have. "Were you born near here?"

She laughed again. "You ask a lot of questions."

He shifted under his blanket, his skin warm from the fire. "I was born in Indiana."

She nodded. "My father told me about this Indiana."

"It's a land of farmers. My parents planted eighty acres of wheat and reared five children. I was anxious to leave, but then I married." He cleared his throat. "Jenny died when she was your age."

"I'm sorry."

"It was a long time ago."

"Perhaps, but some wounds never seem to heal."

He glanced back at her and knew—she'd been wounded too.

"Jack Doyle," she said slowly, like she was practicing his name, "why were this Samantha and her brother alone?"

He squeezed his eyes closed, the events from last week replaying themselves in his mind. He had plenty of excuses. Getting Mrs. Kneedler to a doctor, fear of the snow, exhaustion of his mind and body. But none of them seemed right to him now.

"I left them behind," he said slowly. "Their father was going to die, and I wanted them to come with our company. Samantha wouldn't leave him. I knew she wouldn't do it, but I felt responsible for getting the others to safety."

He hated the words as he spoke them. He hated himself for what he'd done. Glancing at Aliyah, he expected to see disdain in her eyes, but instead he saw empathy.

She looked down at the fire. "It's hard to leave behind those you love."

Had he loved Samantha? He'd respected her determination and enjoyed her company, but he hadn't loved her as he had his first wife. Nor had she seemed to love him.

He leaned forward. "Who did you leave behind?"

She threw a stick on the fire, and it sparked. "My son."

He could feel the pain in her voice deep within him.

He swallowed. "Your son?"

"I didn't think I had a choice, but I had a choice all along. I could have stayed."

"Stayed where?"

Silence was her answer.

He saw the pain in her eyes and shook his head. "You don't have to tell me."

She refilled the gourds with tea. "My mother was from the Cheyenne tribe. My father was an American who worked with the Office of Indian Affairs, but he spent so much time with the Cheyenne people that he looked and sounded like an Indian. When he met my mother, he decided to stay with our tribe." Her voice grew sad. "For a season."

"Do you remember your father?" he asked, his voice a whisper.

She smiled. "I remember his beard. It would tickle my face when he held me. And I remember the wooden horse he built for me. I kept it for years until—"

He wished he could pull her close to him, wash away the sadness in her voice, but he didn't want to frighten her. "Until?"

"We had friends among the other Indian tribes, and we had enemies. My father left when I was twelve and then—" She paused and took a long sip from her gourd. "When I was sixteen, I was gathering herbs near our village. One of our enemies kidnapped me...and their chief kept me as his slave for three years."

Jack didn't mean to gasp, but her words shocked him. His stomach plunged at the thought of her being held captive. "I'm sorry."

"I had my son while I was a slave. They took him away when he was nine months old." Her voice quivered. "It broke my heart to leave him. But the man who called himself my husband rarely let me near him. Visits with my baby were rewards for what he considered good behavior. He and the others thought I would never leave the tribe as long as they had my son."

He bowed his head slightly. "The hardest of choices."

She nodded. "I pray for him every day, that God will protect him since I cannot. And that I can help protect others."

Chapter Nineteen

Alex stood on the wooden planks of the boat landing and scanned the mighty river for any sign of Jack Doyle. Brilliant yellows and oranges from the sunlight danced across the glistening river and the cottonwood timber that lined its banks, but he didn't see any boats paddling down the water.

When Doyle didn't find Mrs. Waldron on the trail, Alex hoped he would hire an Indian guide to quickly paddle him back to the fort, but he wasn't sure how far east the man would walk before he turned around.

When Doyle did return, Alex hoped he could take Mrs. Waldron and her son to the valley and provide a nice home for them through the winter. And then perhaps they could return to the safety of the United States in the spring.

He patted his coat pocket—a new habit since the discovery of the students' gift—and then reached inside it for his watch. It was three minutes past one. A courier had arrived this morning, saying that one of their fur-trapping brigades was expected today with their first bounty of the season. Perhaps they would bring news of Doyle as well.

He glanced up at the folding front gates of the fort and wondered again about the woman resting inside the McLoughlins' house. He hadn't been back to visit her since she woke, but at dinner last night, the governor had said she was recovering quickly.

He wouldn't tell a soul, but he admired the way Mrs. Waldron had put aside her own safety to get her son to a safe place. As a British patriot, he should be pleased if Mrs. Waldron had to return home, but he couldn't find himself feeling anything except esteem for someone who had struggled so hard to survive—and succeeded.

He scanned the river again for Doyle. He admired the man as well—and his determination to find the Waldron family. If Judith and her family were lost in the forest, Alex hoped he would search just as diligently until he found them. Men were supposed to protect their families—current or future.

When he returned to London, it would have been nearly five years since he'd seen the woman he intended to marry. He leaned back against one of the posts, his mind wandering across the oceans to the woman who would be his wife by next fall.

Would Judith appreciate the man he'd become since he'd left London? He'd grown to love the wilderness, and he knew the longing to return to it would be strong. But after they married, he and Judith could summer in the country at his uncle's estate. Perhaps they could winter there as well.

Would Judith still have affection for him? Or had she promised herself to another man when he delayed his return last year?

When Simon suggested that Judith might change her mind, Alex became angry at the question of her loyalties. But the truth was, he wasn't entirely certain that she would be faithful to their promise. She was a woman of integrity, but four years ago, she had also been a woman anxious to marry. Just not anxious enough to accompany him to the Columbia District.

He could not disparage her if she had already married another. But until he knew whether Judith had remained faithful to her promise, he would remain faithful to his.

* * * * *

Early the next morning, Aliyah led Jack back to the river and continued walking west with him. He thought she might turn back to her canyon, but she didn't leave his side. He wanted her to come with him, not to help him so much as to keep him company. It was the first time in months that he'd enjoyed walking.

He kept glancing over at her as they hiked, admiring her confidence in the wilderness, her beautiful smile even when her life had been so hard. She'd lived through hell in her twenty-three years. The fires had burned her, scarred her, but they hadn't consumed her. Instead, it seemed to him that she'd been molded into a woman whose beauty and courage wove through her entire being. She'd escaped her slavery and been living off the land for the past four years. Her son would be raised as his father had been, she said, but she hoped to one day have more children of her own. Children who would never be taken away.

The rain ceased as they walked through the gorge. The air was a crisp cool that reminded him of happy autumn days with Jenny, back in Indiana. After the harvest, life on their farm eased into a pleasant calm of activity, a buzz that lasted through winter. They would retreat to bed early and rise long before the sun to feed the animals and milk their cows. Then he and Jenny would laugh in the winter evenings while he'd played his harmonica, and they'd sing together late into the night.

Samantha never would sing with him.

Aliyah told him stories about her tribe, of leaving their earthen homes to roam for buffalo on the Great Plains each summer and how her mother had struggled to learn pieces of English so that she could speak with the handsome government man whenever he visited their tribe. Aliyah told him how her mother taught her the value of community and how her father's legacy taught her the value of freedom.

That night, after he and Aliyah built their fire, he dug his harmonica out of his pack and played it.

Aliyah sang along.

* * * * *

Micah played on the floor with the wooden animals he carried in his knapsack. Samantha sat in her bed, propped up by three pillows. Through the window she could hear the sounds of the fort's labor—anvils clanging, hammers pounding, the contents of carts banging, men calling to one another as they worked.

A fire blazed in the ornate fireplace, pumping warmth across the small room. The room was decorated with a simple sophistication. Her bed had four posters and green curtains tied back with ribbons—Madame McLoughlin had said the curtains were to keep out the bad air. At the base of the bed stood a washstand and a white basin that bore the blue Hudson's Bay Company coat of arms. White wainscoting bordered the bottom of the room, and the walls above it were adorned with striped maroon wallpaper. Lace curtains draped over the window, which looked out on the piazza and the massive double doors of the fort's front gate.

She'd expected roughly hewn cabins and Indian lodges inside the fort, like the ones she'd seen at Fort Laramie and Fort Hall, but Madame McLoughlin was a very elegant woman, demonstrated in her eye for the finest decor. And in the gentle yet firm way she cared for Samantha, like her mother cared for her before she became ill.

Madame had insisted that Samantha continue resting for several more days after her journey as Micah enjoyed his new playmates. Madame also assured her that Micah would never be allowed outside the fort's gates without Samantha's permission.

Samantha tried to enjoy the peace and security while she had it. All her money was gone, along with her clothing, but after she bathed in the washhouse, Madame McLoughlin supplied her with a burgundy calico dress. Then she sent her servant Annabelle to her with steaming bowls of broth, fresh bread, and a promise for roasted meat and vegetables when Samantha's stomach was ready.

While Samantha was anxious to be out of the bed, part of her didn't want to leave this room. She knew she couldn't rely on the McLoughlins' hospitality forever, but she had no place to go and no money with which to buy land or tools to build a home. She didn't even have anything left to trade for supplies.

She patted Boaz's head. They'd made it this far; somehow they would continue on together. Once Jack returned, maybe he could help them settle in the valley. They would never marry, but perhaps he could help her and Micah build some sort of simple lean-to until she could build a cabin. She could work as a seamstress or wash clothes or even cook food for the bachelors like Lesley Duncan who'd traveled west. Or maybe the Kneedlers would take her in for a season. Madame McLoughlin said that Mrs. Kneedler had been in much better health when she left the fort.

Voices shouted outside her room, and she looked beyond the window. A crew of men on horses hauled big bundles through the front gate, and a good dozen children scampered behind them.

Micah ran to the window. "Those men are the trappers," he said.

"How do you know?"

"Alex told me."

She leaned closer. "What else has Mr. Clarke been telling you?"

"All sorts of things." He shrugged. "He thinks you're my mother, you know."

She nodded. "I suppose we should correct him."

Micah paused. "I don't remember much about Mama."

She blinked, looking back at the fire. He wouldn't have many memories of their mother. She'd become bedridden when Micah was three. Aside from their trip to the fair, when they all thought Mama was getting well again, she remained in the bed until she passed on.

"She was so kind, Micah. She loved to laugh, and she loved to make you laugh."

He held up an elephant. "My animals and I used to play on her bed."

She ruffled his hair. "There was nothing that made her happier than playing with you and your animals."

His face grew serious. "Can I still pretend that you're my mother?"

Most of their company was already in the Willamette, and no one at the fort knew that Micah was her brother. Perhaps it would be better if those at Fort Vancouver continued thinking he had a parent instead of a big sister watching over him.

"I won't lie to Mr. Clarke or anyone else who asks," she said. "But I won't correct them now either."

She slid off her bed and walked slowly to the window, looking outside. Mr. Clarke was among the men who welcomed the trappers back. He was an unusual man—dressed as a fine gentleman and yet comfortable with the rugged fur trappers who each seemed to need a good bath and shave.

The worlds between the wealthy and the workers—the three classes known as officers, tradesmen, and laborers, according to Madame McLoughlin—seemed quite convoluted here. Not only did everyone at the fort seem to need one another, but they seemed to recognize this need.

Just as the people in their company had done as they crossed into Oregon Country. Everyone had been treated as equals because they all needed one another to survive.

"It's always a celebration when one of the trapping parties returns."

Samantha turned to see Madame McLoughlin. She was a large, tan-skinned woman dressed in a navy-blue merino gown. Her graying black hair had been swept back under a blue cap. In her hands was a tray with two plates of thinly sliced meat, bread, and seasoned carrots. Two glasses with milk were beside it.

"I thought you might be ready for some real food tonight."

Samantha smiled. "Very ready."

She set the tray on Samantha's bed. "You should still take it slow."

The tantalizing aroma made her stomach growl. It would be hard to eat slowly.

Samantha set one of the plates on a small table for Micah, and then she thanked God for their meal. As Madame McLoughlin watched, Samantha took several small bites. The food tasted better than anything she'd had on the journey. Until this moment, she hadn't remembered how good food could taste.

Madame McLoughlin sat on a chair. "You are feeling better."

"Much better."

"Where are you planning to go when you are well?"

"I'm hoping to go to the Willamette."

Madame McLoughlin glanced down at Micah and then looked back to her. "What happened to the rest of your family?"

"My mother died before we came on this trip, and my father—" She choked for a moment on the words. "He died on the trail."

"My father died when I was very young, too young to remember him." Madame paused. "Are you planning to marry this Mr. Doyle when he returns?"

She shook her head.

"Some people say women have to marry to survive in this country, but I hope you'll marry for affection as well, as most of the women here do."

Samantha looked out the window again, at the buildings near the front gate. "Where are all the women?"

"Most of the native women stay in their apartments during the day and sew clothing or do laundry for the men, while others make nails for the company. Every adult is employed in some way."

"Do you enjoy living at the fort?" Samantha asked.

"It is a good life, though sometimes my soul stirs to get beyond these walls and back onto the land." Madame's gaze moved toward the window. "My mother was Chippewa. I often want to be out in the woods that she loved."

"I can imagine you love it like she did."

The older woman nodded. "Do you have much wilderness where you come from?"

"I lived in an Ohio town with thousands of other people, but my father loved to hunt. When I was younger, I would go with him."

"When you were older...did you go to school?"

She nodded.

Madame McLoughlin rubbed her thick hands together. "Every woman—every child, for that matter—should receive a good education."

"I would agree with you."

"We've had about ten teachers pass through here in the last five years." Madame McLoughlin paused. "Or maybe it's been a dozen; I've lost count."

Samantha glanced down at Micah, suddenly worried about the children he'd been playing with each day. "What's wrong with the children?"

"Nothing's wrong with them. You just can't pen them up—at least not for long. But then again, children were never made to be penned up, were they?"

"I suppose I never thought about it before."

"You should think about it. There will be more Americans coming, and their children will want to be outside. The wilderness calls to us here, beckoning young and old alike to roam through it."

Samantha took another bite of the carrots and savored it. "I do believe the vegetables taste better in Oregon."

The woman laughed. "Everything tastes better here."

Chapter Twenty

A knock jolted Samantha awake. She'd been sitting in a rocking chair near the window all morning, watching a team of laborers unload barrels from a parade of carts, and she must have fallen asleep. She glanced around the room, but neither Micah nor Boaz was there.

The person knocked again.

"Come in," she said, and the door opened.

Annabelle, Madame's servant woman, stepped inside. Her dark brown hair was coiled at the nape of her neck, and she looked to be about ten years older than Samantha. "Doctor McLoughlin asked me to deliver something to you."

"What is it?"

She held out a small piece of paper. "I believe it is some sort of letter."

Samantha held out her hand, and the woman placed a letter addressed to Samantha in her palm. She opened it.

Please come visit me the moment you arrive in the valley.
You won't believe the news I have! I miss you dreadfully.
Lovingly yours,
Lucille

The letter fell into Samantha's lap. Thank God, her friend had survived the journey.

She looked up at Annabelle. "Thank you for giving it to me."

Annabelle turned to leave, but Samantha stopped her. "Have you seen Micah?"

She nodded. "He's eating in the bachelor's mess hall."

Samantha's heart sped up, the thought of her little brother among all those strangers making her shudder. "Is he safe?"

Annabelle laughed. "Unless he's a bear or a beaver, he couldn't be any safer."

"Is Boaz with him?"

"I suppose."

Samantha tried to relax.

Madame McLoughlin had told her that Micah somehow managed to recover from their journey without a single extra day in bed. A bath in the washhouse and a clean set of clothes seemed to be all he needed to integrate into this new life.

She took a deep breath. The people in the fort had taken good care of him while she was recovering, and Boaz would protect Micah as well. As long as he didn't wander off alone, outside the palisades...

Annabelle wrung her hands together. "I almost forgot."

"What is it?"

"Madame McLoughlin asks you to join her for the evening meal."

"I would be delighted," she said with a smile, and then her smile began to fade. "But I should eat with Micah."

Annabelle smiled. "I'll bring him a meal and stay until you return."

She nodded, pleased at the idea of conversing with her hosts for the evening.

After Annabelle left, Samantha read Lucille's written message again, wondering at her news. She missed Lucille dreadfully as well. She had been here for only a week, but loneliness poured over her like Oregon's steady rain.

She glanced out the window again, at the double front gates through which people came and went all day. She may feel alone, but

Fort Vancouver was hardly a lonely place. Indians came through the gates as frequently as the French trappers, British gentlemen, and the laborers from places like the Sandwich Islands.

Then through the front gate walked a stunning Indian woman dressed in a light buckskin dress, and Samantha stared at her, surprised to see a woman among all the men. This woman's light brown hair was braided, her skin a milky tan color. And she was smiling at the rugged man who'd walked through the front gate beside her.

Jack.

The woman was smiling at Jack, and he was smiling back at her. The worry that had creased his face for months was gone; he looked relaxed. It was the first time in a very long time that she'd seen Jack enjoying himself.

Both Jack and the woman carried large packs on their backs, and Samantha leaned closer to the window, watching the two of them as they stopped to speak with a laborer. When the man pointed toward the house, Samantha ducked behind the curtain. Over the past week, part of her had been anxious to see Jack, while another part had been worried about their reunion and what he expected of her. Clearly, he had moved on in his expectations.

She should feel jealousy at the sight of the man she'd once thought of marrying talking with such a lovely woman, but she felt happiness for him instead. And a new sense of freedom for herself. Jack had wanted her to trust him, but she realized now, with a terrible jolt, that she didn't trust him. Perhaps she never had.

Not that he wasn't an honorable man. He simply wasn't the right man for her. She couldn't trust him with her life or her heart, not after everything that had happened.

But maybe this woman would.

She brushed her hands over the buttons that lined the front of her dress, the ruffled burgundy dress Madame McLoughlin had given her. No dirt stained it, no tears shredded it, and it was free of the permanent coating of dust that had settled over the dresses she'd worn on the trail. Her hair was pinned back in a neat knot, and she patted it gently.

The woman Jack had known was muddy, tired, and irritable. The woman he would see today was clean, rested, and smelled of rose water. Yet she doubted that how she looked or what she said to him would sway his feelings toward her. Nothing he said would change her mind either.

There was a knock at the door, and she took a deep breath before she told Jack to come inside. The door creaked open slowly, and he peeked his head through the doorway.

Brown stubble shadowed his face, and when he took off his dingy hat, his long hair was tangled over his collar. His eyes wore a look she didn't recognize. Gone was the admiration she'd seen on the trail whenever he looked at her, back when she was streaked with dirt and her dress was torn. Gone was the man who'd made her laugh as he played his harmonica, the man who'd poured out his compassion when Micah was lost.

Instead, Jack Doyle looked at her as if she was a stranger.

Perhaps they really were strangers. She thought she knew Jack, but even after seven months of traveling together, perhaps she didn't know him at all.

"How are you?" he asked.

"Much better."

He untied his pack and lifted out a bundle wrapped in a burlap bag. "I found your cart."

Her breath caught. "What did you bring?"

"Some clothes, a bag of your father's seeds, your Bible and—"

She clapped. "*The Pilgrim's Progress*?"

Frustration clouded his face. "No, I—"

"It's all right, Jack." She pulled the bundle toward her. Pulling out Mama's wool shawl, she cradled it in her arms. "Thank you for bringing all this."

"I wish I could have brought more."

"It's more than I ever expected to see again."

He glanced back at the door, as if he was nervous to be alone with her. She pointed to the wooden chair across from her. "Please sit."

His hands were clutched together as he sat, his gaze resting on his lap. When he spoke, his words were barely above a whisper. "I didn't know what to do about your father. I wasn't thinking clearly."

She reached out and patted his hand. "You did what you had to do. You were the leader."

"The snow—" He looked up at her. "I thought it might snow for days."

"You didn't know it would turn to rain."

He looked up at her. "I didn't want him to die."

She took a deep breath. "I know."

"He's buried now."

Tears flooded her eyes, relief filling her that Jack had given her father a proper burial.

His gaze wandered out the window, to the lady waiting in the piazza.

Samantha dabbed her eyes with her handkerchief and then joined Jack in gazing out the window. Men had gathered around the woman, talking to her, but they didn't seem to worry her. Perhaps because Jack was nearby.

"She's lovely."

His gaze darted back to her. "Samantha—"

She lifted her finger to her lips, stopping him with the shake of her head. "You don't need to explain."

"Aliyah buried your father."

She blinked. "Aliyah?"

He nodded. "She wanted to help you."

She looked back out the window at the beautiful woman in the white dress. She looked like an angel. "This woman—I think she brought us food. And a blanket."

He looked out the window again. "She had a son once—" He paused. "She wanted you and Micah to be safe."

"Please tell her thank you."

He nodded.

"I'm happy for you, Jack."

He glanced back at her. "What?"

"She seems to be the perfect companion for you."

He continued to stare at her. "We're not—she's not my companion."

A smile played at Samantha's lips. "But I think she might be someday."

He sighed. "I meant for you and I to marry, Samantha, but—"

She stopped him. "You don't have to explain."

He stood and put his hands into the pockets of his long coat.

Samantha brushed her hands over the bundle in her lap. "Aliyah will help you to heal."

He cleared his throat. "What are you and Micah going to do?"

"We'll figure it out."

"Perhaps you could come stay with us—with me."

She shook her head. "That would never work."

He walked toward the door and then turned back. "Did Hiram leave you some money?"

"He left us plenty," she reassured him. She didn't tell him that she'd lost all of it in the river.

"I wanted you to know…" he started and then hesitated.

"What?" she asked.

"I did not vote to kill the dogs."

She caught her breath, surprise mixing with relief. Jack had stood up for what was right. "You only wanted me to trust you."

He nodded. "One day you'll love a man, Samantha. A man you will trust."

She hoped he was right. One day she hoped to marry a man she trusted with her life and her heart.

He lingered a moment longer at the door, and she waved him forward. "Go, Jack."

He put on his hat, tipping it toward her, and then he left.

Tears streamed down her cheeks as she watched him walk into the courtyard, taking Aliyah's arm to lead her away from her admirers. Samantha cried not because she wanted to marry Jack, but because everything was changing around her. She'd expected change, welcomed it, even, but she hadn't expected to lose so much on their journey.

She had expected to build a new life, not to put back together the broken pieces of their old one.

She opened the bundle and brushed her hands over the Bible that had been in the Waldron family for more than a hundred years, reading the names of her ancestors on her father's side.

Closing her eyes, she drifted back to the day that she, Papa, and Micah had left Missouri with the Loewe party. They'd packed everything so carefully in that wagon, full of anticipation and hope for the future. Papa was more alive than she'd ever seen him as they floated across that first river; Jack was confident as the newly elected lieutenant. Back then, she'd even trusted Captain Loewe's confidence to guide their entire company safely to Oregon.

Now all the others were gone. Those who hadn't lost their lives during the journey were off like Jack, preparing new homes for the future. Their wandering was finished, but her wandering was far from over.

What was she supposed to do without any money or a way to earn an income while she cared for Micah? Perhaps they would offer her a position in the kitchen or cleaning Bachelor's Hall. She would work hard at whatever job they gave her. If she asked, perhaps they would let Micah attend school with the other children.

She glanced outside again. Alexander Clarke was greeting a group of trappers at the front gate of the fort. If anyone could help her, she guessed it would be Mr. Clarke, but he hadn't visited her again.

She opened the Bible in her lap and found another verse Mama had liked Samantha to read to her when she was on her sick bed.

Trust in the LORD with all thine heart; and lean not unto thine own understanding. In all thy ways acknowledge him, and he shall direct thy paths.

She didn't understand all that had happened. She didn't know why she was here. But God had directed her and Micah's path. He had led them here.

She would have to trust solely in the Lord.

* * * * *

Alex helped the trappers unload their heavy bales in the newly built warehouse. The trapping party would celebrate for a night or two before they headed back out to their camp. They had nearly forty thousand pounds of pelts to send with him when he returned to London, but the committee was anticipating at least sixty thousand. Alex hoped the other parties would return soon, before the ship came from England in the spring to collect the fur. He wanted to arrive in London victorious, the ship filled with the expected annual supply.

He imagined his uncle would plan a large gala to welcome his nephew home, but Alex was no fool. Those in attendance would be more interested in the arrival of the furs than in Alex's arrival, although they would feign interest because he was the president's nephew.

Now he wasn't sure exactly where home was—here in the Columbia District, or over at his uncle's home on Grosvenor Square, or near London's shipyards in the East End where he'd lived as a boy.

He stepped out of the warehouse and his gaze wandered to the white house again. He couldn't seem to stop himself from wondering about Mrs. Waldron. She'd shown such courage in her willingness to journey so many miles, but he couldn't seem to find the courage to walk back up those steps and politely knock on her door to inquire about her health.

But it was more than cowardice that stopped him. He feared himself and his growing admiration of this woman. Samantha Waldron was a lovely widow still mourning the loss of her husband. If he went to inquire about her again, it would seem as if he were taking a risky step toward breaking his promise of faithfulness to Judith.

The front door of the house opened, and Alex watched as a man strolled confidently outside. It was Jack Doyle.

Alex stepped forward as Doyle greeted an Indian woman at the side—the same woman who had directed Alex to Mrs. Waldron and Micah. Doyle took the woman's elbow, and she went willingly with him toward the front gate.

"Doyle," Alex called out, hurrying toward the man. "Where are you going?"

He turned quickly, releasing the elbow of the native woman. Alex saw fear in the woman's eyes before Doyle whispered something to her. She nodded and then stepped outside the gate.

"Where are you going?" Alex repeated.

"To the Willamette."

Alex pointed back at the house. "What about Mrs. Waldron and her son?"

Doyle eyed him curiously. "Micah?"

Alex nodded.

"Micah is her brother."

Alex swallowed. "I thought her husband died on the trail."

Doyle shook his head. "Their father died."

Their father?

Alex blinked. "Where is her husband?"

"Samantha's never been married."

Alex swallowed hard. It made more sense. Samantha Waldron likely was as young as she looked—maybe nineteen or twenty—and yet she had shown such courage.

A sudden uneasiness prompted Alex forward. Miss Waldron couldn't stay here.

"Are you taking them to the Willamette with you?"

Doyle shook his head. "Samantha doesn't want to go with us—with me. I'm not going to fight her any longer."

"You should fight harder."

"Samantha will survive just fine without my help."

"She must go with you," Alex said. He sounded desperate now—and perhaps he was.

"Samantha doesn't want me to take care of her."

Alex looked at the woman standing by the double gates and saw the European in her. For a moment, he flashed back to a memory of his mother after his stepfather left them. She was never the same after the man who'd vowed to love her for life walked out the door and never returned. "Are you going to take care of her?" He gestured to the Indian woman.

"If she'll have me."

Alex leaned back against one of the palisades, crossing his arms. "The men here often marry Indian women and then leave them a few years later to marry others."

"My first wife passed away a year after we married," Doyle said. "When I marry again, it will be for life."

Alex studied the man for a moment. He believed Doyle was telling the truth.

"Go with God," Alex said.

Doyle nodded and then turned toward the Indian woman.

He never looked back.

Chapter Twenty-One

When the bell rang at six, Alex hung up his frock coat on a rack before he joined the other officers for the evening meal around McLoughlin's table. He glanced through the open doorway in the hall, to the smaller dining table where Madame McLoughlin entertained her female guests. There were four ladies gathered with her, all of them native or mixed-blood wives of the officers.

Miss Waldron must be dining in her room again tonight.

He breathed a sigh of relief. Doyle's revelation had shaken him this afternoon. He wasn't exactly sure how to talk to Miss Waldron now that he knew she had never married. It shouldn't make a difference to him, but for some reason it did.

The large dining room was in the middle of the house. A hallway led from the front door to the dining room and then spread out like a *T* to reach the bedrooms and both parlors. Miss Waldron's room was located off the left hallway, but he dared not even glance that direction for fear of seeing her.

McLoughlin motioned him to a seat beside an empty chair. Candlelight flickered on the white-and-blue Queen's Ware and reflected off the silver. Before him were platters of venison, chopped greens, and fried potatoes.

He greeted the man across from him as he sat down. When he glanced up again, all the men's heads were turned, looking to his left.

Miss Waldron stood at the arched entryway in a burgundy dress, her hair dangling in neat curls on both sides of her head. She smiled boldly at the men and then strolled to the empty seat beside Alex. When he didn't stand, she pulled the chair out herself and sat down.

All the men looked at McLoughlin, and Alex's mouth gaped like the rest of theirs. Never before had they entertained a woman at this table.

He cleared his throat and then whispered. "What are you doing here?"

"Madame McLoughlin invited me to dinner," she replied, not even bothering to dip her voice to match his.

"But—" he started.

"Welcome," McLoughlin said, an amused smile on his face. "We're glad to have you."

Several of the men bobbed their heads in agreement.

She glanced around the table. "Where is your wife?"

"She's eating in the other dining room."

Miss Waldron looked at Alex and then back at McLoughlin. "Other dining room?"

"We spend our dinners talking business," Alex said. "The women become bored."

She looked confused. "Why would business bore them?"

Alex did not have an answer. He had always assumed that Madame McLoughlin and the other women chose to separate themselves to discuss whatever it was that woman liked to talk about. Back in London, men and women ate together at dinner and then separated after the meal, but here in the Columbia District, business and social gatherings were conducted differently.

Before the governor spoke, Miss Waldron pushed back her chair as ribbons of red streaked up her cheeks. "Am I in the wrong place?"

McLoughlin shook his head. "Stay with us," he insisted. "We would like to hear your stories."

Alex stood up and scooted her chair back under the table.

"I'm not sure I have much to say."

"Tell us about your journey," McLoughlin prompted.

And so she did. She told them about the lightning storms over the plains, the clouds of mosquitoes that almost carried them away, the deaths of her friends and then of her father on the trail. She told them stories about Indians who'd tried to trade for her, the springs of soda they'd found bubbling up from the earth, the Hudson's Bay Company traders who charged forty dollars for a barrel of flour at Fort Hall. She told them about the captain who wanted to kill their dogs and about the grizzly that had attacked their camp.

"What happened to the bear?" Alex asked.

She took a long sip of water before she spoke again. "I shot it in the head."

Murmurs rippled like waves across the dining hall, and she managed a bite of food before the men began pestering her with questions. Yes, she had walked the entire way. They had cut their wagons into carts to cross the Blue Mountains and then abandoned their carts altogether to walk through the gorge. Yes, she had traveled the last week without any assistance from men, although an Indian woman had brought them food. No, she didn't regret coming to this place she called Oregon, but she deeply regretted the loss of her father on the trail.

Alex listened to her stories, in awe like the other officers.

"Were you not afraid?" he asked after the other men began talking.

"Terrified."

"You took incredible risks."

"Sometimes risk is foolish, I suppose." She paused. "But sometimes it is faith."

* * * * *

Madame McLoughlin never entered the Fur Shop, so when Alex watched her walk into the warehouse so late in the evening, fear gripped him. The men stopped their work for a moment, seemingly paralyzed at the unprecedented visit of the governor's wife. Then they all began working harder.

Madame scanned the room, which was crowded with piles of cheap furs on the floor and more valuable pelts hanging from beams. When she found Alex, she motioned him forward with one hand.

Had something happened to Doctor McLoughlin...or to Miss Waldron? He put down the daybook and rushed toward her. Hopefully no one was injured—and hopefully there were no more Americans at their doorstep.

"Good evening, Madame," he greeted her. "May I assist you with something?"

She clutched her hands together, her plump cheeks forged into a smile. "I have the best news."

He glanced around the room. The trappers might be pretending to work, but he knew they were listening. The best news to a woman might be the worst news to his men.

He directed her to the door, and they stepped onto the dirt walkway. "What is it?"

Oil lanterns flickered above them, the light illuminating the wide lines of Madame's smile. She clapped again. "I've found a teacher for the children."

He blinked, wondering why this news prompted her to personally deliver it at such a late hour, but he was glad that the children would have someone instructing them. "That is splendid indeed," he replied. "Where did you find him?"

Her eyes twinkled. "It's not a *him*."

He paused, his gaze wandering to the big house. How was he supposed to respond? He knew exactly what she was going to say, but many in their company wouldn't be pleased at the notion of a woman—and an American—teaching their children. And he didn't want to subject Miss Waldron to a room full of ruffians, either. "You didn't offer Miss Waldron the position, did you?"

"Of course not. I knew she'd be reluctant to take it."

"She is a wise woman."

"That's not wisdom, Alexander. It's nonsense. She is educated, and she takes excellent care of her brother."

"But he is well beha—"

Her eyebrows climbed, and he stopped his words. It would be a poor choice to insult the children in front of the governor's wife.

She continued. "You must persuade her to take this position."

"Me? She will not to listen to me."

"Of course she will. You're the one who rescued her from the river."

"And now you want me to use my influence to manipulate her—"

She stopped him. "Miss Waldron needs a position, and we desperately need a respectable teacher. I hardly think we are manipulating her."

"What did your husband say about this idea?"

Her smile dimmed a bit. "I'm going to need your help in convincing him as well."

After Miss Waldron's performance at dinner earlier that evening, it probably wouldn't be difficult. "I shall speak with your husband."

She nodded. "You won't regret it."

Chapter Twenty-Two

A Canadian man named Louie—or was it Huey?—stepped into Samantha's room. He was an inch taller than her, and though he looked to be only a year or two older than she, he had a sandy-colored beard that draped over his collar. In his hands he held a bunch of wildflowers and colorful leaves.

She glanced at the bouquet. "Where did you find such pretty flowers this time of year?"

He shrugged, tossing the flowers toward her, and she added them to a vase full of flowers already on her bedside table.

"Thank you."

He leaned back against the door frame. "I'm wondering if you'd like to marry me."

She coughed, turning quickly to straighten the flowers. Back in Ohio, men and women courted for months and sometimes years before they spoke of marriage, but here it seemed to be acceptable to propose upon first meeting.

"I don't believe I'm ready to consider marriage at this time," she said as politely as possible.

He gave a slight bow and rushed out of the house without another word.

Samantha smiled as she arranged the flowers in the vase that Madame had loaned her. His was the third bouquet she'd received since she had taken dinner with Doctor McLoughlin and his officers last night. Several suitors back in Ohio had brought her flowers, but here the men kept knocking on her door all day, and she wasn't sure what to do about it.

She couldn't keep the men's names or nationalities straight. They were from around the world, and many of them hinted that they were ready to begin their travels again with a wife. Others said they wanted to settle at the fort and start a family. Some, like Louie, even stated outright that they wanted to marry her.

She tried to respect each of the men and their offers. Plenty of people married out of necessity, back in the United States as well as here, and sometimes she wondered what was wrong with her. She could simply take one of the proposals and marry, for Micah's sake if nothing else. But she couldn't bring herself to marry a man for mere convenience. She wanted to love her husband, like Mama had loved Papa.

She prayed that she would never be so desperate that she'd have to marry a man she didn't love.

She arranged the autumn blooms and sat back on her chair. Peace seemed to settle over the room as she savored the aroma of the flowers. If only her heart was at peace as well.

She had never imagined being in Oregon without Papa. Now she'd not only lost him, but she'd lost her means to provide for Micah and herself. Every morsel of food they ate and every stitch of clothing they wore were provided by the McLoughlins. And she had no prospect of ever repaying their generosity.

Micah bounded into the room. "Can Pierre and I go to the gardens?"

"Who's Pierre?"

He sighed. "My new friend."

"Why isn't Pierre in school?"

Micah shrugged. "He said the teacher ran away."

Where could one possibly run to around here?

She stepped to the window and saw dozens of people milling in the piazza on this Friday morning. All day long they went in and out of the wide gates, trading furs and working the land outside. The gardens, Madame had told her, were on the north side of the tall palisades that fenced in Fort Vancouver and kept her and Micah safe.

She shook her head. "I don't want you to go outside the fort."

"We won't go alone," Micah said before he blew his long hair out of his eyes. "The cook said she would take us. She has to pick beets for supper."

Panic surged through her. What if he wandered off like he had on the trail and got lost in the wilderness? What if an Indian stole him? What if another wild animal, like the strange one on the river, threatened him?

There were too many unknowns in this new land. "You need to stay inside the gates."

"But Sam—"

"After what happened on the trail—"

Someone cleared his throat by the door, and she looked up at Mr. Clarke. "He'll be fine."

"Alex!" Micah shouted, running to him.

"It's Mr. Clarke," she said, correcting her brother before addressing the man in the doorway. "I'm sorry. We called most of the men in our wagon party by their first names."

Mr. Clarke smiled, placing his hand on the boy's shoulder. "I am not offended."

Micah turned back to her. "Alex says I'll be fine."

She stepped toward him. "I don't mean any disrespect, sir, but little has been '*fine*' in this wilderness. If something happened to Micah…"

She couldn't bear to think what would happen if her brother wandered off again.

"He is not going into the wilderness. He will be visiting the governor's personal gardens." Mr. Clarke smiled. "The only animals that venture into the garden are deer and rabbits, and when they do, they end up on our dinner plates."

She studied the gentleman in front of her, the man who had risked his life to rescue them. Surely he wouldn't let Micah do anything that would endanger him further.

"Are you certain?"

"Nothing is certain, Miss Waldron, but it is just as safe in the gardens as it is inside these walls."

"Please—" her brother begged again.

Her gaze traveled back out the window. She had assumed they were safe in the fort, but there was probably nowhere in this wilderness that was completely safe. Neither of her parents would want her to keep Micah trapped inside these walls forever.

"Would you feel more comfortable if I took them?" Mr. Clarke asked.

She searched his face for a moment. "You don't mind?"

"I would be honored to do it."

She knelt beside her brother. "You stay with Mr. Clarke and the cook."

He crossed his fingers over his heart. "I will."

"And come tell me when you return."

"Would you wait for me outside?" Mr. Clarke asked Micah. "I must speak for a moment with your sister."

Micah nodded and stepped toward the door. Then he turned. "Are you married, Mr. Clarke?"

Samantha glared at her brother.

"Not yet, but I will marry when I return to London next year."

"Who are you marrying?"

Alex shifted on his feet. "A woman named Lady Judith Heggs."

"Are you certain?"

Alex's smile seemed forced. "You had better hurry along, or Cook will pick the beets before we get there."

Samantha stared at the empty doorway, talking more to herself than to the man in front of her. "He doesn't even like beets."

Alex laughed. "Did they not tell you that everything tastes better here?"

"That's what Madame McLoughlin said." Sighing, she slipped into her chair. "We were told a lot of things about Oregon."

"I realize that much of it is exaggerated, but one cannot find better food." He glanced around the room and chuckled. "Or flowers."

"Where are the men getting them?"

"Some flowers grow wild until winter, but the men are likely hiring children to take them from McLoughlin's garden."

"Will Madame be upset?"

"She may pretend to be upset, but she will probably be amused."

He pulled the second chair toward him and sat across from her. She tried to read the expression on his face. Hesitation. Distrust. Perhaps someone had sent him to tell her that she'd relied on the McLoughlins' hospitality long enough and it was time to leave. Or that she'd embarrassed all of them at the dining table.

She wrung her hands. She knew it was time for her and Micah to find a place to live on their own, but they no longer had even a sliver of canvas to sleep under. Nor a penny to spend. All that was left from their cart was what Jack brought them, the Noah's Ark pieces, and her brother's clothes.

She blinked. Mr. Clarke had referred to her as Micah's sister.

"How did you find out Micah was my brother?"

"Jack Doyle told me." Mr. Clarke leaned forward, his piercing eyes studying her. "Miss Waldron, I am here with a proposition."

Her thoughts seemed to collide in her head. Now that he knew she wasn't recently widowed, was he going to propose marriage as well?

That didn't seem right. He'd just told Micah he was engaged to marry another.

She sat up straighter. "What is your proposition?"

"Until several months ago, we had a teacher for our children, a British man by the name of Warren Calvert. He was here on a temporary basis until our new teacher arrived from London."

She listened slowly, trying to process his words. What did this have to do with his proposition? "Micah said their teacher ran away."

"He is correct. Calvert decided he was not keen on life inside our fort."

"The poor children."

"Right." Mr. Clarke cleared his throat. "Doctor McLoughlin places a high value on educating our children, but no one here is, uh, qualified to teach."

"Qualified—or willing?" she asked.

He sighed. "Certainly not willing, and likely not qualified either."

She reflected on his words. "What is your proposition, Mr. Clarke?"

"We wondered—" He cleared his throat. "Would you teach our children until our new teacher arrives?"

She glanced out the window again. "When will the ship arrive?"

"Sometime this spring."

If she did teach these children, she and Micah could continue to live on their own, at least until the new teacher assumed his position. She could provide for them instead of relying on the gracious hospitality of their hosts.

"How many children?"

"Twenty-three," he replied. "Ages five to fifteen."

She took a deep breath. It was one thing to care for her brother but quite another to teach twenty-three children in one room. But if she didn't want to marry soon, she really had no other good option. She would have to learn how to teach.

"It will be a difficult position for anyone, especially for—" He stopped abruptly and cleared his throat.

"You don't approve of my teaching?"

He shook his head. "I have never seen you teach."

She didn't tell him that she never had. She'd taught Micah plenty the past few years, but she'd never taught in a classroom. "Do you disapprove of me because I'm an American or because I'm a woman?"

"I do not disapprove of you personally, Miss Waldron. These children are an unruly group. I do think we need a man to temper them before any teaching is done. We have had so many teachers…"

A slight smile crept up her lips. "'Unruly' doesn't frighten me."

"I wonder, Miss Waldron," He leaned toward her. "What does frighten you?"

She glanced out the window, at Micah and his friend walking away from her. "Losing someone else I love."

He cleared his throat.

She turned back to the man whom she hoped was becoming a friend to her. "Please call me Samantha."

Mr. Clarke edged forward on his seat. "The McLoughlins have personally requested that you consider this position and that you continue living in their house. The company will provide you and Micah with board and a small stipend in the form of credit at the Sale Shop."

"Could—" she started, almost afraid to ask for something else when he'd already offered so much. "Could Micah attend the school as well?"

"Of course."

She took a deep breath. Perhaps it would be good to spend the winter here before settling near the Kneedlers and Lucille and the others. "I would like to go to the Willamette in the spring, even if the ship hasn't arrived."

He smiled politely. "You will teach until then?"

She nodded. "I'll teach them."

He stood up, his hat in his hand. "Thank you, Miss Waldron."

"Samantha," she whispered as he walked out the door.

* * * * *

Micah and Pierre ran toward the back gate of the fort and Alex walked slowly behind them carrying a large willow basket for the elderly cook. No one seemed to know her real name, but she was a heavyset, mixed-blood woman who had cooked for the McLoughlins since the governor took over the post at Fort Vancouver. Her limp was pronounced, yet she didn't complain during their short walk. It was good for her, he supposed, to spend some time outdoors.

"Do they know they're both orphans?" she asked, nodding toward the boys.

"I'm not sure."

"A sad story, that one," she said, her eyes focused on Pierre.

"Indeed." Alex had known Pierre's father, a loud Frenchman who could entertain entire trading parties with stories of his adventures—until one of his adventures took his life. Pierre's mother had died when he was born.

Sadness flooded every orphan's story, but at least Micah had a sister who cared deeply for him. Miss Waldron would protect him from those who might want to cause him harm.

Cook carefully limped around a rut in their path. "Yet he doesn't stop, does he?"

Alex laughed. "Just like you."

She clucked her tongue. "No old leg is going to stop me."

A light wind brushed over them as they stepped outside

the fort and walked toward the McLoughlins' neatly planted kitchen garden.

Sprawling to their west were barns, an orchard, fences that harbored the fort's livestock, and seven hundred acres of grain and vegetables. To the east, beyond the kitchen garden, lay miles of forest that stretched toward the gorge.

The fertile land outside the fort was bulging with bounty all year. He didn't know the names of most of the plants ahead of them, but he had the deepest appreciation for the way Cook prepared them for dinner.

He would miss the clear air and fresh food when he went back to London. He'd miss the reliance they each had on the land to provide for them. He'd miss McLoughlin, Simon, and the other men he'd befriended over the years.

And he'd miss Samantha Waldron.

He swallowed hard, shocked by his thought. How could he miss her? He'd only just met her. He admired Miss Waldron—that was all—admired the way she cared for her brother. Admired her passion and strength and the way she didn't seem to concern herself with conforming to society's mold.

Micah grabbed his hand, dragging him forward. "Come look at this."

He glanced down at the boy's hand, feeling quite awkward. He'd seen plenty of the fort's women holding the hands of their children, but he didn't know what to do now that one had taken his hand.

Cook urged him on. "Go with him."

He cleared his throat. "What is it that you would like to see?" he asked the boy.

Micah tugged again. "It's a surprise."

The cook laughed as Micah pulled him past a gazebo and between raised wooden beds that flourished with leaves in a variety of shades and shapes.

At the end of one of the rows, Micah stopped him and pointed at what looked like lettuce. Three mollusks had crawled onto a leaf, white slime stretched in sticky threads behind them along with a trail of holes bearing evidence of their feast.

Micah's eyes were wide as he watched them. He looked up at Alex. "What are these?"

"Mollusks."

Pierre rolled his eyes. "They're slugs."

Alex thought about correcting the child, and then the thought amused him. Thankfully he no longer was responsible for educating the children. Pierre could call them slugs if he wanted to.

The cook yelped over his shoulder.

At first Alex thought the woman might run away, but she plucked one of the mollusks off the leaf and hobbled with commendable speed to the forest. Then she came back to dispose of the other two.

As she worked, the boys raced through the beds, searching for more slugs along with toads and snakes, and Alex laughed as he watched them play. Micah reminded him a bit of himself when he was seven—except there had been no gardens where he lived.

As a child, Alex had spent his afternoons exploring the London's docks, wondering what exotic places the ships had visited and where they would be going next. The sailors hadn't liked children playing at the docks, so he often hid behind barrels or crates to watch the ships. At the time, he was certain he would be a sailor when he grew up.

His uncle quickly put an end to the idea of his sailing—that is, until Alex boarded a ship for Fort Vancouver. He hadn't enjoyed the actual journey nearly as much as he'd anticipated, but he had enjoyed exploring this untamed land. He'd always yearned for adventure, he supposed.

Pierre leaned down and picked up a red frog with black spots, the creature squirming to flee from its captor. The boys examined the frog with wonder. And Alex watched the children with wonder as well.

Micah knelt down by a plant. "What is this?"

Alex shook his head. "I have no idea."

Micah looked back at up at him. "Papa left us seeds to plant."

"Do you miss your papa?"

Micah nodded slowly. "I was going to help him farm."

"You would make a good farmer."

Micah grinned. "So would you."

Alex laughed. "I do not know the first thing about farming."

Micah's grin grew serious, and he knelt by one of the garden beds. "You dig a hole, like this." He pushed the dirt away to make a hole. "And you put a seed in it."

Alex tried to match the solemnity in Micah's face. "And it just grows?"

Micah shook his head. "It needs lots of sun and water."

"We certainly have enough water around here. I am not as confident about our sunshine."

Micah glanced across the gardens. "But look at all the plants."

"I suppose we do have enough sun then."

The land was fertile enough, but Alex knew there was plenty of skill involved in farming. Yet Tom Kneedler and other Americans managed to grow food when they had never done it before. Kneedler even claimed to have harvested a good crop over the summer.

What would it be like to farm this land? To grow wheat, corn, carrots—even cherry and apple trees out of a bag of seeds?

He shook his head. It was pointless to dream about the possibilities.

But still he was curious about how well the Americans were faring as they farmed the Willamette. Before he left for London, perhaps he could see for himself what drove the Americans to this valley.

Chapter Twenty-Three

Samantha sorted and then rearranged the items Mr. Calvert had left on the desk. There was a small box of chalk, an eraser, five books, a quill pen, and a brass inkstand. There was also a tablet filled with scribbled notes, but the handwriting was so sloppy that she couldn't read it.

It was still twenty minutes before the students were expected to arrive, at half past the six o'clock morning bell. Alex said she would teach for two hours and then breakfast with the children in the mess hall before returning to the classroom.

As she waited, she thought again about the things she'd like to teach the older children in particular. If they were already well-schooled in their addition and subtraction and Murray's grammar, they could progress to multiplication and division. The younger children, she would teach how to read.

Rain beat against the windows, and a fire burned in the stove to warm the room. Micah sat quietly in the front row, waiting for the other students to arrive, as he fidgeted with the brass buttons on his new shirt.

She'd written her own notes for the day on a slate, beginning the day with prayer. Alex said that Doctor McLoughlin required all students to be in class, but she still feared a mutiny, especially when the boys realized they would be under the supervision of a female.

What would happen if none of the children came this morning? She couldn't lose this position before she'd even started. When the children arrived, she wouldn't let any of them see her fear.

She wrote her name across the blackboard behind her desk in flowing cursive and then stepped back to critique her work.

Miss Samantha Waldron

She erased it and rewrote *Miss Waldron*. Perhaps the students might respect her more if they didn't know her first name.

She took a deep breath as she scanned the twelve crudely carved desks in front of her. At each desk was a bench for two students to sit—twenty-four children, with Micah. If their class grew, perhaps some of the younger students could sit three to a bench.

Mr. Clarke had provided a list of the students' names, but many of the names she couldn't pronounce. Yet. Today she would learn the names of her students and their academic abilities. Then tomorrow morning she would begin to teach.

Even though she'd never taught, she'd certainly been in school back in Ohio long enough to learn a thing or two about how to operate in a classroom. Today she would simply implement and imitate the best teacher she'd ever had, Miss Randolph. That woman could tame a shrew.

The bell rang in the courtyard, and seconds later the door opened. She stood up straight, feigning complete confidence in her new role, but instead of a student, the clerk named Simon walked inside.

Simon took off his hat, holding it to his chest. "I just wanted to see if there'd be anything you needed this morning."

She glanced down at the stove already warding off the morning chill. "No, thank you," she replied. "We're just waiting for the students to arrive. Mr. Clarke said they would be here a little after six."

He laughed.

"Did I say something funny?"

He shook his head. "I've never heard anyone refer to him as *Mr. Clarke*."

"What do you call him?"

"I call him Alex, but most people call him by his official title, Lord Clarke."

Lord Clarke? She had messed up his name as well.

"I'm sure it will be a fine first day for you and your students," Simon said, though his tone lacked assurance.

She glanced beyond the window, looking at the rear gate of the fort that led to the gardens. Everyone except Madame McLoughlin acted like they were sending her into a lions' den, but she was more afraid of failing the children than of the children themselves.

And she desperately needed this position until spring.

She glanced back at the desks, and Simon was still there, watching her.

She nodded at him. "We will have a fine day, and I hope you will as well."

After Simon left, the minutes slowly ticked past the hour of six, but none of the children arrived.

Micah fidgeted on his bench. "Where are they?"

"I'm sure they'll come," she replied, though her voice sounded about as confident as Simon's had.

She sat on her wooden chair, scanning the notes she'd already memorized. Then she picked up Mr. Calvert's copy of *The Vicar of Wakefield* and flipped through the pages.

Should she find Mr. Clarke—Lord Clarke? She put the book on the desk. She didn't care what the others called him. Simon called him Alex, and she would as well.

Perhaps she was supposed to collect the children herself. Alex had only said that school started after the bell. She'd assumed that the children would come when the bell rang.

She glanced back at the clock. It was now thirty minutes past six.

Maybe she should have asked Simon to retrieve her students.

* * * * *

Children finally trickled into the classroom one or two at a time, most of them arriving shortly after the hour of seven. Samantha sat at her desk, pretending to be engrossed in the vicar's story as she waited for the seats to fill. The students laughed and talked like they didn't notice their new teacher or the lateness of their arrival.

Samantha kept her eyes on the book's pages.

Perhaps none of these children would respect either an American or a woman. Maybe she should snatch Micah and run out that door as Mr. Calvert had done.

But where would she run?

She lived at Fort Vancouver, if only for a season, and she would have to do the work assigned to her—and do it as well as she was able.

When all the seats in front of her were filled, she snapped the book shut. Some of the children glanced up at her, pretending not to be interested, and yet she could see the intrigue in their eyes. Others didn't appear the least bit interested as they bantered with those around them, throwing a small leather ball back and forth across the room.

Micah squirmed on his bench,

She stepped forward, catching the ball in midflight. Then she tucked it into her apron pocket. "If you would be kind enough not to play catch during class time, I would greatly appreciate it."

"There isn't a kind one among us," one of the older boys quipped.

She faced him, a forced smile on her lips. "And I aim to change that."

A few of the children laughed at her. At first she was grateful that not all the children laughed, until she realized why. Not all of them spoke English.

She leaned back on her desk, studying their faces. "How many of you understand me?"

Half of the twenty-four students raised their hands.

She glanced around the room at those with raised hands. "What do the other children speak?"

One of the girls, about ten or eleven years old, spoke for the group. "It all depends on their mamas. Some of them speak Cree or Chinook or Nez Percé. Others speak French."

Samantha stepped toward the girl. Her messy chestnut hair matched the streaks of dirt on her dress. "Do you know all those languages?"

The girl shrugged. "A little."

"Please explain to the others that this morning's late arrival was unacceptable."

The girl muttered a few sentences, and Samantha hoped she spoke to all the children.

"We will begin again tomorrow morning," Samantha said, and the girl translated again. "I will lock the door promptly at six thirty. Any student left outside will have to answer to Doctor McLoughlin." She turned back around and began to gather her things. "You are dismissed."

After a few moments of silence, the children began to stand up, turning toward the door.

Samantha tapped the book on her desk and they all faced her again.

"I expect each of you to be here on time tomorrow." She straightened her shoulders. "And I want each of you to bring your mother."

* * * * *

Alex eyed the schoolhouse as he supervised the work of a dozen laborers. Hundreds of pelts were being strung over clotheslines in the piazza. Silver fox. Elk. Pine marten. Beaver.

The men pulled the stacks of furs out of the Fur Shop and hung them outside in the sunshine. If they didn't air and then carefully beat the pelts, pests and mildew would destroy them long before they were put on the ship for London.

It was Alex's duty to ensure that every pelt made it to Great Britain intact.

He knew the type of each animal by the color, size, and feel of its pelt. The gray pelts of the wolves were coarse, but they made inexpensive coats for laborers. The darker pelts of the wolverine were for the gentlemen who walked down London's Oxford Street in the rain. The silver fox was extremely soft to the touch, fashionable for ladies' coats, while the badger had long fur, making it perfect for shaving brushes and paintbrushes.

When the *Columbia* came into port, they would bale the fur with cheap tobacco pressed between each pelt to repel insects during the six-month journey back to London. The factories outside London would transform them into hats, coats, and brushes.

As his men worked, Alex's gaze wandered back to the schoolhouse. He'd heard that Miss Waldron had dismissed the children yesterday morning not long after they arrived. He wanted to rush into the school and cane every one of the children for disrespecting their new teacher, but McLoughlin told him to wait. The governor wanted to see what this fiery young American would do on her own.

"Those kids are going to eat her alive," Simon said, walking up to stand beside Alex.

"I am not so sure. She has spirit."

"I don't know about spirit, but she's about the loveliest lady I've ever seen."

Alex bristled. He knew that many of these men were already hounding her with marriage proposals, but he didn't want her to have to marry one of them for provision.

"You had better take care not to make a fool of yourself, my friend."

Simon laughed, clapping him on the back. "*L'amour* always makes a fool of itself."

"You are not talking of love."

"I'm talking about the beauty of desire, something you don't seem to know about."

Alex straightened the pelt of a bobcat. "Anyone can desire, Simon. Integrity is what makes a man."

"You're a true man, my friend, because you certainly don't have any desire to marry your Lady Judith. I don't even think you have a desire to go back to London."

"I most certainly do—"

"Well, that's good, because you'll be there for the rest of your life."

One of the laborers, a man named Paul, strode up beside them. "Have you seen Taini?"

Alex shook his head. He hadn't seen her since the day he had fled the schoolhouse, but he'd heard that she was planning to marry one of the blacksmiths.

"She said she would repair my coat today, but she's not at her apartment."

"Perhaps she went to the kitchen," Simon suggested.

Paul shook his head. "I checked there as well. Cook acted a bit strange but wouldn't tell me where she was."

Another laborer joined them. "She's probably with my wife over at the school."

"The school?" Alex's eyebrows raised. "Why is your wife at the school?"

The man shrugged. "Ask that new teacher of yours. You're the one who hired her."

Technically, he hadn't much of a choice, but he didn't point that out to the man.

"I will return," Alex said.

He walked bristly across the piazza to the tiny schoolhouse by the back gate. He admired Miss Waldron's tenacity as much as McLoughlin did, but every member of the fort was critical to their survival. He didn't know what Miss Waldron intended, but they needed the women to work as much as the men.

Opening the door, he stepped inside the schoolhouse and then stopped abruptly, shocked at what he saw. The room was teeming shoulder-to-shoulder with children and women alike. About forty of them. Some of the women sat on the floor, a child in each lap, while others sat on the benches made for children. And they were all listening to the woman at the blackboard as she pointed to a list of words.

Miss Waldron confidently met his gaze, and all those in the room slowly turned and stared at him. He needed to talk to her, but only a fool would dare to go up against this crew.

He cleared his throat. "Might I speak with you…outside?"

Curiosity filled her eyes. "Certainly."

She stepped down the stairs, looking up at him with eyes that changed from blue to green in the light. "What is it?"

He breathed deeply, willing himself to be strong. "Why are these women in the schoolhouse with their children?"

She crossed her arms. "Do you know that some of these ladies don't know how to read?"

"What does that have to do with—"

"Some of them don't even know how to speak English!"

"Miss Waldron—"

"For heaven's sake," she said, interrupting him again, "call me Samantha."

"Miss Waldron," he continued, "we have hired you to educate our children at Fort Vancouver, not their mothers. All the adults at the fort must work."

She put her hands on her hips. "How do you expect these children to learn English if their mothers can't speak it?"

"Well, I—"

She didn't give him the opportunity to finish. "Not only do the children need their mothers to learn English, but they are completely unmanageable without them. None of them obey me one lick while their mothers are at home."

He lowered his voice, afraid those inside might hear him. "Not all the children have mothers."

She matched his whisper. "No, but they listen much better to their friends' mothers than they do to me."

The brilliance of her idea slowly dawned on him. "So...you can teach these children now?"

She nodded. "And their mothers."

Why hadn't he and the governor considered this before? Perhaps the women could attend school in the morning with their children and then work until dusk.

"I shall ask Doctor McLoughlin for permission."

"No need," she replied, climbing the stairs. "He already gave it."

She closed the school door behind herself, but Alex didn't move. What kind of woman was this who didn't seem to falter in the face of danger on the Columbia or buckle before a man as powerful as the governor?

She didn't even seem to be afraid of those children.

Apparently Samantha Waldron had passed their test.

He was still shaking his head when he crossed the piazza to immerse himself back into his work.

He had to stop thinking about this woman.

Chapter Twenty-Four

The night before Christmas, the fort was lit with candles, its doors decorated with hundreds of ribbons and wreaths. The aroma of evergreen rooted itself on the winter air, reminding Samantha of home—Papa playing his fiddle, Mama roasting a goose, she and Micah stringing popcorn to hang on their tree.

As she crossed the piazza alongside Alex and Micah, she wished God would give her parents a glimpse of how wonderfully He was caring for them in this waiting place.

Papa and Mama would have liked the tall officer who now escorted her and Micah to the Christmas Eve service at Doctor McLoughlin's request. They would have liked his integrity, his strength—and the fact that he allowed Micah to trail him around on Sunday afternoons, visiting the gardens and barns as if he were in need of a herder.

Mama would have liked his refined British manners. Papa might initially have found him too proper, but when he learned how Alex rescued her and Micah from the icy river, Papa wouldn't care one bit about Alex's manners. The important thing was that Alex knew when to discard his reserve in the face of danger.

Micah stopped in front of Bachelor's Hall. "Which room is yours?" he asked.

Alex knelt on one knee next to Micah, pointing up at the second floor. "The third window from the left."

Micah counted the windows until he stopped at Alex's.

Samantha sighed. She'd never given any thought to where Alex lived, but now whenever she passed the hall, she knew she'd find herself looking up at that second floor, the third window over.

Candlelight flickered on some of the windows as their residents moved slowly toward the entrance to the hall.

Alex tapped Micah's shoulder. "How do you like our fort?"

"It's my favorite place in the whole world," Micah said. "But I still want to play outside."

Alex glanced over at her as he stood. "Perhaps one day we can all explore together."

Micah shook his head. "Samantha won't go back outside the walls."

He turned back to Micah. "Doctor McLoughlin said your sister is doing a fine job as a teacher."

Her face warmed at the compliment, but Micah shook his head. "She's too hard."

"I heard she has even been tutoring some of the women after dinner."

She looked looked up at Alex. "They are anxious to learn."

He smiled at her. "It was a good idea to teach them English."

She was grateful for the darkness that hid her blush. "Thank you."

Micah tugged on Alex's hand. "Can we show my sister the Fur Shop before we go to the service?"

"I don't think—" she started.

"C'mon, Samantha," Micah urged.

She took a deep breath. She'd seen plenty of animal skins along their journey, but it didn't mean she could stomach a roomful of them.

"Unless they pose a threat"—she looked back at Alex, trying to rid herself of the images of the bear and wolverine—"I have a soft heart for animals."

He nodded slowly. "Then the Fur Shop would not be a good place for you to visit."

"Please," Micah begged.

Alex rumpled his hair. "We have to protect your sister's heart."

She thanked Alex again, but neither of them moved toward the mess hall. She was well aware that Fort Vancouver was an outpost that dealt primarily with capturing animals and trading their fur, but she had not come to Oregon Country to pilfer animals from the land. She wanted to grow things, raise herds of animals, as her father had wanted to do.

She ran her fingers over the ribbons threaded through a wreath on a post. "When did you decide that you wanted to be part of the fur-trading business?"

He eyed her with curiosity. "I never decided. It is my family's business."

"Are your parents back in London?"

He shook his head. "They died when I was young."

Compassion filled her heart, the aching for her own parents still fresh. "I am sorry."

"My uncle raised me as his son."

They continued walking, and Samantha watched as Alex looked down at Micah and then at her. He could understand her brother's loss and it inspired her, knowing what an accomplished man he had become after his parents died.

"Your parents would have been proud of you," she said.

A smile broke on his face. "I hope they would."

Micah rushed through the door of the mess hall, but she and Alex stopped outside. "How old were you when they died?"

"My father died not long after I was born, and my mother remarried. She died when I was ten." He looked at the candlelight in the window. "I did not know my father's family until after she died."

She saw the grief in his eyes and wondered how long it had been since he spoke about his parents. "Your uncle came for you when she died?"

He nodded slowly. "My aunt and uncle arrived within hours after she passed. They were distraught at the squalid conditions in which

I had been living, but I had never found it dirty or unkempt. It had been home to me."

"You must care for your aunt and uncle a lot."

"My uncle is a great man."

The bell rang to announce the beginning of the service, and several people hurried past them to go into the room. Neither she nor Alex moved.

"If he were here, I'm sure your uncle would be quite proud of you as well."

He looked into her eyes, and their intensity made her stomach tumble. "I fear I have failed him."

"How could you possibly have failed him?"

"By caring for an American."

She took a deep breath, her heart beginning to wonder how much he cared.

He cleared his throat. "Caring for all of the Americans who have come here—their food and supplies."

"Of course." He may try to hide it—and fight it—but it was clear to Samantha that Alex would never let a person, American or otherwise, suffer if he could prevent it. "God created you to care for others," she said softly. "Why shouldn't you care for Americans?"

He shook his head. "My family relies on me to make the appropriate decisions on behalf of the company."

"Don't they know there is One much higher than any company?"

A flutist began to play music on the other side of the door. "They already have a god."

"But not you, Alex. You know the truth."

His eyebrows climbed, and she wasn't certain if it was because of her words or because she had used his first name. He didn't correct her on either account.

"My family's livelihood is being threatened."

"Because the Americans are coming?"

"Partially."

"Then perhaps you should reconsider your livelihood."

He shook his head. "It is too late—"

"Micah and I are not a threat, are we?"

"Micah is not."

"But I—" She swallowed her words, her pulse racing at his implication.

"We have traded fur for hundreds of years. We need this country to trap animals."

She dug her heel into the dirt pathway. "This country is also for growing and harvesting. Perhaps you and your company could raise animals instead of taking them from the land."

"The company has plenty of sheep and mules in the barns." He paused. "When the weather is better, I shall take you and Micah to see the gardens and barns."

"We would like that."

He took her elbow, and goose bumps spread over her skin. "We should join the others," he said, his voice low.

"Thank you," she said.

"I have not done anything—"

She stopped him one last time. "Thank you for caring—for all of us."

* * * * *

Alex opened the door to the bachelor's mess hall, and the aromas of cinnamon and orange peel wafted out into the night air. Miss Waldron stepped into the crowded room and he walked in behind her, the words from their conversation playing in his head, confusing him.

Had he just told Samantha Waldron he cared for her? He tried to recall his exact words as he guided her through the benches.

He didn't care for her, at least not in the way he might have implied. She intrigued him, inspired him—that was all. Perhaps he shouldn't have invited her and Micah to tour the garden and barns, but McLoughlin had asked him to watch over both of them. He was glad to attend to the boy who'd lost his father as well as the woman who loved her brother.

Alex's mother had loved him when he was a child, but his aunt hadn't wanted an orphan in their home. Lady Clarke had never liked Alex much—she had always desired children of her own to carry her husband's name and title. But she'd never had children, so she allowed Lord Clarke to pretend that he had a son.

Thank God she had done it. Without his uncle's influence and direction, he might never have left the East End. Or he might have become a sailor and spent the remainder of his life as a miserable wretch.

Perhaps in some small way he could help Micah as well.

Miss Waldron pointed to her brother sitting in the midst of the clerks and their wives on the fourth row. There were two seats reserved to the boy's right, for his sister and Alex.

They joined Micah as Doctor McLoughlin read the Scripture for Christmas Eve. Then Alex held the candle for Micah and Miss Waldron as they took the bread and cup together. As they prayed, he glanced at the bowed heads of the beautiful woman on his right and the boy on his left.

Then Alex closed his eyes as well.

It was almost as if they were a family.

Chapter Twenty-Five

Instead of snow, January and February brought torrential rain to Fort Vancouver, so much so that Alex hadn't been able to take Samantha and Micah to visit the barn animals or the gardens. Alex had said that March usually brought several days of sunshine, but as the rain continued to drown the fort, she wondered if it would ever end.

Samantha buttoned her new dress, made from the emerald-green muslin she'd purchased at the Sale Shop. Then she glanced at herself in the looking glass above the washbasin as she prepared to leave for the church service that met down the hallway in the dining room.

She'd tried to make the dress before Christmas, but she'd been so busy with the school that she hadn't had time. Two of her students, wives of the officers, finished it for her as a gift, and they had even embroidered white flowers on the sleeves and hem.

She shook her head, trying to erase the pleasantness of her Christmas memories with Alex. She admired the man's commitment to his promise to marry a woman in London, but the thought of Alex married to another made her heart sad. She had hoped...well, it didn't matter what she'd hoped.

She enjoyed their times together when he would escort her and Micah to church. Doctor McLoughlin and the other officers liked to do things here with decorum. All the ladies were escorted to services by their husbands, and McLoughlin thought she and Micah required an escort as well.

But Doctor McLoughlin had left yesterday to travel for several weeks, checking on the operations at Fort Colville. She doubted Alex would come today, and she didn't fault him for it. The church service was conducted but thirty paces from her room. She hardly needed someone to take her there.

She adjusted the tie around Micah's neck and smoothed back his hair. "You look like a gentleman," she said.

He puffed out his chest. "Like Alex?"

She sighed. "Exactly."

"You can call me Lord Micah Waldron."

She laughed. "All right, Lord Waldron."

"I like Alex," he informed her and then grinned. "I think you should marry him."

"I can't, Micah. He's marrying someone else."

"But he hasn't married her yet."

"You wouldn't want him to break his promise, would you?"

He stood straighter, eyeing her with seriousness. "Yes, I would."

She shook his head. "No honorable man breaks a promise."

"I still wish he'd marry you."

Someone knocked on the door.

"Hush," she whispered to Micah before she opened the door.

Even with Doctor McLoughlin gone, Alex had come for them. He stared at her for a moment and then dropped his gaze. She thought he might comment on her new dress, but he only held out his arm for her. In his other arm was some sort of package.

No matter what Micah said, no matter how Madame McLoughlin hinted, Samantha had refused to entertain thoughts about a marriage to Lord Alexander Clarke. But as she took his arm this morning, she couldn't seem to help herself from thinking about what it would be like to marry such a man.

There was no one else at the fort quite like him, with his strength of character and his confidence. He may not be able to teach children, but his men followed him around like Micah did, as if he were the king of England. Everyone at the fort respected him and his leadership, and they even seemed to respect his decision to wait so many years to marry a lady back in London.

Perhaps one day another gentleman, a man like Alex, would arrive from the United States or even from Great Britain. A man who wasn't married or engaged. Until then, Samantha would do what she'd come to love—teach the woman and children at Fort Vancouver how to speak and read English. Until she left for the Willamette, that is.

Her stomach clenched with a mixture of excitement and anxiety at the thought of leaving the fort. When the ship arrived from London, everything would change again.

She closed the door behind Micah, and the three of them stepped toward the dining room and the low din of voices traveling down the hall.

Micah rushed ahead of them, but Alex stopped in the hallway.

"I have something for you," he said.

She eyed the brown paper package in his hand. "What is it?"

He held out the package. "I thought you might enjoy this."

She carefully tore back the paper and found a copy of *The Pilgrim's Progress*. She looked up at him, surprised. "Where did you get this?"

"I brought it with me from London," he paused. "The night I—the night you arrived at the fort, you spoke about the Celestial City. I thought you might like it."

Tears welled in her eyes, and she tried to blink them back. "I do."

He stepped forward, but her legs wouldn't cooperate, immobilized first by shock and then by gratefulness for his gift. He had no idea what it meant to her.

He took her elbow as she regained her footing and then guided her quietly into the dining hall. She followed Alex toward a chair and sat between him and Micah, the gift clutched in her lap.

She didn't want to marry any other man. She wanted this man.

She sang the first hymn softly, Alex's voice strong beside her. Then he stood to read from the text in Philippians since Doctor McLoughlin was gone.

"'Not that I speak in respect of want: for I have learned, in whatsoever state I am, therewith to be content. I know both how to be abased, and I know how to abound: every where and in all things I am instructed both to be full and to be hungry, both to abound and to suffer need. I can do all things through Christ which strengtheneth me.'"

During the past year she had been hungry; she had been weak. She had suffered need, and yet God had provided for her. He'd strengthened her.

As the winter turned into spring, she needed His strength even more to say good-bye to the man that she knew in her heart she loved.

She brushed her fingers over the gift he'd given her. How could she possibly say good-bye to him?

The front door of the house banged open, and she heard footsteps pounding across the entryway. Everyone turned and looked as a messenger bolted into the room.

Alex scowled at the interruption. "What is it?"

"A courier has arrived, sir."

He didn't move. "What did he say?"

"The *Columbia* is in Baker Bay."

Several of the men around them stood, but Alex sank to his seat instead.

She leaned over, whispering to him, "What's the *Columbia*?"

His voice sounded hard. "The boat from England."

Her heart fell. It was the boat that had come to take Alex home.

* * * * *

Alex wasn't on the ship yet, but as he stood on the wharf, his stomach rolled.

His heart belonged in this wilderness, not in London.

And his heart belonged to a woman living here as well.

His mind wandered back to Miss Waldron's light touch on his arm during church, of her inquiry about the *Columbia*. He'd seen the sorrow in her eyes—the same sorrow he'd felt at the thought of leaving this district, at the thought of leaving her and Micah.

He had learned in this wilderness how to be content, as the Scripture from Philippians directed, when he was abased and when he abounded. He had learned to be content up until that day on the river when he lifted Micah from the water and carried his sister to the fort.

Now he must learn to be content with or without Samantha Waldron.

He desperately needed God's peace, the peace that passeth all understanding.

Rain drizzled over his hat this afternoon, streaming down his cloak, as he waited on the landing with the other officers. He had to stop himself from entertaining thoughts about Miss Waldron. She was an American. She was leaving for the Willamette soon.

She was not the woman he had promised to marry.

The *Columbia* had been stuck out at Baker Bay for almost a week now, at the mouth of the Columbia River, but the waters had calmed enough for them to travel upstream. Another courier had arrived by canoe this morning to say that the ship would finally arrive at Fort Vancouver today.

Rain continued to soak his hat and cloak, but he stood tall with the rest of the men. Officers and laborers alike had toiled hard all week, cleaning and baling the remaining pelts. They had prepared 185 bales for this trip, each one weighing about 300 pounds. The total weight was 54,000—not as much to transport back as in previous years, but still a respectable amount. Once his uncle understood the increasing difficulty of finding and trapping animals in this district, he would be pleased with their harvest.

Alex knew he should care more about what the shortage of animals meant for the future of Hudson's Bay Company, but at this moment, all he could think about was the fact that he was leaving this beautiful country...and a beautiful woman.

Grosvenor Square would be his home now, Judith his wife.

For the rest of his life.

The years ahead would be planned out for him in the precise way of every true gentleman. In the Columbia District, life was unpredictable and messy, but in London, there would be little unpredictability. After four years in the wilderness, he should be glad of it, but the truth was, he would miss being here more than he ever imagined.

A weathered mass of sails appeared around the bend, and the crowd of men around Alex cheered at the sight of *Columbia*. The ship sailed toward them, and the sailors waved as she anchored by the landing.

A door opened, and the gangplank stretched between the wharf and boat. A dozen men poured out of the ship, many of them pale and thin. One of them knelt and kissed the wooden planks on the landing. Alex scanned the men as he greeted them, wondering if one of these was the new schoolteacher.

The clerk beside Alex gasped, and he turned to see the profile of a woman in the doorway, her blond hair a wiry mess. At first, Alex thought one of the passengers—perhaps the new schoolteacher—had brought his wife.

His mouth dropped open.

This wasn't just any Englishwoman.

Lady Judith Heggs had arrived at Fort Vancouver.

Chapter Twenty-Six

Samantha turned the page of her book, seeing words on the page but not reading the story. She thought of Alex's face when he heard the news of the *Columbia*'s arrival. Instead of excitement, she'd seen disappointment.

Perhaps he didn't want to go home. Perhaps he felt as if he didn't have a choice. Perhaps a letter might arrive on this ship with news that his betrothed had married another. She hoped beyond hope that it meant he wouldn't be on the ship when it left.

Sighing, she turned another page.

Just because her heart longed for Alex didn't mean that his longed for her. The proposals from the other men had dwindled with her rejections, but a few of them still persisted in asking for her hand. She didn't want to marry any of the other men. She wanted Alex.

The ship was coming today; the bales of fur were ready to transport. Madame said it would take only three days at the most for the men to load them. Soon Samantha would have to say good-bye.

Her stomach turned.

She glanced out the window of the parlor and saw Alex walking toward the house alongside three drenched gentlewomen and a gentleman.

Had the new teacher brought a wife? And who were the other two ladies?

Samantha closed her book and smoothed her skirt. The women

would certainly want a bath and a good meal after their long journey. Perhaps she could keep herself busy by helping Cook.

The door opened, and Micah stood to his feet, scattering the animals from his Noah's Ark collection around him.

Alex's gaze found hers, and she'd never seen such a distraught look on his face. He looked lost, as the boy long ago must have felt when his mother died. She wished she could rescue him this time.

She glanced at the ladies and gentlemen with concern and then looked back at him.

He took a step toward her. "Miss Waldron, I would like to introduce you to the woman I'm to marry, Lady Judith Heggs."

Samantha opened her mouth to respond, but the shock seemed to paralyze her. No words came out.

Micah reached for her hand. "But my sister is supposed to—"

"Micah," she said, stopping him, "will you please fetch Madame McLoughlin?"

He groaned but left the room without another word.

Alex's future wife was no longer waiting for him in London. Nor had she changed her mind. She was here, right in this room, coming for the man she would marry. And even though she was soaked, she was still quite beautiful in her bright blue day gown with its pointed waist and bell-shaped skirt molded over layers of petticoats. Her blond hair hung drenched over her narrow shoulders, but her skin was a smooth ivory, and her blue eyes matched her dress.

Samantha glanced down at her plain burgundy dress and wished she could hide in her room. There was no comparison between her, an American schoolteacher with a small store credit to her name, and this wealthy English lady, the picture of nobility and fashion.

"It's nice to meet you, Lady Judith," Samantha managed, bending her knee in what she hoped was an acceptable curtsy.

The woman nodded, shivering.

The older gentleman beside Lady Judith held his top hat in his hands, and the white-haired woman next to him wore a brown cape over her gray dress.

Alex motioned them forward. "This is Lord Stanley, the Earl of Derby, and his wife, Lady Stanley. They are friends of my aunt and uncle, and they have graciously escorted Lady Judith here."

"It's a pleasure to make your acquaintance," she replied, hoping she had responded like a lady.

"And this is Miriam, their ladies' maid."

Samantha greeted the maid before her gaze found Alex. He glanced over his shoulder as if to see whether there was anyone else he was supposed to introduce.

"Would you kindly guide us to the bath?" Lady Stanley asked.

Samantha nodded, stepping away. She would do just about anything to get out of this room. "Let me draw baths for all of you in the washhouse."

Lady Judith's teeth chattered. "Where is the fire?"

"It is in the other parlor," Alex said, guiding her and the others to the hallway.

He turned, looking back at Samantha, and she saw the regret in his eyes. But it wasn't his fault. He had been truthful with her from the beginning. She'd always known he was to marry, and yet she'd given her heart to him—unwillingly, perhaps, but completely.

After they warmed by the fire, Samantha escorted the three ladies to the washhouse. For a moment, she wished she were back on the trail before Papa died. Back when everything was filled with wonder and hope.

Back when her heart didn't hurt so badly.

She wanted to be genuinely happy for Alex, as she had been for Jack, but God help her, she was only angry. If Alex looked at Lady Judith the same way Jack had looked at Aliyah, she would have done her best to be happy for them. But Alex didn't look pleased. He looked miserable.

Samantha opened the door to the washhouse, and Lady Judith eyed the four stalls with bathtubs. "Are you going to draw our baths?"

"Yes, ma'am," she replied, hating the way she sounded.

Yes, Alex was an English gentleman. Yes, she had become too familiar with him in this land that stitched together the lives of the poor and the wealthy; the officers and the laborers; the British, French, Indians, and Americans. Alex may have questioned the propriety of the Americans coming here, but he had treated her as an equal. As a lady.

She stepped back outside to obtain hot water from the kitchen.

She was close to finishing her journey to the Willamette, but her heart still wandered. Where it would settle, she didn't know.

* * * * *

A fire roared in the parlor as Alex paced across the room. He'd stood on the wharf like a dolt, staring in shock at the woman he was supposed to marry and then forgetting the names of his uncle's loyal friends.

Judith hated being on the water. Never once had he suspected that when he didn't return last year, she would make the grueling voyage from England.

After the women left for the washhouse, Lord Stanley had retired to the guest room he and his wife would share on this side of the house. Stanley had said he had pressing business to discuss with Alex but that it would have to wait until he recovered from the journey. Alex hoped Stanley would need a day or two. He had yet to recover from his own shock.

Rain pelted against the dark windows, and he stopped pacing and stirred the fire.

The look on Miss Waldron's face when he brought Judith to the house made his heart crumble. He'd refused to entertain thoughts of whether she might return his affections, but seeing her tonight, the wounded look on her face… He hadn't meant to encourage her feelings—or his own feelings, for that matter—but still he felt as if he'd deceived her.

He didn't know what he was doing.

He'd planned to meet Judith back in London, five months after he left Miss Waldron.

Skirts swished in the hallway, and he turned to see Judith. Her hair was still damp but pinned back neatly in a style he didn't recognize. She wore a gray evening dress with ivory lace, and her neckline dipped low, exposing her bare shoulders. Her waist had been cinched to a degree that now appeared abnormal—sickly, even. Had he ever found this corseted shape attractive?

None of the women wore such finery here, nor would they dare display their skin in such a suggestive manner. It was only the beginning, he guessed, of what would look odd to him in London.

He stepped forward, trying to speak calmly. "I hope you had a pleasant journey."

She laughed derisively.

"What are you doing here, Judith?"

She tried to step forward but teetered, her sea legs still adjusting to the land. Springing forward, he took her hand and led her to a couch. She arranged her skirts as she sat, her eyes scrunching into a pout. "I thought you would be delighted to see me."

"I am delighted, of course." He tried to sound convincing. "Delighted—and surprised."

"I received that dreadful letter from you last year." She tugged at one of her sleeves. "And I was quite unwilling to wait yet another year to marry."

"I was planning to come home this spring."

Her eyebrows slipped up. "Your plans have proven unreliable."

"You must forgive me for last year. There was much I had to attend to before I could return to London."

"Certainly I have forgiven you. I would not have spent five months aboard that accursed ship had I not."

His gaze traveled to the window and the miserable weather accosting them. "I am sorry the weather has not greeted you properly."

"No one has greeted me properly." She brushed her hands over her skirt. "What has happened to you, Alexander?"

He searched for an answer, but so much had happened in the past hours that he wasn't quite sure of her question. "What do you mean?"

"You no longer speak like an English gentleman." She critiqued his clothing with her gaze. "Nor do you dress like one."

He glanced down at his striped trousers, white linen shirt, and waistcoat. "I am dressed in the proper fashion for this district."

"London would be aghast."

He looked away from her, toward the fire. Not only would London seem strange to him, he would seem strange to London.

It was no wonder his speech had slipped, living as he did among the voyagers and natives, and it was impossible to keep up with the changing fashions when he'd been gone for so long. Nor had he cared to.

He stirred the fire again before he turned back to her. "How are your parents?"

"Quite anxious for our marriage."

He nodded. "And my uncle?"

Her eyes widened. "Have you not spoken to Lord Stanley?"

"He retired quickly to his room."

"You must speak with him, Alexander. At once."

"I can hardly awaken him."

"Then first thing tomorrow—"

"Certainly."

He sat down in the chair beside her, leaning forward. "Is my uncle unwell?"

"Lord Stanley should discuss it with you."

Annabelle appeared from the hallway, carrying a tray with a teapot and four teacups. Judith looked as if she might hug the servant woman as she poured her a proper cup of tea. She took a cautious sip, and then Alex saw the hint of a smile cross her face. At least they imported the queen's tea and Annabelle had learned how to brew it.

He took a long sip of his own tea, curiosity sprouting in him. "Did my uncle send you here to ensure that I return to London?"

"No one sent me." She set down her teacup. "But I believe the news shall please you."

"I am not sure I can handle any more excitement."

"I am not sure I shall be able to board that miserable ship again." He swirled the remaining tea in his cup. "We could stay here."

She looked so horrified that he almost laughed. "No sensible woman would remain here."

Alex nodded. Perhaps that was why he enjoyed Miss Waldron's company so much. She didn't bother with sensibilities.

Judith stood. "Where shall my lady's maid and I spend the night?"

There was one guest room left in the McLoughlins' home, and it was meant to house a single guest. "I am afraid your accommodations will be sparse. We were not prepared to entertain any women from the ship."

"A decent bed is all I require."

He didn't say that he doubted she would find her bed decent.

She stepped toward the doorway and then turned back to him. "Are you not the slightest bit pleased to see me?"

He leaned forward, taking her hand. "I apologize. I have never been a keen recipient of surprises." This was the woman he was going to marry. Surely the affection would grow between them. "And this wilderness is no place for a lady."

Her lips turned up in a stiff smile. "I have no intention of staying in the wilderness."

He leaned back. "Of course not."

She stood by the entrance to the hall. "Are you not eager to return home?"

His heart and mind felt as if they warred against one another. In doing what he thought was right, was it possible that he may not be doing what God required of Him? He didn't believe Simon's theory of desire, but he did believe that God placed desire in the hearts of His servants. His desire was to stay here.

"I am eager to do what is honorable."

"I would expect nothing less of Alexander Clarke."

Chapter Twenty-Seven

"Boaz!" Micah called as they walked through the fort, and then Samantha shouted their dog's name.

Boaz had been wandering off more lately, roaming outside the gates during the day, but he always came back before the bolt-and-brass padlocks clamped them together at night.

The McLoughlins had been gracious in allowing Boaz to sleep in the room she shared with Micah these past five months. Madame in particular seemed to understand the importance of keeping their small family together. But tonight Boaz hadn't returned home.

Micah shouted for him again as they wandered from building to building. She tried to keep her mind on finding Boaz, but it kept wandering back to this afternoon and the arrival of Lady Judith at the fort.

Jealousy rose inside Samantha, and she hated herself for it. She'd known that Alex was engaged to marry. She'd known that he was going back to England on this ship. But the reality saddened her in a way she hadn't expected.

He would never consider her as anything other than a teacher for the fort's students, and as far as she knew, that time was limited. About twenty-five men had come off the ship, and one of those was probably the new teacher.

Rain soaked her hair and face as she walked, but her clothing was protected by a new coat made from the pelt of a wolverine. Alex had wanted to make sure that neither she nor Micah would again be exposed to storms as they had been on the river.

Micah reached for her hand, tugging her forward. "We have to find him."

The gates were already closed for the night, as was the postern, the small door in the front gate, but she and Micah diligently searched inside the fort, calling Boaz quietly in the rain so they wouldn't disturb anyone's sleep.

Eventually they found themselves back on the McLoughlins' porch.

Micah's tears mixed with rain on his cheeks. "Where did he go?"

She hugged him. "He'll probably be waiting outside the gate in the morning."

Inside their room, she kissed his forehead as he lay on the trundle and tucked the blanket over his slight frame. And she prayed for Boaz to return as Micah drifted off to sleep.

Leaning back in her chair, she stared at the dark ceiling. She should sleep as well, but her mind raced instead. She needed Alex. She needed people like the McLoughlins. It was clear now that she couldn't live in Oregon on her own, no matter how hard she tried.

But she didn't only need Alex. She loved him—in such a different way than she'd ever cared for Jack. The thought of him leaving, of never seeing him again, made her ill.

She got into her bed. They would find Boaz, and then she and Micah would finish their long journey. Now she would have to rely on Lucille and her other friends in the Willamette. It was time for her and Micah to make their own way home.

* * * * *

Samantha and Micah walked slowly to the schoolhouse for the last time. The new schoolteacher had indeed arrived on the *Columbia*, a Mr. Bevins, who would begin teaching tomorrow morning. Even though she'd known this day was coming, it would still be hard to say good-bye to her pupils—both the children and their mothers.

Though not nearly as hard as it would be to say good-bye to Lord Clarke.

Her eyes wandered to the wing of the big house where Lady Judith slept, and she felt like running all the way to the Willamette.

She and Micah would leave as soon as they were able, the next morning perhaps. As soon as Boaz returned. This fort had only been a waiting place for them, as the land of Beulah had been for Christiana before she crossed over to the Celestial City.

Micah looked back at the front gate, and she knew he was still searching for Boaz. But there was no sign of their dog. The men had opened the gates an hour ago, and she'd fully expected Boaz to come bounding inside at first light. There had been no one, animal or person, on the other side.

She squeezed Micah's hand. "Surely he'll come back later today."

Micah nodded, but doubt had settled into his eyes. His world was fracturing today: Alex was preparing to leave, he had to say good-bye to his school friends, they were preparing to travel once again into the unknown, and now their beloved dog had failed to come home,

"We can't leave without him," Micah insisted.

She shook her head. "We won't."

March rain dripped around them, a seemingly endless deluge. The days were still short and gray, the sun hiding itself behind the clouds during the few hours it crossed their horizon. She longed to feel the sunshine on her arms, her face. She longed to be outside these palisades, roaming the countryside again.

She hadn't left this fortress since they arrived, but today she wanted to run far away, on the other side of these walls.

Officers and laborers alike were carting barrels of fur down to the boat landing, but she didn't dare survey the crowd moving in and out of the gate. She was afraid she might see Alex among them.

The bell rang as she stepped into the classroom. It was already full of her students and their mothers, all of them looking as mournful as she felt. Mr. Bevins had been hired to teach only the children of the fort, but she hoped he would teach the mothers as well. If he didn't, at least now the mothers could help the children with their lessons—and make sure they attended school.

Her eyes filled with tears as she said her good-byes to all of her pupils. They had all worked together the past four months; they'd taught her about this new life, and she'd helped them learn the basics of a new language.

Micah bounded up the steps when they got back to the big house that afternoon, searching again for Boaz, but their dog still hadn't returned. Lady Judith was in the parlor with her maid, however. Adorning the mantel and end tables were an assortment of grasses, decorative branches, and wreathes made of evergreens and winter berries. They were a pretty alternative to flowers, she supposed, when flowers couldn't be found.

Madame McLoughlin joined them in the parlor, a platter with a pot of tea and three cups in her hands. "The men are all vying for Miriam."

"Perhaps you should stay here," Samantha suggested, smiling at Lady Judith's maid.

A gasp escaped Lady Judith's lips, but Samantha saw the slightest of smiles on Miriam's petite face. She was probably a year or two older than Samantha, and she was quite pretty with her slender figure and pale green eyes. No wonder the men were smitten.

"Where are the Stanleys?" Samantha asked.

Madame McLoughlin glanced as Lady Judith as if she expected her to respond. When she didn't, Madame spoke. "They've been resting all day. It was a long journey."

Madame set the platter on the coffee table, and Miriam reached forward, pouring it for them.

"Would you like tea?" Miriam asked.

Samantha shook her head, backing toward the door. She couldn't stay here, making polite conversation with her Ladyship.

"I'm so sorry." She nudged Micah's arm. "We need to search for our dog."

They rushed outside, but she hesitated at the fort's back gate. It was the first time she'd been outside the walls since they arrived in November.

Micah nudged her forward, his knapsack perched over his shoulder.

They walked together into the muddy gardens, shouting for Boaz around the outer wall, and then took the path up to the village where Micah said many of the laborers lived. They passed green fields, acres of orchards and vineyards, stables, a sawmill, barns, dairy houses, hundreds of animals, and a blacksmith shop.

She hadn't realized a whole world existed outside the fort's walls.

The two of them searched for hours, calling Boaz's name, but their dog didn't respond. With the sun hidden by the clouds, it was impossible to know what time it was. Darkness came upon them quickly, and she hurried Micah back to the fort.

There were still fifty yards from the back gate when she watched the double doors close for the night. She and Micah shouted, running toward them before they were locked, but it was too late. She pushed on the doors, but the bolt was already in place.

She nudged him forward. "We need to hurry to the front gate."

She and Micah ran as fast as they could, circling the outer wall. Doctor McLoughlin was strict about not letting people come and go in the late hours in order to alleviate theft, but the watchman couldn't leave her and Micah out here in the night.

The wind blew harder now, rustling the trees behind her and sending leaves swirling around her cloak. The front gate was closed, so she jiggled the handle on the postern. It was also locked.

She pounded on the small door, praying the watchman would hear her. She didn't want to think about hiking back up to the village tonight with no lantern.

Micah joined her in the pounding until someone shouted from the other side. "Who's there?"

"It's Samantha Waldron," she shouted back in the wind. "And my brother."

The lock rattled and Daniel finally opened the door, a lantern swinging in his hand. "Don't you know you're not supposed to be out this late?"

"Our dog ran away," she said.

Daniel glanced over her shoulder at Micah rummaging through his knapsack.

She shook her head. "We didn't find him."

"It's dangerous in the dark—"

She stopped him. "We're well aware of the dangers."

Samantha stepped through the open doorway, but Micah lingered by the door, cinching his knapsack shut.

"Come along," she insisted.

Micah peeked out the door one last time, and then he shut it. The watchman motioned her and Micah forward and escorted them back to the big house. Daniel stepped up onto the porch, but even after Samantha opened the door, he didn't leave.

"Thank you for bringing us back safely," she said.

His neck strained to look around her. "Do you think Miss Miriam is still taking callers?"

"I don't know."

"Would you mind inquiring for me?"

"Aren't you supposed to be watching the gate?" she asked.

"I'll only stay for a few minutes," he said. "Just to give my regards."

She stepped into the sitting room and found Alex and Lady Judith, Alex reading aloud. The thought of them spending every evening in their home together overwhelmed her for a moment. Her eyes blurred until they found Miriam, who sat quietly in a rocking chair listening to the story.

"You have a caller at the door," she said.

Miriam blushed, and Samantha could feel the heat swelling in her own wet cheeks when Alex looked at her. "By all means," he said, "send the gentleman in."

His eyes didn't leave her face, and she studied the floor for a moment before she looked up at him. When she met his gaze again, he was almost pleading with her. "Would you like to join us?"

Lady Judith cleared her throat. "Certainly Miss—"

"Waldron," Samantha finished for her.

Lady Judith's eyes were on Alex. "Certainly Miss Waldron has other obligations this evening."

Part of her wanted to run back to her room and bury herself under her covers. She didn't want to be here with Alex and Lady Judith, nor did she want to hear the watchman try to impress poor Miriam.

But she wasn't going to run. She could sit with them for an hour or two. For all she knew, this might be the last evening she would spend with Alex before he left for London.

"I must get Micah to bed first," she said.

After Micah climbed under his covers, she kissed his cheek. He prayed that God would bring Boaz back to them…and then he prayed that God would bring Alex back to them as well.

Chapter Twenty-Eight

The candle flickered in the darkness as Alex packed his belongings into his camphorwood cassette. After Miss Waldron arrived in the parlor tonight, Judith talked incessantly about their upcoming wedding and all who would attend. She had already selected a date for the fall and delivered an invitation to Her Majesty.

Miss Waldron didn't speak often, but still the differences between the two women were stark. Both had endured difficult journeys to travel here, but there was no joy in Judith's heart for this new place. Granted, the skies had dumped buckets upon buckets of water since her arrival, and she couldn't see its beauty. But even if she saw the flowers and gardens and snow-covered mountains, he doubted that she would love this country as he did.

He had paced the piazza for an hour after he bid good night to the ladies.

Affection might grow between a man and woman who scarcely knew each other, but how was he supposed to marry a woman whom he no longer liked?

Someone knocked on his door, and he glanced up at the clock on his wall. It was after ten.

Most everyone at the fort should be asleep after working all day in the rain to load the ship. Perhaps the night watchman had seen his candle and was checking on him.

He opened the door, and there before him was Lord Stanley, shivering in the cold. He quickly hurried the man into his room.

"You should not have come out so late."

"I would have come earlier," Lord Stanley countered, "but the voyage was most disagreeable for Lady Stanley and me."

The lord unbuttoned his cloak, and Alex hung it on a peg before he offered the man a chair.

"I have news for you, from London."

Alex sat across from him. "Lady Judith said you might."

"Unfortunately, it is not pleasant news that I bear."

Alex leaned forward. "Please tell me what happened."

"Lord Neville Clarke is deceased."

Alex fell back against his chair.

"The doctors said it was the poor condition of his heart."

His uncle was dead. "How long ago?"

"Eight months past."

His hands trembled. "How is my aunt?"

"As well as can be expected."

"So you have come to make sure I return to the committee..." Alex's voice trailed off.

Lord Stanley hesitated. "In your absence, the committee inquired about your lineage. There was some question, you see, about your father."

"My father was the Duke of Clarke. Lord Neville Clarke's brother."

Lord Stanley retrieved a letter from his coat pocket and slipped it to Alex to read. Alex opened the crumpled sheet.

It was a letter from the Duke of Clarke, the man he believed to be his father, dated the year Alex was born. It said that his wife was expecting but the child was not his. The duke had been abroad in the year his wife conceived this child.

Alex's hands trembled as he hastily handed back the letter. "Did my uncle know this?"

Lord Stanley slowly nodded his head. "The duke gave it to him before he died."

And yet his uncle had taken him in, groomed him to take his place on the committee, made him his heir. Alex shook his head in disbelief, unable to speak.

When he did, his voice was a whisper. "Who gave you this letter?"

Lord Stanley looked at his hands.

"Who gave it to you?" he repeated.

"Lady Clarke."

"But why would my aunt…" he began, and then he stopped. "I see. I am no longer the heir, am I?"

"In the past year, Lady Clarke has befriended a distant cousin of yours." Lord Stanley hesitated. "They have developed some sort of agreement."

"This cousin will inherit the title and the property?"

"He will."

Alex cringed. The next heir had presumably promised his aunt a greater share of Uncle Neville's money than she would receive in her dower. And Alex would receive nothing from his uncle's estate.

"Did the committee discover the name of my real father?"

"Your father is believed to be a street performer named Fulton Knox."

His stomach clenched. "I believed him to be my stepfather."

"Knox has been dead sixteen years now."

"Is there then no place on the committee for me?"

Lord Stanley slowly shook his head. "They have nominated Lord Dodds."

"Of course."

There was no reason to return to London.

He set the letter by the candle, raking his fingers through his hair. He'd miss his uncle, the man who'd given a little boy hope to continue living despite the grief that had threatened to consume him. He'd miss the man who had rescued Fulton Knox's son from poverty and shame and who always had confidence in him.

Judith had said the news in his letter was good. She must know that his uncle was dead. How could she consider that *good*? "Does Judith know this?"

"Only about your uncle's death."

Alex swallowed hard, closing his eyes. Judith must still think he would become the president of the committee. Perhaps that was why she'd boarded the ship, to make sure not only that he would return, but that she would be secured in the position of president's wife.

He looked at the dark window and watched rivulets stream down the pane. What would Judith do when she discovered the truth? Could he dare hope that she would change her mind?

He escorted Lord Stanley to the door.

"I am sorry to be the bearer of such bad news."

Alex nodded. "I am sorry that my uncle is gone. But I thank you for coming in person to tell me." He closed the door and walked back to his chair.

It felt as though the world had split open under his feet and he was falling without any idea where he would land. But even as he fell, a new thought began to seed in his mind.

He was free now—free of all the expectations of the committee. Free to find a position he enjoyed. Free to live his life in the way Sovereignty directed.

He could remain at Fort Vancouver and continue working for McLoughlin. Perhaps Judith wouldn't have to get back on the ship. He could fulfill his obligation and provide for her here.

Rain pattered harder against the window, seeming to drown out his thoughts. If he stayed here, his work would change. He was at Fort Vancouver at the request of his uncle, the president of the committee. If he wanted to stay, would the current president allow him to do so?

McLoughlin had probably been sent a letter from the committee to explain the pending change in leadership. Once McLoughlin returned from his trip, he might not permit Alex to stay here.

He stood up, hope dawning on him again.

What if he could stay here in the wilderness? Was it possible? He could build a house and plant seeds. He could learn how to harvest crops and raise animals instead of trap them.

Like the Americans.

There was another knock on his door, and he cringed. Had Lord Stanley neglected to deliver all of the bad news?

He moved slowly toward the door and opened it, but instead of Lord Stanley, Miss Waldron stood on the other side, dressed in her long coat and moccasins. Tears brimmed in her blue eyes, and her lips trembled. Compassion overwhelmed him at the sight of her tears.

Her gaze pleaded with him, but he didn't know what was wrong. He wanted to take her in his arms as he'd done at the river. He wanted to rescue her from the pain she'd borne so resolutely and continued to bear.

He reached for her hand, grazing her fingers, but he pulled back before he held it. For heaven's sake, couldn't he be as kind as McLoughlin without showing his affection for her?

Tucking his hands behind his back, he leaned toward her. "What happened?"

"Micah—" Her voice shook. "He's gone."

He glanced down the hallway. "Where did he go?"

* * * * *

The burden Samantha carried was so heavy, she could scarcely walk. The weight of it pressed firmly against her lungs, stealing her breath away. She was too terrified to consider the possibilities of what could happen to her brother.

She pulled her hood over her head and forced herself forward as they slogged across the muddy piazza, propelled by Alex's lantern light and his assurance that they would find Micah.

Micah never left the room at night. He didn't even go out in the daylight without permission.

I'm sorry, Mama.

She'd tried her best to keep him safe, for two thousand miles overland and then for five months here at the fort. Micah loved Boaz as much as she did. She should have guessed that he would try to sneak out and find him. If only she'd taken the slightest precaution, locking the door to their bedroom. If she'd locked it, she would surely have heard him leave their room.

But she hadn't heard the door open. She hadn't even known he was gone until she'd awakened from her sleep and reached down to check on him in the trundle. Her hands searched for his arm below her, as they did most nights, but tonight he wasn't there.

She'd bolted upright in her bed.

She had hoped it was a bad dream, but now she and Alex were out in the cold, in the rain. Micah was gone, and she didn't know where he went.

Alex thought Micah had to be inside this fortress, but she had a terrible feeling that he'd gotten out. If he had wandered far— dear God, she didn't know what would happen to him.

Alex checked the front gate first, and the lock was secure. Daniel was asleep in the small hut beside the gate, and Alex shook him. The man woke with a start, looking between her and Alex. "What is it?"

"Have you seen Micah Waldron?"

The man shook his head. "I haven't seen anyone out except you tonight."

"He is not in the big house."

The man grabbed his gun like Alex had done. "I'll help you look."

The watchman slipped between the buildings as Samantha eyed the locked gates. She started to turn away but then stopped. Stepping forward, she pushed on the postern. It swung open.

Alex swore and then reached down, picking up something that had kept the door cracked open. She watched him examine it with his light, and then he held it out to her. Her fingers wrapped around the wooden object, and then her tears flowed. It was Micah's wooden elephant.

Anger bubbled inside her along with the fear. Micah hadn't waited to make sure the door was closed. He'd waited to prop it open. Her brother had planned all along to go back out tonight and find their dog.

She fell back against the palisade. "Micah's out there."

Out in the wilderness that never ended. Out with the wild animals and the unforgiving rapids, with endless forests and dangerous cliffs, with natives who might steal him away.

The sight of his body, crumpled up at the bottom of that cliff on the trail, rushed back to her. She began to slide to the ground, but Alex caught her.

"I am taking you back to the house."

"This door is supposed to be locked," she said.

"Daniel must not have checked it after he visited Miriam."

She pounded his chest. "You said Micah would be safe outside."

"Not alone."

She felt sick. "I'm going to find him."

"It is not safe for you either, Miss Waldron."

She grabbed the lapels on his cloak, clinging to him. "I can't leave him out there—"

He held her in one of his arms, lifting the lantern to illuminate her face. "Micah is in trouble because he went to find your lost dog. If you go, I am afraid… If you get lost searching for him…" His voice broke. "I must search for him alone."

The anxiety in her heart began to taper.

Alex wasn't going to leave Micah out there alone to fend for himself. She could trust this man to do everything he could to find her brother.

"What can I do?" she asked, begging him for a task.

"You need to return to the house."

"I can't—"

"You must trust me," he said.

She took a deep breath.

"And pray that God will guide me to him."

She slowly released his cloak. "I will pray, Alex."

Then he hurried through the door.

Chapter Twenty-Nine

Giant trees loomed above him, their branches draping over Alex's head like hundreds of fingers trying to capture him. Rain crashed against the leaves, drowning out any other sound, and the darkness was so thick he could barely see his next step in the lantern light.

One hand held his lantern, dripping from the rain, and his other hand clutched his gun. He knew Miss Waldron would be faithful in her prayers, and he was glad of it. He'd never been outside the fort alone at night—their company's fur parties always traveled in the safety of a brigade. He needed the guidance of the Holy One to find this boy.

Only God could find a child out here.

He stopped for a moment, trying to decide which direction Micah would have traveled. Miss Waldron said they'd already been to the village this afternoon, so he didn't repeat that path. And he doubted Micah would have gone back down to the river. So Alex hiked east toward the gorge, hollering the boy's name as he climbed over boulders and fallen trees.

He could find his way back to the fort—all he needed to do was walk south until he reached the river and then turn west. But Micah wouldn't know how to get back.

Alex trod carefully through the woods. Hopefully the wild animals had hidden themselves away in caves tonight to stay dry.

How far would the boy travel to find his dog? If he was as persistent as his sister, Alex figured he might travel all night.

He wouldn't stop searching until he found the boy.

* * * * *

Samantha clung to Micah's elephant for the remainder of the night, praying as she'd never prayed before that her brother wouldn't meet the much bigger "elephant" on the trail, that God would protect him and Alex wherever they were.

Morning dawned slowly, chasing away the rain, but Samantha didn't move from the sofa, didn't stop praying. The servants bustled through the house to prepare breakfast, but she didn't budge until Lady Judith and Miriam emerged from their room.

Miriam greeted her, and she blinked as she looked up at the maid, wishing to find consolation in a friend.

Should she tell Lady Judith that Alex was gone, out searching for Micah? Her mind bristled at the thought of how her Ladyship might respond. She couldn't stomach the woman's coldness, and she didn't want to answer any questions about why she had walked across the piazza to ask for Alex's help instead of knocking on Madame McLoughlin's door.

The truth was, she hadn't once considered asking anyone else for help. The moment she realized Micah was gone, she'd thrown on her cloak and moccasins and rushed to Bachelor's Hall. Second floor, third window from the left.

This morning she wrapped her fur cloak over her calico dress and walked outside into fog that clung to the buildings. The front gate was already opened, but she didn't walk toward it. She turned to the back gate, hoping to see Alex and Micah walking toward her, but there was no one.

She wandered through the gate, out into the gardens. Fog dipped over the arbors and settled on the plants. She couldn't see the trees yet, but she heard something in the distance, something that sounded like a bark.

She cupped her hands, yelling, "Boaz!"

Her dog bounded toward her, crashing into her open arms. She toppled over as she clung to his neck.

"Where have you been?" she scolded, burying her head into his fur.

She sat up and examined his right back leg. The fur was mangled and bloody, as if he'd gotten stuck in a crevice or some rocks.

It didn't matter what happened, she supposed. She was glad he was home.

She lifted her head again, scanning the fog behind him. Her heart ached for a man and boy to emerge behind Boaz. She stood waiting, praying they would follow him home, trusting the Lord with all her heart. But no one else came through the trees.

* * * * *

Forty men fanned out from the fort after breakfast. Madame McLoughlin reassured Samantha that these men knew how to track all manner of creature. They could certainly locate her brother.

What neither of them dared to question was whether they would find Micah alive.

Samantha sat under a gazebo in the gardens, watching one of the men disappear into the forest. She'd told Madame that she wanted to join the men in their search, but the older woman's wisdom cut through the rubble of Samantha's scattered mind. When Micah returned, as Boaz had done, she needed to be here to care for him.

She groaned as she waited, the ache in her chest returning.

Why hadn't she stopped Papa from coming to Oregon?

She should have told him that Micah was too young, that they should wait a few years. Papa had wanted them to be one of the first families out here, but in doing so, he'd given up his life. And if Micah were lost too, even his legacy would be gone.

She couldn't bear to think about Micah crossing the river before she did, joining Papa and Mama on the other side of those heavenly gates. She wished she could be content for Micah to join their parents, but she couldn't muster the slightest bit of joy at the thought of losing her brother. She wanted him to live his life on this earth and grow to be a man. She wanted him to carry on Papa's legacy. She wanted them to be a family.

"Trust Me."

Did she really trust God, after He took her father from her? Did she trust Him enough to care for Micah?

Her body trembled at the thought of letting Micah go, at the thought of him hurt or stuck some place as Boaz had been, of him calling out to her when she couldn't hear him. She balled her legs to her chest, begging God for relief from her fear, begging Him to rescue Micah.

She'd thought she could protect Micah from harm, but she wasn't the Sovereign One. God's messengers were their only real protection until their Father called one of His children home.

"He's Yours," she whispered, giving Micah back to the One who loved him much more than she ever could. But even as she released him to their heavenly Father, she pleaded for His mercy. She prayed that He would guide Alex's steps and show him where Micah was.

If Micah hadn't been found by nightfall, she would wrap Boaz's leg and send him out with one of the men. Perhaps he would find Micah again, as he had done at the canyon.

Until then, she would continue to pray.

* * * * *

Alex didn't stop walking, not even when night faded into dawn. The cold had crawled into his limbs and burrowed so deep within him that his bones seemed to have frozen. But no matter how much his body hurt, he refused to quit.

He doubled back and forth through the forest, searching behind boulders and shouting into the trees. Surely Micah would have grown tired soon after he left the fort, lying down somewhere to rest. And if he were asleep, his blond hair would glow like candlelight in the deep browns and greens of the forest.

He couldn't stop searching until he found the boy, for Miss Waldron's sake and for his own. He'd almost begun to think of the three of them as—well, as a family.

He swallowed hard at the thought. It was almost as if Micah were his son.

God, help me.

Grown men with guns and knives died out here. A boy with nothing except his knapsack would be prey to too many horrific things to consider.

He had to focus on rescuing Micah, not letting his mind wander to all the possibilities.

He called out Micah's name again, his voice almost hoarse, and then he rested against a tree. What if Micah had gone back to the fort, like Samantha and he had done when Doyle was searching for them? Micah could be with his sister, eating a hot breakfast by the fire or resting under a stack of warm blankets in bed.

He hoped Micah had already found his way home.

Perhaps he should turn back and check with Miss Waldron. If he hadn't returned, he would pack some food and resume his search.

Alex stepped backward, turning toward the river, and when he did, he saw a wooden figure similar to the one he had seen lodged in the fort's door.

His heart pounded as he leaned over and picked up the carved giraffe off the mossy rock. He scanned the trees around him.

"Micah!" he shouted, straining his voice.

He quickly trekked forward through the shrubs and tangled trees, searching for him. There would be no returning now, not without Micah.

He stopped again. There was no wooden animal this time, but at his feet was a blue knapsack. And there, in the trees in front of him, was a tepee.

He picked up the knapsack, surprised by its heavy weight, and set it on a rock. Then he slipped behind a tree and surveyed the village. There were five tepees clustered together near a stream, and in the center stood a birch-bark lodge. Beside the lodge, coals burned inside a ring of stones, but he didn't see anyone tending the fire.

If only McLoughlin weren't off at Fort Colville. The natives respected the governor, but most of them merely tolerated Alex out of deference for McLoughlin. He wished he could walk into the village and use his hands to sign for their help, but he would probably frighten them. He didn't care to frighten any tribe of Indians, especially when he was alone.

Two Indians ducked out of one of the tepees, and Alex gasped. Between the two natives, he caught a glimpse of Micah's hair.

He didn't recognize the men, but they were Flatheads, and they wore shirts made of wood rat skin, long buckskin leggings, and shell ornaments around their necks.

How could he approach a tribe of Indians he didn't know? The Flatheads were usually peaceful, but they might kill him, along with Micah, out of pure fright. He clutched the gun at his side.

Should courage restrain him now, or should it propel him forward?

Perhaps he should return to the village and gather the women who knew these tribes well to come and plead for Micah. But if he left, the Indians might travel away with Micah or, God forbid, perform a ritual that would steal Micah's life.

This was exactly why they shouldn't bring children into the wilderness.

Minutes passed, his eyes fixed on the lodge as he formulated a plan. Miss Waldron communicated well with the native women in the school even when she didn't speak their language. He might lose his life in the process, but he would have to attempt to do the same as she had done. He certainly couldn't leave Micah here alone.

Taking a deep breath, he left Micah's knapsack on a rock and stood tall, walking confidently toward the lodge.

God help him save this boy.

Chapter Thirty

The hours seemed like an eternity as Samantha waited with Boaz in the garden. Madame McLoughlin delivered the noon meal to her. Every time she saw the tip of a hat, her heart leaped, but the men who returned to the fort shook their heads in resignation. There was no trace of her brother.

She squeezed the elephant in her hand.

They may not know where Micah was, but God did. Even in the tangled overgrowth of this wilderness, He could see Micah. She crossed her arms, rocking on the bench as she continued to pray.

Boaz stood up, his ears arched back. She didn't hear anything, but she watched the trees, expecting to see another of the laborers appear. This man, though, was taller than the others. And in his arms he carried something.

A boy.

Boaz barked, and together they raced toward Alex. Micah didn't look up at her as she expected.

Had he already traveled through the pearled gates?

She breathed deep, trying to trust God when she didn't understand.

She reached out, lifting Micah from Alex's arms. His knapsack fell to the ground.

Her brother stirred and rested his head against her shoulder, and her heart filled with gladness at the life that remained in him. She quietly thanked God that he was alive.

"Is he injured?" she asked, holding her brother close to her.

Alex shook his head. "He is very tired, though."

"How far did you carry him?"

He shrugged. "A ways."

Mud caked Alex's cloak, and his brown hair was coated with leaves, just like Micah's. Yet he looked so handsome to her. This British gentleman who'd reprimanded her for traveling here with her brother had rescued Micah yet again.

The other men had given up, but not Alex. His tenacity overwhelmed her. His gruffness was only a prickly cover to a heart pliant with compassion. This dear man had stayed up the entire night, and he hadn't come home until he found her brother.

This time she didn't long to sink into his arms. She wished he could sink into hers, as Micah had done.

Tears flowed down her cheeks. "Thank you, Alex."

"It was my pleasure."

"You—" She started. "Twice you've saved his life."

Alex picked up the knapsack and tried to smile at her, but she could see the exhaustion in his eyes, in the trembling of his arms. "And his knapsack," he quipped as he held it up. "Your brother is quite smart. He left out his animals for me to find."

She pulled Micah closer to her as Alex tossed the knapsack over his shoulder. "This must weigh as much as he does."

She smiled. "He carries all his treasures with him."

"He must be quite the wealthy young man." Boaz nudged Alex's leg with his nose, and Alex put his hand on the dog's head. "You caused a lot of trouble today."

Samantha turned, moving back toward the fort with Alex and Boaz. "Where did you find him?"

"It is a long story."

Micah stirred again, and she smoothed her fingers over his hair. "Why don't you tell me while you eat?"

He nodded, the weariness heavy in his eyes.

She could wait as long as necessary for the story, long enough for him to change into dry clothes, eat, even sleep if necessary. She was just glad both of them were home.

Home.

Oregon Country had become home to her.

They walked quietly, side by side, through the open gate and to the big house.

Her heart overflowed.

* * * * *

Alex opened the door for Miss Waldron and Micah so the three of them could enter the big house. His skin still felt frigid, his bones tumbling inside him like ice, but he was grateful beyond words that Micah was safe. The natives hadn't wanted to give up this boy, but God in His graciousness and power had helped him persuade them.

Micah was free.

Alex was cold and exhausted, but he was glad to be here with Micah and Miss Waldron. So very glad.

Miss Waldron nodded toward the hall. "I should put him to bed."

He walked her to her room, opening the door for her. "Do you need me to assist you?"

The look she gave him was one of admiration, and it swelled within him, bolstering him.

"Thank you, Alex," she said again as she lowered Micah onto the trundle bed. "I will care for him while you change into dry clothes."

He hesitated. "Perhaps we can dine together in the next hour."

She nodded, and her smile warmed his skin.

He backed away from her, bumping into the doorpost. Then he

closed the door and hurried down the hallway, preparing to go to his quarters.

After he changed, he would ask Cook to prepare a hot meal for him and Miss Waldron along with some porridge for Micah when he woke. Renewed vigor replaced his exhaustion at the thought of sharing a meal and his story with her. He could stay up for hours more as long as they were together.

He turned the corner of the hallway, passing the sitting room. And he stopped.

Judith was sitting on the sofa, her hands folded neatly in her lap.

Alex stared at her, horror cresting in him. All he'd thought about since last night was Micah—Miss Waldron and Micah.

He'd forgotten that he was engaged.

Judith looked perfectly pristine as her head turned slightly to meet his eyes.

"There you are," Judith said. "Madame said you had been out all day."

The look she gave him was much different from Miss Waldron's. Her gaze could freeze his bones back into ice.

He shivered inside his cloak. "I am, indeed, back."

He waited for her to inquire after Micah's well-being, but she did not. Instead, her gaze fixed on his muddy cloak. Then she turned to Miriam. "Go draw him a bath."

The weariness returned to him.

"There is no need," he said with a shake of his head. "I can care for myself."

Judith's sigh was drawn long. "You must stop this nonsense, Alexander. When we return to London, you mustn't stay out all day and soak yourself like a dog. You must at least act as distinguished as your uncle and allow the servants to do things for you."

Would he be going back to London? He wasn't so certain.

She sat up straighter. "Did Lord Stanley speak with you?"

"He did."

Her lips eased into a smile. "The president of the London committee must act like a gentleman."

His clothing may be filthy, his body cold and tired. He may be hungry enough to eat an entire goat in one serving, but first they needed to be honest with one another, before the ship departed for England. He stepped toward her, standing taller.

"I am not going to be the president," he said, his voice strong.

"Of course you are—"

He shook his head. "They have nominated Lord Victor Dodds to take the presidency."

She sank against the sofa, her mouth dropping in shock. "That is not possible."

"I'm afraid it is. But I should be able to find another position—"

She interrupted him. "On the committee?"

He shook his head, not quite sure how to deliver information that he hadn't had time to process for himself. As he watched her, he could see the change in her eyes. Doubt drained into anger—disdain, even. She desired this marriage as little as he did. If they married, they would both be miserable.

"The ship leaves tomorrow." She rubbed her hands together, panicked. "We have a long journey ahead to sort this out."

He eyed Miriam in the corner, where she studied the book in her hands, and then he looked back at Judith.

How could he tell Judith that he didn't want to return to London? That he would fulfill his obligation to her if she really desired it but that he didn't think either of them would be happy in this marriage? When they had agreed to marry, he had expected to become president of the committee one day, and she had aspired to be the president's wife.

He leaned back against the wall, water puddling on the carpet under him. "Do you want to marry me?" he asked.

She shot him a furious look and then glanced back at Miriam. "What a preposterous question."

"Because I am not going to be the president of the committee. I am not even going to be on the committee. I must find my own way in this world, whether it is here or in London. And if I marry, I hope my wife and I will be able to find this new way together."

"There is no *way* to find, Alexander. My father will speak with Lord Dodds upon our return." Her voice trembled. "They *must* keep you on the committee."

He took a deep breath. "I am afraid I've lost more than my position, Judith. I have lost my title and inheritance as well."

His words seemed to crash around her, around them. Her mouth fell open. "But you—you are now the Duke of Clarke."

He shook his head. "Apparently my father was a street performer on the East End."

"Ludicrous," she announced. "We will fight this."

"There is nothing to fight."

"I came all this way…" Her voice trailed off as she stood.

"I am sorry, Judith."

She stepped toward the door. "I must think."

"Of course."

* * * * *

Samantha kissed Micah on the forehead and slipped out the door, wearing her new muslin dress. Even though Alex had invited her to join him for supper, she knew he might be resting instead. She couldn't fathom how exhausted he must be—but she still hoped he and Lady Judith might be waiting for her. She could suffer through the woman's glare for an hour, if only to hear the story of Micah's rescue.

The moment Lady Judith began discussing their wedding ceremony, however, she would leave.

Candlelight flickered down the hallway from the dining room, and she almost turned and escaped back in her room. She'd taken Alex for granted during the past five months, his escorting her to church services, his playing with Micah, his strength during the storms. If something happened to Micah again, whose door would she knock on? The other men brought her flowers, but none of them cared for her and Micah like Alex did.

A dish clinked in the dining room, and she took a deep breath before she strolled inside.

Her heart leaped with gladness when she saw Alex there, waiting for her, alone. He pulled out a chair and motioned for her to sit in it.

She smiled. "Are you sure I'm not supposed to be in the other dining room?"

He returned her smile. "I am certain you are in the right place."

She glanced toward the hall on the other side of the room. "Where is Lady Judith?"

He shrugged. "Packing her things, I believe."

Sadness passed over her again, and she fought to resist it. Alex had to leave with her. Samantha's longing would only wound them both. "Is she sad to return to London?"

He smiled again. "Hardly."

She sat down, and he walked around the table, pulling out a chair to sit across from her. She unfolded her cloth napkin, straightening it in her lap, and for a moment she felt quite like a proper Englishwoman as she sat tall against the high-back chair, courting a proper English gentleman.

Was there any harm in pretending, just for the night, that she was Lady Clarke?

After he said grace, he served her a winter squash soup, followed by boiled turkey sprinkled with thyme and dinner rolls spread with fresh butter. She savored the food with gratefulness for God's bounty and His mercy. Micah's return was a miracle. A gift from God.

She ate a few bites of turkey and then set down her fork.

Alex watched her in the candlelight, and her heart fluttered in the intensity of his gaze. It was good that he was leaving on the ship tomorrow. She didn't want him to go back to London, but she thought she could bear his departure. What she couldn't bear was his remaining any longer while he belonged to another.

He refilled her water glass, his eyes still on her face. "How did you do it?"

She took a deep breath. "How did I do what?"

"Walk two thousand miles across this country, through the wind and the rain."

She looked over at the mirror on the wall and saw her reflection. She still resembled the woman who'd left Ohio a year ago, but she felt nothing like her. The journey West was now a blur to her—of campfire smoke, endless walking, brutal sun, and parched lips. It was also the triumph of accomplishing what seemed to be impossible, the beauty of waking each morning to the joy of her community, the hours spent with her father before he died.

She barely remembered the wind and the rain.

"We had no choice but to keep walking. We simply put one foot in front of the other, for two thousand miles."

He leaned forward, and for a moment she thought he might reach for her hand, but he folded his together. "You amaze me."

Her cheeks warmed. "Thank you."

Heaven help her, Alex had to stop talking to her like that, had to stop looking at her like he might love her too. She fidgeted with her napkin in her lap. They had to talk about something else.

She took a deep breath. "You were going to tell me where you found Micah."

He pushed back his plate, his gaze drifting to the flicker of candlelight. "He was in an Indian village."

Her skin crawled. "An Indian village?"

"They had not harmed him."

She pulled at the napkin at her lap. How did Alex know they hadn't harmed him? Harm sometimes buried itself deep inside a body and emerged later in anger and fear. "Were they planning to hurt him?"

"I don't know." He paused. "They believed he was the son of a god."

She leaned back against the chair and imagined the Indians looking on her brother with wonder, the blond boy seemingly dropped into their midst. If they knew about the fort, they might have wondered if he came from there, but perhaps it didn't matter.

"You should have seen him," Alex reassured her. "He was so brave."

He leaned forward again, his voice intent. "He didn't even cry until we were far away from the village."

The thought of Micah's tears made her heart sink again. "How did you get him away?"

"Apparently they wanted my gun even more than they wanted the son of a god."

"You traded your gun?"

He shrugged. "I can get another."

She took a deep breath, marveling again that God had sent this man into their lives when they needed him so much. "You are a hero, Alexander Clarke."

He shook his head. "I am no such thing."

But in her heart, he was a hero to Micah and, most of all, to her. "Others falter in the face of danger, but when someone is in need, you keep pressing forward."

She could see the conflict in his gaze as he searched her face. He was an honorable man, the honor threaded through him as tightly as the stitching on Mama's prized shawl. She wouldn't do anything to entice him to break his promises.

"I need to tell you—" he began, but his words were interrupted by a cough from the hallway.

She turned to see Lady Judith there, glaring at both of them. Heat climbed up Samantha's cheeks again.

"I'm quite sorry to disturb you both, but Lord Clarke and I must talk."

Lord Clarke.

Samantha stood quickly, tossing the cloth napkin onto her chair. Alex was so very different from her. He may be her hero, but he was also nobility and wealth and prestige. Everything she was not. She had to stop thinking that there might be more between them than a thread of mutual respect. She couldn't even pretend there was friendship.

"I'll miss you," she whispered, not caring if Lady Judith heard her.

Then she turned and fled to her room.

Chapter Thirty-One

Samantha shook Micah's shoulders gently. "Wake up."

He rolled over, and she looked down on him with a heart full of admiration and gratitude. He had grown up so much during the past year, and she was proud of his bravery and a bit envious of his ability to rest well after his world crashed around him.

She'd slept only four or five hours, her body succumbing to her exhaustion, but then she'd awakened again before dawn. All she could think about was Alexander Clarke—Alex nodding a formal good-bye before he boarded the ship. Alex with Lady Judith on his arm as they left the landing. Alex waving to his fellow officers before the ship disappeared around the bend.

She couldn't say good-bye, couldn't watch his cursory wave to her before he left. She couldn't pretend they were acquaintances merely taking different paths in their life. Their paths would never intersect again. This was good-bye for a lifetime. She thought she would be able to bear it, but after last night, she knew she couldn't.

She shook Micah a little harder, urgency boiling in her. They had to leave the fort right away. "You have to get up," she insisted.

He groaned, but he slowly sat up on his trundle.

In the early morning hours, she had packed their few things in two packs to strap to their backs. Now she wrapped Boaz's leg and strapped a light load onto his back as well. She took with her their family's Bible and a bag of sea biscuits in her pack . Part of her wished she could take Alex's copy of *The Pilgrim's Progress*, if only as a reminder of Mama, but it would also remind her too much of him. She had to say good-bye to any hope of a life with him, just as he was doing with her.

"Where are we going?" Micah whispered.

"We have to finish our pilgrimage."

After she helped Micah strap on his pack, she glanced around the room. Quickly she reached for Alex's book and stuffed it into her pack. She would have to say good-bye later.

Micah clutched her hand, his knapsack balanced over his shoulder, as they moved quietly out the front door with Boaz.

If only they had their gold from Papa. Then they would be guaranteed for life in the Willamette. But now, it was a gamble whether or not she could stay with the Kneedlers or with Lucille. And whether she would even be able to find them.

Still, she had no choice but to go.

She hated to hurry Micah after his terrifying experience yesterday, but they couldn't stay. Nor would she subject Micah to the pain of saying good-bye to Alex. He admired Lord Clarke more than any other man.

The front gate slowly opened, and she glanced back at the big house one last time. She didn't want to leave without saying good-bye to Madame McLoughlin or Annabelle, but one day she would come back for a visit, long after Alex was gone.

Micah tugged on her hand before they stepped outside. "Can't we stay a little longer?"

She shook her head. "It's time to finish our journey."

They stepped onto the path outside the palisades and walked slowly toward the river.

"But I like it here," he said.

"You'll like it in the Willamette too. The Rochesters will be there, and the Kneedlers. You remember Katherine Morrison, don't you?"

He groaned. "Katherine's just a baby."

"I'm sure her dad would appreciate your entertaining her."

"You're not going to marry her father, are you?"

"Well…" She'd never really considered someone else besides Jack and then Alex. "Do you not like her father?"

"It's not that." He turned and looked behind them again. "You're supposed to marry Alex."

"Unfortunately, not everything works out the way we want it to."

"I don't want to leave Alex."

She stopped and hugged him. "Neither do I."

She brushed tears from her eyes and then, holding her head high, she and Micah and Boaz marched down to the landing. As they walked, she glanced up at the clouds hovering in the morning sky, but they held no threat of a storm. The river flowed steadily this morning. Calm.

She had one last obstacle before Alex and Lady Judith came down to the landing. She had to figure out how to get back across the river.

Several laborers were already on the dock, loading the remaining crates onto the boat. She stopped one of the men who'd brought her a bouquet of flowers shortly after she arrived at Fort Vancouver.

"Louie?"

He blinked "My name is Huey."

"Ah, Huey." She pointed to one of the bateaux on the shore. "Could you please row Micah and me to the other side?"

He shook his head. "I have to help get this ship loaded up before they leave."

She thought for a moment. She didn't have any money to pay him, but she still had credit at the Sale Shop. "You can have my store credit," she said. "I'm not planning to come back."

He stopped. "How much do you have?"

When she told him, he eyed the boats. "Does Clarke know that you're leaving?"

"It doesn't matter," she said. "He's leaving today as well."

Huey glanced down Boaz. "Your dog will tip the boat."

She shook her head. "He won't."

"I don't know—"

"Never mind. I can row us across." She set her pack in one of the small boats. "After the ship leaves, would you come retrieve the boat?"

"McLoughlin will have my head if something happens to you."

"We're no longer the governor's responsibility."

Huey handed his load to another worker and climbed into the boat that held her pack. "I'll take you."

The journey across the river was nothing like their first trip. Alex had been so brave back in November, coming after them in that horrible storm. She would never forget his reaching for Micah, risking his life to pull her brother out of the river. Then he'd carried her all the way back to the fort.

Tears filled her eyes at memories both beautiful and agonizing. She wasn't leaving Alex, she reminded herself. He was leaving her.

She shouldn't be angry with him for fulfilling his promise, but she was angry with him anyway. In his honor, he was choosing to leave her and Micah behind.

Micah turned around twice in the boat, his gaze questioning her. She smiled to reassure him even though she didn't feel the least bit assured that she was doing the right thing for them. But she couldn't go back. Fort Vancouver was just a resting place. It was time for her and Micah to finish this journey.

The bateau slid onto the bank, and Huey hopped out before Samantha, helping her to the ground. His hand clutched hers for a moment longer as he searched her face. "You sure you won't marry me?"

She arched up on her toes and kissed his coarse beard before she stepped back. "My heart belongs to someone else."

"I understand," he replied before he tipped his hat. Then he turned quickly to row the boat back across the river.

As she and Micah stood on the shore, her brother's hand in hers, they looked at the ship as it prepared to leave port. They would walk slowly today, following the Willamette River south. Home. Alex had said it was less than a day's journey to the settlement.

Micah tugged her hand. "I want to watch him leave."

"I can't."

"Please," he begged.

Perhaps she could watch from afar, where Alex couldn't see her. Where she couldn't see him waving good-bye.

She unrolled a red-and-green wool blanket from her pack, one she'd bought with her teaching wages. Then she spread it on the ground.

Micah sat beside her, snuggling up against her arm. Boaz lay down on the grass beside them. "Can we go visit Alex someday?"

"You'd have to swim."

He lifted his head. "I can swim."

"A very long way." She put her arm around her brother. "Alex said you were very brave when the Indians took you."

"They fed me."

"What did you eat?"

"Cooked moss and acorns."

He followed her gaze to the ship.

"You are a true explorer, Micah." Her brother had overcome tougher challenges in his seven years than most men did in a lifetime, and yet he was resilient. Nothing, it seemed, would stop him.

Papa would be proud.

He sat a bit taller. "An explorer and a gentleman."

She laughed. "I believe you are."

"I'm sorry I left without telling you," he said.

"I almost died of fright."

"I didn't mean to scare you." He reached out to pet Boaz. "I couldn't lose him too."

"I understand, Micah, but the next time you want to search for him, we'll do it together. I can't lose you either."

He nodded. "Next time we'll go together."

She hugged him. "Do you still like it in Oregon Country?"

His head pumped up and down. "Very much."

"Because we could go back East in the spring."

This time his head went side to side. "I want to stay here, in case Alex returns."

She couldn't bear to tell him yet that Alex wouldn't be returning, at least not as the same man they knew and loved. London would probably change him. Marriage certainly would.

The ship moved forward, slowly cruising toward the ocean. She and Micah sat quietly as it sailed toward the river's bend.

"Good-bye, Alex," she whispered.

Go with God.

Her legs trembled as she stood, but she refused to collapse. Alex had made his choice to begin a new journey, and she must choose to do so as well.

If only there was a way she could live in the Willamette without having to marry. She and Micah could learn to make it on their own.

* * * * *

The crowd on the wharf cheered after the ship departed. The pelts were out of the fort's warehouses, on their way to London, and men and women alike would celebrate for the rest of the day before they began their work anew, trading and storing the furs for next year.

Alex didn't move from the landing until the ship carrying Lady

Judith, Lord Stanley, and Lady Stanley was beyond the bend. If he moved, he feared his heart might burst with joy.

For the first time in his life, he was as free as the Americans who traveled West. Free to work where he chose. Free to marry whom he chose. He no longer had to hide his feelings from Miss Waldron—from *Samantha*—though, admittedly, he'd done a poor job of hiding his affection last night. But he no longer had to pretend. If she would have him, he would take her in his arms as he had when she collapsed at the riverbank. Except this time he wanted to tell her that he loved her.

Alex raced from the river, toward the big house, to find Samantha.

When Judith finally absorbed the news that he'd lost his fortune along with his title, that he was nothing but the illegitimate son of a street performer, she left without another word to him. Lord Stanley explained the next morning that while Judith's father still held his title, his fortune was nearly gone. Judith desperately needed to marry someone who could provide for herself and her family.

Alex felt sorry for her for the pressure she faced to care for her family. Perhaps Lord Dodds was unmarried. Then she could still be the wife of the committee's president.

Alex may no longer be addressed as "lord," but he had no intention of changing his surname to Knox. The Americans in the Willamette wouldn't care about his name. He could choose to be Clark, without the "e," if he wanted. He could choose to be a farmer as well.

He pounded on Samantha's door. When no one answered, he hurried out to the gardens.

Judith's maid had refused to go back to London with her mistress. Apparently Miriam wasn't so enthusiastic about another five months on the ship...and Daniel, the night watchman, had asked for her hand in marriage.

Judith had seemed more distraught about the loss of her maid than she had about the loss of her prospective husband. Alex had heard her pleading with Miriam, offering her all sorts of promises if she would board the ship, but like Samantha, Miriam never showed up for the departure of the boat. Daniel seemed to be missing as well.

Perhaps Lady Judith and Lady Stanley could take turns as maid.

Alex didn't find Samantha and Micah in the garden so he went to the schoolhouse, but it was empty as well.

Strange.

When he hadn't seen Samantha at the landing, he'd assumed that she and Micah were resting after their exhausting day yesterday. Perhaps Simon had seen her.

He walked toward the Sale Shop, but before he opened the door, he heard one of the laborers arguing with Simon inside.

"She said I could have her credit," the man spouted.

"I don't care what she told *you*," Simon replied. "I need her to tell me."

"But she's gone."

Alex pushed open the door and stepped inside. Huey Osant, one of their carpenters, was standing across the counter from Simon with both fists on the countertop.

Alex stepped forward. "Who is gone?"

Both men turned, and Huey's eyes filled with surprise. And then fear.

"Who is gone?" he repeated.

Huey cleared his throat. "Samantha and the boy."

Alex clutched his fists. "Where did they go?"

"Across the river."

Alex grabbed the man's collar, pushing him up against the wall. "What do you mean, they went across the river?"

"I told her you wouldn't like it if she left."

"Told her?" Alex raged. "Why didn't you *stop* her?"

"I couldn't. She insisted on paddling herself across the river."

He shook his head. Samantha had almost drowned on that river. Why would she insist on leaving on her own? He relaxed his grip on Huey's collar. "What did she say when you told her I wouldn't like it?"

"She said it didn't matter, that you were leaving first."

Simon's hand was on Alex's shoulder; he released Huey's collar. He brushed his hands on his pants. "Did you take her across?"

Huey nodded. "I didn't think you or McLoughlin would want her to go alone."

"And because she offered him her store credit in return," Simon said.

Huey shrugged. "I needed a few things."

Alex wanted to strike something—Huey Osant, in particular— but hitting this man wouldn't help him find Samantha.

What if another Indian tribe decided they wanted both the son and the daughter of a god? What if another wolverine tried to attack them? As far as he knew, Samantha no longer had a gun to protect herself or Micah. If an Indian tribe took them away, he'd never be able to follow their tracks.

Why did she have to run?

"I asked her to marry me," Huey continued, staring at Alex. "But she said her heart belonged to someone else."

The man's words emboldened him, calming his fury. Perhaps she had run for the same reason he'd decided to stay. Perhaps she did love him as much as he loved her.

His heart raced. "What did they take with them?"

"They both had packs...and their dog was carrying supplies on his back too."

At least they had Boaz.

He turned away from Huey, toward Simon. "I must buy another gun."

"What's wrong with yours?"

"I traded it."

"Wasn't that your uncle's gun?"

He shrugged.

"You must have traded it for something special."

Alex flashed back to yesterday, to Micah looking up at him in the midst of the Indians as if he fully trusted that Alex knew what to do to rescue him. He would have done anything to keep Micah safe. "It was worth the trade."

Simon shooed Huey out of the store, and then he helped Alex find a rifle.

"I'm going to need some other supplies too," Alex said. "For a journey."

Simon's eyebrows arched. "Where are you going?"

He felt almost guilty saying it. "To the Willamette."

Simon threw his head back and laughed. "I believe you might be turning into an American."

Alex stiffened at first, and then he joined his friend in the laughter.

Simon handed him sea biscuits to eat, candles, an extra blanket, and a twist of tobacco.

"I don't chew tobacco."

"But it's better to trade tobacco than your new gun," Simon said with a wink. "Who's going to be in charge while you're gone?"

Alex took the bundle into his arms. "I am no longer an employee of the company."

Simon eyed him. "What do you mean?"

"When McLoughlin returns from his trip, he'll discover that I am a free man."

"You're even talking like an American."

He laughed again. "I suppose I am."

Simon siphoned black powder into a horn for him and handed it over the counter. "Now all you need is an American wife."

Chapter Thirty-Two

Tears of joy trickled down Samantha's cheeks when she saw the chinked cabins clustered together at the base of the Willamette Falls. She and Micah had done it. A year after leaving Ohio, a year of walking and waiting and not knowing what would happen next, they had reached the end of their pilgrimage.

She stopped for a moment by the river, surveying the beautiful paradise in front of her. The valley was lush with green from the winter and spring rains, a blue ribbon of river cutting through it. The mammoth waterfall bent like a horseshoe, white mist spraying overhead. To her left, a sea of vibrant blue and violet flowers mixed with orange blossoms, and beyond, as in a perfect landscape painting, dark forest blended with the flowers and grass.

In the distance, she could see the snowy peak of Mount Hood. The giant, overseeing it all.

Papa would have liked it here.

There were about thirty homes in the valley near the falls. Some of the houses looked like makeshift shelters, while others looked permanent with fences and gardens. There were no palisades around the homes, as at Fort Vancouver. Perhaps the valley was a safe place for her and Micah to live.

They walked past a woman tending her garden, and Samantha stopped to speak with her. The woman couldn't have been more than twenty-two, and she wore a brown dress, her hair tangled in the sweat on her face.

The woman studied her for a moment. "Where did you come from?"

"Ohio—almost six months ago. I've been living at Fort Vancouver."

The woman stuck out her stained hand. "I'm pleased to make your acquaintance."

Samantha shook her hand. "Do you know Lucille McLean?"

"No, I don't."

Samantha's heart started to plunge again. Perhaps Lucille hadn't made it the entire way to the Willamette after all.

"I only know one Lucille, honey," the woman continued, "but her last name's not McLean."

Samantha caught her breath. "What is it?'

"Morrison."

Samantha clapped her hands together as she thanked the woman. This must be what Lucille was hinting at in the letter. Lucille had not only survived the journey, but perhaps Katherine had a beautiful mama now—and Titus a wife.

She guided Micah away from the garden, and they followed the woman's directions to a cabin fifty yards away from the river. A pelt hung in the doorway in lieu of a door, and there was a small window in the front, its shutters folded back.

"Hello?" she called into the front room.

"I'll be right there!" Lucille's voice called back to her.

Lucille glanced out the window and shrieked when she saw Samantha and Micah. She ran outside and wrapped her arms around them both, hugging them tightly.

"You're here." Lucille held on to Samantha's hands as she looked at her. "I can't believe you're finally here."

Samantha smiled at her friend's enthusiasm. Perhaps she and Micah weren't so alone.

"Oh, we have to tell my parents and the Kneedlers and Jack and Ali—" She stopped, seemingly horrified at her own words.

"It's all right," Samantha said. "I assumed Jack was going to marry."

"He seems quite happy." Lucille paused. "Did you know I married as well?"

Samantha smiled again. "I figured it out."

Lucille pulled back a long pelt and welcomed them into her home.

A crudely carved table sat in the front room, and a fire smoldered in the hearth. The room was sparsely decorated, with only tin dishes lining a shelf along the wall and gingham curtains framing the windows. Katherine had been playing on the swept dirt floor with a corncob doll, but when she saw Samantha and Micah, she rushed to Lucille and clung to her skirt.

"Titus is out planting a field with my father. They both work from sunup to sundown, but Katherine, here, keeps me good company and sometimes my parents let Shep come visit us too." She pulled the girl even closer to her, and Katherine beamed. "Jack told us you stayed at the fort, and he told us about your father. I'm so sorry."

"Thank you."

"I wanted to come visit you at the fort, but we haven't stopped working since we arrived. I kept praying that you'd make it here safely." Lucille studied her a moment longer. "You look exhausted."

"I haven't had much sleep lately."

"I'm afraid there's not much sleep to be had here either."

Samantha glanced around her friend's new home again. She hated to admit it, but now she was the jealous one.

"You have a lovely home."

"It's all temporary," Lucille explained as she looked with Samantha around the room. "Just until Titus can build us a better house this summer, with a real parlor and a front door and maybe four or five rooms instead of two."

"It's a much better place to live than a tent."

Lucille laughed as she reached out and took her hands. "I haven't missed my tent, but I've sure missed you, Samantha. You always make me laugh."

It had been a long time since she'd laughed, as well.

As the woman talked, Micah knelt on the floor beside Katherine and opened up his knapsack. He pulled out his wooden animals, and Katherine squealed like her mother had minutes before, diving for a lion. When Micah made it roar, she laughed with delight.

Lucille nodded toward the children playing. "I sure wish you were here to stay."

Samantha hesitated, trying to muster enthusiasm in her words. "We are here to stay."

Lucille clapped her hands. "Katherine and I will both have friends."

Samantha smiled. She was grateful for her friend, but the thought of this new life felt empty without Alex. Would it ever feel like home without him?

As the children played, Lucille made dandelion tea for her on the cookstove that was dented from the trip. "Titus is going to get me a real stove as soon as he is able."

"He sounds like he is a good husband to you."

Lucille nodded, the familiar smile easing across her face, both calm and warm. "He treats Katherine and me like royalty."

She added a spoonful of honey to sweeten the tea then handed a tin mug to Samantha. "Titus bought the honey from another family, but he said we can keep bees next year."

Samantha sipped her tea. "Are you glad you came?"

"Sometimes I long for the familiar." Lucille's voice grew wistful. "But we knew that nothing would ever be the same again when we first crossed the Missouri River, didn't we?"

Samantha nodded. She supposed they did.

"Our neighbor said the warm sun will come again soon, and when it does, it will stay for months."

Samantha looked back out at the late afternoon sky speckled with clouds, and then she glanced back down at the children. "You're a good mother to Katherine, I can tell."

Lucille smiled again. "I love her like she's my own daughter."

Samantha nodded. "I understand."

The women talked about their journey and how the Loewe party had traveled east to the Whitman Mission before they went west. At The Dalles, they hired rafts to travel down the Columbia. Lucille said that the last portion of their journey was the hardest.

Two more people had died before they got to the Willamette—Marcia Kohler drank bad water, and little Charlie Hamlin fell off a wagon and was run over by a wheel. Charlie had often followed Micah around their camp when they stopped on Sunday afternoons, as Micah had done with Alex. Charlie and his dog.

Perhaps Alex was right; this was no journey for a child. The adults took the risks willingly, but the children did not.

Samantha told her about losing Papa and then about how they'd lost most of their things in the river. She told her about the McLoughlins and her work as a schoolteacher, but she didn't say anything about Alex.

"What are you going to do now?" Lucille asked.

"I'm not sure."

"Titus will let you live with us."

"Thank you," she said. The cabin was comfortable but too small for her and Micah to join them. "But we couldn't impose on your new family."

"I wish you could live with my parents, but their home is even smaller than ours."

"Maybe I could stay with the Kneedlers...."

Lucille shook her head. "They are living with their son and his family until he can build them a separate house."

Samantha took a deep breath, exhaustion weighing down her spirits.

She couldn't build a house on her own. Even if some of the men did offer to help, she didn't have any money to her name for supplies.

Lucille patted her hand. "You can stay here until you decide where you'll go next. The Rochesters and the Oxfords are preparing to go back East with Captain Loewe in the next week."

"But they just arrived!"

"It's been a long winter for several of the families," Lucille said. "A few people have asked to purchase their homes, but maybe one of them would sell their house to you and Micah."

Samantha looked back out the open window, at the falls crashing into the river. She had no money with which to buy a home—or anything to put in it if she did.

"Is there work here for women?"

"Oh, there's plenty of work, but no one has much money to pay for it. I wash Lesley Duncan's clothes every week, and he's paid me with these three chairs."

"Maybe I could teach school."

"A school is a wonderful idea," Lucille replied. "But I think Micah is the only child of school age."

"What about mending clothing?" she asked, thinking of the women at Fort Vancouver.

Lucille sighed. "Mrs. Rochester has been taking in clothing to mend, but she rarely has work. That's why they are returning East. Doctor Rochester doesn't have enough patients to keep him employed either."

"But there will be more people coming," Samantha said. One day the doctor would have enough patients to tend to. One day there would be enough children for a school.

"The doctor doesn't think it will be soon enough. He says they can't afford to wait another year," Lucille said. "But Jack has decided he wants to be a doctor instead of a farmer—I suppose in part because we lost so many people on the journey. Rochester is training him to take his place."

Perhaps she should turn around and go back East with the captain. She wanted to be here, but she was fooling herself to think that she and Micah could make it without help. She'd wanted so badly to be independent, but now that she was, she didn't know how she could support herself and Micah.

Panic surged through Samantha's chest, and for a moment it felt like she couldn't breathe. Perhaps she could go and beg Captain Loewe to let her and Micah return with him. She cringed at the thought of being with the captain for the next six months, but she would do what she must. They might be able to stop and get her cart—if it was still there—but she would still need money to purchase oxen and food. It had taken Papa a lifetime of savings to bring them here. The little she'd earned was back at the fort in the form of store credit, and even if she returned for supplies, she had already promised the credit to Huey. Perhaps when they got back, Grandma Emma would reimburse the captain. Boaz might have to stay here, but Lucille and Katherine could care for him.

"Do you have any other ideas?" Lucille asked.

"I could start a garden with Papa's seeds." She took out the small bag and put them on the table. "But I don't even know what they are."

Lucille smiled. "Maybe they're cherry trees."

It would be *years* before she could harvest cherries—if they even grew in this country.

She thought for a moment, her smile matching Lucille's. "Maybe they're something even more exotic, like oranges."

"Or blueberries."

Samantha licked her lips. It may take a few years, but it would be wonderful if her father did bring seeds for blueberry bushes.

Lucille brushed her hand over the bag. "If only you could grow gold with those seeds."

She sighed. "If only—"

Micah looked up at them. "You can grow my gold seeds."

Both the women laughed.

"Why are you laughing?" Micah asked.

She stopped her laughter. "I like that thought, being able to grow gold."

Her brother shrugged and returned to his playing.

Lucille eyed the clouds building in the sky. "I'd better get my clothes off the line before it rains."

Samantha stood up. "I'll help you."

Lucille patted her hand. "You stay right here and rest your legs."

"I don't mind helping."

"It would be more helpful if you could keep an eye on Katherine."

Samantha didn't argue with her friend. She sat back on her chair, her eyes fighting to stay open as Katherine and Micah played. Micah reached into his weatherworn knapsack and pulled out his elephant. Katherine laughed when he made a trumpet sound.

Samantha's gaze fastened on his knapsack.

Was it possible?

She looked back at her brother, the teasing gone from her voice. "What do you mean, you have gold seeds, Micah?"

He shrugged again. "The seeds that are in my pack."

"When did you get gold seeds?"

"I helped you carry them, remember?"

Her mind flashed back to those moments before they'd crossed over the Columbia the first time. Micah had asked if he could help her carry something. She'd told him he could take the seeds, but he hadn't had time to get anything out of her pack…had he?

Never once had she thought to ask if he'd taken something.

Her voice trembled. "Do you have the seeds in your knapsack?"

He nodded and hopped up to open his bag. He pulled out a small burlap bag almost identical to the one that held Papa's seeds and cradled it for a moment. When he gave the bag to her, it sank in her hands.

No wonder Alex said the knapsack was heavy.

She slowly opened the tie, and there before her was Papa's gold.

Her hands shook as she looked back at her brother. "Why didn't you tell me you had this?"

"You told me to take the seeds."

"I suppose I did."

"But you never asked me to give them back."

A laugh escaped from her lips, and she covered her mouth with her hands.

"Papa told me to help you."

"You have been more of a help than you can imagine," she said as she gathered him into her arms. Her heart felt as though it might burst with gratitude.

They wouldn't have to return East. With the gold, she could hire some of the men to build them a home, and later she could start a school. Surely there would be more children coming West soon, and Katherine and the other little ones from their party would need to go to school one day.

Maybe she could even open her doors to some of the native children who didn't have parents—or whose parents wanted them to go to school.

Maybe she and Micah could thrive out here on their own.

She laughed again, hope surging in the place of her panic.

Then Alex's face slid back into her mind, his strong smile as he sailed out into the Pacific Ocean. He was starting a new life with the woman he'd marry. There was a grand wedding awaiting him on other side of the world. And an important position, as well, that would impact all those who lived at Fort Vancouver and probably those who lived here in this valley.

She shook her head, trying to rid herself of the memory of his handsome face. It might take months for her heart to recover, but she couldn't continue to torture herself with the memories.

She secured the bag of gold in her lap.

With God's help, she and Micah would find their own way in this new country. When all seemed hopeless, He continued to provide for them.

Chapter Thirty-Three

Alex had wanted to leave for the Willamette the afternoon he'd found Samantha and Micah missing, but he had felt obligated to leave his former superior and post with professional dignity. He could no longer work for McLoughlin, but he wanted to wait and thank the governor for all he had done even as he passed the torch of his position to a successor.

Alex hadn't earned much of a salary while he was at Fort Vancouver—he hadn't needed much—but now he'd spent all of his and Samantha's store credit on supplies for his new life. And he gave a little of his credit to Huey Osant in exchange for a gift he planned to bring with him. Simon allowed Alex to use Samantha's credit but, with a wide smile on his tobacco-stained lips, made Alex promise that he would take the supplies to Samantha.

Eight days after Samantha and the ship left, McLoughlin returned to the fort and then sent Alex off to the Willamette with a long oration and a toast.

Alex told him he might return if he couldn't succeed at farming. But McLoughlin didn't seem to think Alex would be coming back to the fort, at least not to stay.

Without any money saved, Alex was at the mercy of the governor for the mules and the food he carried with him toward the valley. The mules swam across the river while two laborers paddled Alex and his supplies and left him on the other side.

It had felt unusually warm for April when they crossed the river, but as he hiked south, the sun alternately hid behind the clouds before it appeared again in grand form. Willows and low shrubs grew along the river, and flocks of geese flew overhead.

Samantha, he had no doubt, had followed this river right to the other Americans who would care for her. But what would those Americans think about a Brit living among them? The British had used this land and taken from it, but with the exception of the land around Fort Vancouver, they hadn't tried to tame it.

With God's help, he could plant food on his own and harvest it. He could raise animals and hunt and learn how to build. He even could raise a family as Tom Kneedler and his wife were doing.

He walked faster, guiding the mules along the river.

Would Samantha be glad to see him?

She had told Huey that her heart belonged to another. Alex wanted to believe that she left the fort because she loved him as much as he loved her. That she couldn't say good-bye.

But what if he was wrong? With the arrival of the new teacher, Samantha's work at the fort was complete. What if she left simply for the life she'd traveled almost two thousand miles to begin?

Maybe she didn't love him at all. Maybe she was glad for him to go.

If only he had something to offer her and Micah beyond what McLoughlin had given him—even a bit of his uncle's inheritance to buy them a house and some land.

A grand rainbow emerged on the other side of the Willamette, and the colors filled him with hope. He knew this wilderness well, and Samantha was the most determined woman he'd ever met. If she would have him, they could work hard to build a new life. Together.

If she wouldn't marry him…

He couldn't allow himself to dwell on that thought. He couldn't go back to London, and he didn't want to live in the Willamette without her. McLoughlin might let him work for another year at the fort, but Alex suspected that it wouldn't be long before the committee removed the governor from his position. If they released McLoughlin, Alex doubted they would keep him in their employ either.

In the distance he saw smoke above several houses, and he stopped the mules, taking another deep breath and praying that Samantha and Micah had made it here safely.

At one of the houses, a young woman and her daughter greeted him at the door.

"Do you know a woman by the name of Samantha Waldron?" he asked.

"Of course I do." The woman tilted her head. "But how do you know her?"

"I met her at Fort Vancouver."

"And you came all the way down here looking for her."

He nodded. "I have come to ask her to be my wife."

With a big smile, the woman directed him to the house where she said Samantha lived. He crossed the grassy field, eyeing a small wooden home with a split-rail fence circling it. Then he took a deep breath and knocked on the front door.

When it opened, he bit back a gasp.

There in front of him, with a hammer in his hands, was Jack Doyle.

Stunned, Alex stared at the man. "I am sorry—I thought this was Miss Waldron's house."

"It is."

"What—what are you doing here?"

Doyle lifted the hammer. "Just fixing up a few things. What are *you* doing here?"

Alex didn't answer his question. "I thought you married."

"I did," Doyle said with a laugh. "My wife is in the garden out back."

His heart seemed to stop. He was too late. Samantha had thought he was on the ship back to London. She thought he was getting married.

Of course she had married as well. She had to provide for Micah. He never should have waited for McLoughlin to return to leave the fort. He should have discarded his professional obligations and come right after her. Instead, he'd driven her into the arms of someone else.

Alex took a step away from the house. "Please tell her I said hello."

Doyle clapped him on the shoulder, pushing him toward the garden. "Go tell her yourself."

* * * * *

Samantha dug a hole with her hands, in dirt that was as black as night.

"That's too deep," the woman kneeling beside her said. "Like this." Aliyah dug about two inches deep and sat back.

Samantha lifted the burlap bag in her hands to the sky, to honor her father, and then she carefully untied the leather strap to take out one of Papa's seeds.

Micah drew in closer, watching her fingers. She rifled through the seeds, letting them sift through her fingers, and then she pulled out one of them, hiding it in her hand. With Micah and Aliyah watching, she slowly opened her fist.

Her eyes grew wide as she examined the red seed in her palm. It looked like a…

She glanced first at Micah and then at Aliyah. The three of them burst into laughter.

Papa had surprised them with beans.

The bag was filled with an assortment of bean seeds, probably enough for her and Micah to have bean soup for the rest of their lives.

Perhaps she could sell her harvest to those who decided to move East next year.

She handed the kidney bean to Micah, and he carefully positioned the seed inside the hole. Then she pushed dirt over it and kissed the tiny mound.

Micah giggled at the ring of dirt around Samantha's lips, and she laughed with him as she wiped it off with her forearm.

"Now it will grow," Aliyah declared, and Samantha believed her. She'd learned much about Aliyah in the past week, learned that she knew more about growing things than anyone Samantha had ever met. And she learned that Aliyah adored her husband of four months.

Samantha glanced around at her almost an acre of garden, imagining what it would look like ripened with Papa's beans and the Rochesters' plants.

Papa's gold had purchased this house before the Rochesters left, and she had plenty of gold remaining to build a one-room school. She and Micah could live—thrive even—in the Willamette on their own.

Micah wrestled with Boaz as she dug another hole in the dirt. Her new friend complimented her on her work, and Samantha smiled at her.

By the fall, Aliyah had confided, she and Jack would be parents.

How blessed Samantha was that her guardian angel now lived in a home just a half mile down the river instead of in a cave.

Her mind wandered again to the man she had wanted to marry. She hoped that one day Lady Judith would realize what a blessed woman she was to be married to Alex. People could change and grow. Lady Judith could certainly learn to appreciate and love the man she'd married.

Now Samantha had to focus on what she believed God had called her to do.

She turned to Aliyah. "What would you think about starting a school together?"

Aliyah's eyes widened. "What do you mean?"

"I'd like a school where both English and native children could attend."

Aliyah paused. "What would I do?"

"Help me teach them."

The smile on her friend's face grew. "I think I would like that very much."

Boaz barked and began running toward the house, and Micah turned around quickly. Then he hopped up to his feet. "Alex!" he shouted as he ran toward the house.

Samantha's head jerked up; her heart lurched at the name. She froze on her knees, not daring to turn around.

"Who is it?" she whispered to Aliyah.

"It's a man," her friend whispered back as she glanced over Samantha's shoulder. "One of the officers from Fort Vancouver."

She caught her breath. "Is he wearing a black frock coat?"

"He is." Aliyah scooted closer to her. "And he's watching you."

Her heart felt as if it was tumbling out of control. Alex wasn't on his way to London with Lady Judith. He was right here, in her garden.

Perhaps the ship had returned...or perhaps he hadn't gone at all.

Perhaps he and his wife had decided to settle in the Willamette.

If so, she would hurry to catch up with the Loewe party. Submitting to Captain Loewe for the next five or six months would be paradise compared to living near Lord and Lady Clarke for an entire year.

Aliyah watched her face for a moment and then stood. "Come along, Micah."

"I'm staying right here."

Samantha couldn't say anything, not even to reprimand her brother for his disrespect.

Then she heard Alex's voice, low and strong. "Why don't you go get the gift I brought for you, Micah? It's inside a bag on the lead mule."

"How will I know it's for me?"

Alex laughed. "You will know."

She heard shuffling behind her as Aliyah coaxed Micah toward his gift at the front of the house. Then she heard Alex whisper her name.

She took off her bonnet and stood, turning slowly.

Lord Alexander Clarke stood before her, looking quite regal in his frock coat and top hat. She couldn't breathe.

"You're supposed to be on that boat," she said, her voice trembling. "Going to London."

"London is no longer my home."

"But Lady Judith—"

He stopped her. "She did not want to stay here."

"You were supposed to marry."

He shook his head. "I did not love her, nor did she love me."

She brushed her hands over her yellow apron, streaking dirt down the front of it as he stepped closer to her. The pounding of her heart seemed to echo in her ears.

"Why do you Waldrons keep running?"

"Micah and I—" she whispered. "We had to finish our journey."

He reached for her hand, and her heart leaped as he wrapped his strong fingers over hers and placed them on his heart. "The trail ends right here, Miss Waldron. With you and me."

"If you don't call me 'Samantha'—"

He leaned forward and drowned her words with his kiss. Her body warmed in his embrace, her skin fluttering at his touch. Strong and tender. Powerful and passionate.

Alex Clarke hadn't gone to London. He was here, and he wanted to be with her.

Micah ran toward them, and Alex released her. In Micah's arms was a beautifully carved ark.

Her eyes grew wide. "Did you make that for him?"

He shook his head. "A friend made it for me."

"It's perfect," Micah said.

"You can use it the next time you try to cross the river."

Micah set down his gift and wrapped his arms around both of them. Alex leaned down and lifted the boy with one arm. The other he put around Samantha. "I no longer have an income, or a position for that matter, but we can find our way together, can't we?"

Samantha smiled. "I have a surprise for you."

He kissed the top of her head.

Micah grinned. "Does this mean you're going to marry her?"

"If your sister says it is all right."

Tears trickled down her cheeks. "It's fine with me."

Alex looked into her eyes, and she never wanted him to look away again. "Is there a reverend around here?" he asked.

Samantha laughed. "I believe we can find one."

He leaned close to her. "Will you marry me, Miss Waldron?"

She put her hands on her hips. "Only if you'll stop calling me 'Miss Waldron.'"

"All right." He paused, leaning closer as he whispered in her ear, "How would you like to be called Mrs. Clarke?"

"Samantha," she insisted.

He smiled. "I think I'll just call you *Sam*."

Author's Note

The Americans didn't stop coming to Oregon Country. In 1843, more than nine hundred men, women, and children emigrated in what is now known as "the Great Migration."

During the next twenty years, approximately three hundred thousand Americans traveled West on the Oregon Trail. About thirty thousand of them lost their lives to accidents, drowning, and cholera—one grave, it is said, for every eighty yards of the trail.

In 1846, the United States and Great Britain settled their dispute over the control of Oregon Country by dividing the land. The British took control of the wilderness north of the 49th parallel in what is now known as British Columbia. The United States took ownership of the land to the south, including what is now Oregon, Washington, Idaho, and parts of Montana and Wyoming. Oregon became a US territory in 1848, and in 1859 it became the 33rd state.

Wagon trains on the Oregon Trail were each run like a democratic country with an elected captain and a manifesto of rules. There are multiple accounts of dogs being killed as well as people being left behind.

The first organized company of wagons set out for Oregon Country in May of 1842. The captain of this party, Elijah White, insisted on executing the dogs in their party for three reasons—because they were keeping the party awake at night, because of the fear of drawing Indians, and because of the fear of rabies. As a result, the wagon train split into two factions.

There is no lack of books and firsthand accounts from men and women who kept diaries while traveling on the Oregon Trail. This is a huge blessing as a researcher; however, it is also a challenge because some of these accounts are contradictory. For example, some people wrote about an Indian path along the Columbia River that pioneers walked, while others wrote that there was no such path. In later years, emigrants either paid Indians to guide them on rafts from The Dalles, or they took the Barlow Road ("road" being a very loose term) around Mount Hood and down into Oregon City.

By the spring of 1844, Doctor John McLoughlin had spent $31,000 of company money (equivalent to about one million dollars today) along with a large sum of personal funds to help American pioneers who'd lost most of their belongings on the journey. Many of them never paid him back. Doctor McLoughlin was forced into retirement in 1846 and later became a citizen of the United States, building his home in Oregon City near the falls.

While Madame Marguerite McLoughlin's father was a Swiss partner in a fur-trading company, history differs on the origins of her mother's Indian family. Her mother was probably from the Cristeneaux (Cree), Ojibway, or Chippewa tribe.

Less than two hundred years ago, the American West was a vast wilderness, home to many nations of Indians. None of the information in this book is intended to be disparaging to any people group. While I hoped to capture the facts of history as accurately as possible, this American Tapestry novel was intended to focus specifically on the determination of American men and women who traveled overland to Oregon as well as the Native Americans and British who aided them in this journey.

My greatest hope is that the story truthfully reflects what many of the pioneers experienced as they lost loved ones and possessions in their journeys west and then worked diligently to create new, thriving lives in the beautiful country called Oregon.

In the winter of 2007, my husband, two daughters, and I immigrated to Oregon via airplane. We'd heard about the rain in the Pacific Northwest, but when we woke up on our first morning in Portland, we were shocked to not only find ourselves in the midst of a snowstorm, but to see bicyclists traversing the snowy roads. Not even a snowstorm stops a determined Oregonian.

While we were sipping soft drinks on the airplane and then soaking in the hot tub at our hotel, my saintly father drove our moving van filled with furniture and boxes over the icy pass into Oregon. There were no oxen for him to feed or rivers to forge, but when our moving van struggled to make it over the mountains, my dear father probably felt like discarding a few pieces of furniture along the trail. Then the fuel line sprang a leak, and he had to wait for the delivery of a new moving van—from San Francisco—before reloading all our things and reattaching the trailer to my Honda so he could finish the journey.

Did I mention that my father is a saint?

After six years in Oregon, we've come to love our home state—enjoying the lush green of the forest next to our house, sledding near Mount Hood in the winter, taking Sunday afternoon drives through the Columbia River Gorge, watching sea lions play off the coast, hiking the beautiful hills and rocky cliffs above the Pacific, and picking mounds of organic fruit each summer. We love the sunny days when our neighborhood emerges en masse to soak up the sunshine together, and we enjoy those rainy days cuddled up with books or playing games around the fireplace.

While crops may not grow in a single day, it is true that almost everything grows well in Oregon. Even my husband Jon and I, who are notorious for killing plants, have enjoyed the bounty from our little garden of tomatoes, herbs, and lettuce. As for the cantaloupe and red peppers—let's say that most Oregonians are better gardeners than us.

Oregonians are truly a unique people, forged from a unique past. They are fiercely protective of their land even as they enjoy all that the land offers. It's been almost two hundred years since the first wagon train floundered through the Blue Mountains. Because of the hard work of its people in taking care to preserve its fertile land, the beautiful state of Oregon continues to flourish.

And the Dobson family is honored to call this state our home.

Thank you to all the people who helped this East Coaster learn about Oregon's rich history.

Cheri Garver at the National Historic Oregon Trail Interpretive Center near Baker City, for answering my many questions. Becky Smith and Jim Keetch, the fabulous wagon master, for taking my daughters and me on an unforgettable journey at the National Oregon/California Trail Center in Montpelier, Idaho. If you are interested in learning more about the Oregon Trail, these centers are incredible places for both adults and children to explore.

Randy Howarth and Robin Kirkpatrick, for sharing a bit of their family history with me. Scott Daniels, the reference librarian at the Oregon Historical Society, for helping me with my facts. Any errors are my responsibility.

I'm also grateful for the many people who continue to walk and often run with me along this writing journey. Thank you to:

Rachel Meisel, my amazing editor, friend, and coach, for your consistent encouragement and expertise, and for gifting me with the seeds to grow this story.

Natasha Kern, for your honesty, wisdom, and direction—you are such a blessing to me. Susan Downs and Connie Troyer, for polishing this story and catching the many things I missed.

Pinn Crawford—you continually amaze me with your ability to track down any resource. Thank you for locating so many wonderful old books about Fort Vancouver and the Oregon Trail.

Leslie Gould, Nicole Miller, Dawn Shipman, and Kelly Chang for reading the first chapters of this book over and over and for all your input to help shape this story. Thank you to Nicole and Dawn as well for helping bring Fort Vancouver alive in my mind's eye.

Michele Heath for offering me both your insight and your friendship. My trouper of a friend, Allison Owen, for braving the cold December night as we explored Fort Vancouver by candle-light. Sheila Herbert, my English friend, who graciously answered my questions about Great Britain's history and explained customs quite foreign to me.

Kevin, Amanda, Jake, Shannon, Aaron, Grey, Joseph, David, Mari, and Michael, who let me sip peppermint tea until late at night as I wrote in their coffee shop. I appreciate each of you so very much.

Dad and Lyn Beroth, Kristy Colvin, Tosha Williams, and Jodi Stilp for your prayers and for carrying me across the finish line.

My adventurous daughters, Karly and Kiki, for traveling eighteen hundred miles with me to explore the remnants of this trail. It is such a delight for me to watch you grow in the beauty and love of Christ.

My wonderful husband, Jon—I couldn't have written this book without you! Thank you for loving me and our whole family.

Most of all, I'm grateful to my heavenly Father and His messengers, who direct the steps of every pilgrim on their journey home.

With joy,
~Melanie

About the Author

 Melanie Dobson is the award-winning author of eleven novels, including seven historical romances for Summerside Press. In 2011, Melanie won ACFW Carol Awards for *Love Finds You in Homestead, Iowa* and *The Silent Order*, and in 2010, *Love Finds You in Liberty, Indiana* was chosen as the Best Book of Indiana (fiction). Melanie's next historical romance, an American Tapestries™ novel about the Revolutionary War, will be published in October 2013.

Melanie is the former corporate publicity manager at Focus on the Family, and she worked in public relations for fifteen years before she began writing fiction full time. Born and raised in the Midwest, she has lived all over America and now resides with her husband and two daughters near Portland, Oregon. Read more at MelanieDobson.com.

AMERICAN TAPESTRIES™

Each novel in the American Tapestries™ series sets a heart-stirring love story against the backdrop of an epic moment in American history. Whether they settled her first colonies, fought in her battles, built her cities, or forged paths to new territories, a diverse tapestry of men and women shaped this great nation into a Land of Opportunity. Then, as now, the search for romance was part of the American dream. Summerside Press invites lovers of historical romance stories to fall in love with this line, and with America, all over again.

NOW AVAILABLE

Queen of the Waves
by Janice Thompson
A novel of the *Titanic*
ISBN: 978-1-60936-686-5

Where the Trail Ends
by Melanie Dobson
A novel of the Oregon Trail
ISBN: 978-1-60936-685-8

COMING SOON

Always Remembered
by Janelle Mowery
A novel of the Alamo
ISBN: 978-1-60936-747-3

A Lady's Choice
by Sandra Robbins
A novel of women's suffrage
ISBN: 978-1-60936-748-0